HIDDEN DEEP

Book One of The Hidden Trilogy

Amy Patrick

Cover design by Cover Your Dreams
Formatting by Polgarus Studio

Print ISBN: 978-0-9904807-7-8

Visit http://www.amypatrickbooks.com/ to sign up for Amy's newsletter if you would like to receive news and insider information on The Hidden Trilogy books and release dates.

CONTENTS

CHAPTER ONE
NOT HYPOTHERMIA

The first time I saw him, everyone convinced me he was a hallucination caused by hypothermia. It was the second time that really messed me up.

* * *

It was only noon, but I couldn't wait anymore. The need to get out there had been growing stronger every day. With everything my mom had going on, maybe she wouldn't give me an argument this time. The screen door slammed behind me with a loud creak and double-bouncing bang.

"Ryann? You going out?"

I exhaled loudly then turned and faced my mother as she followed me out onto the back porch. She was dressed in her new red interview suit, a face full of going-

1

somewhere makeup, and her hair up in clips where she'd been straightening it in sections. She'd rushed to the door in her stocking feet, causing a fresh run to start near her big toe.

"I left a note on the counter. Just going for a walk— you know." I shrugged. *No big deal.* Glancing down, I nodded toward her foot. "You'd better change those."

"Shoot!" She hiked up her skirt and started ripping off the pantyhose. "What the heck am I doing? I haven't worked in sixteen years. They're going to laugh me out the door."

She wobbled to one side, off balance. I reached out to steady her. "They'll love you."

Mom wrinkled her nose, brushing off my reassurance. "You're right. How could they not want such a strong job candidate? Thirty-six, living with my mother again, and did I mention the part about no work experience? Don't ever get yourself in this situation, Ryann. Depend on you—no one else—"

"Mom." I interrupted before she could launch into the full mantra. "They're going to love you."

She balled up the ruined stockings and gave me a doubtful smile, the shallow lines on her forehead deepening. Her eyes closed for a long moment, and she let out a resigned sigh. "Why do you want to go tromping around in those buggy, thorny woods every day, Ryann? You know I hate it."

"I won't go far. I'll probably be back before you even get home."

I knew exactly what this was about. In my mother's mind, I was still six years old, likely to wander off and get lost, and this time, never return. There was a pause, and I could see the surrender forming behind her eyes.

"Well... spray yourself so you don't get eaten alive." She picked up a can of insect repellant from the porch railing, thrusting it at me. "And stay on the trails. And don't be late."

"*You* don't be late." I took the can and smiled at her, already backing down the porch stairs. "And good luck."

Stepping out into the pine-scented heat was a relief. We'd moved way out into the sticks, but we hadn't left the tension behind in town. A giddy sense of freedom swept me up, and I practically ran to get to the trees bordering my grandma's house. My home now, too, as of three days earlier.

I'd come here for visits my whole life. Now it was a little more permanent, which was fine with me. I'd always loved this place. The hot clinging air, the rambling log house, and especially the deep, dense woodland surrounding it. The locals would probably think that was kind of strange, since most of them remembered when I nearly died out here.

Sticks snapped under my sneakers as I walked, listening to birdsong and whining insects. All familiar and welcoming. And a familiar feeling wrapped around me as well. Of hoping for... something. I wasn't sure what.

I'd promised not to go far, and I didn't intend to, but once I got going, it was too tempting to keep on walking, exploring deeper into the woods. The further I went, the lighter I felt. The sensation was like exhaling after holding your breath for way too long. Anyway, if I'd kept my promise and stayed on the trail, I never would've found this place.

The spring-fed pool was so clear I could see the large flat rocks and green plants lining the bottom. Leaves pirouetted from the surrounding trees, landing and floating on the glassy surface. Sunlight streamed through the treetops in little pockets, making a kaleidoscope pattern on the moss and springy wild ferns growing along the water's edge. It felt like my own magical discovery.

My t-shirt and shorts were plastered to me at this point, and my skin actually felt thirsty. Late May in Mississippi is not for wusses. Looking at the clear water, the idea of an outdoor bath started to seem too delicious to resist. It was kind of crazy—I mean, I hadn't exactly packed a swimsuit for my little nature walk. Whatever. I could use a minute or two of crazy in my life right about now.

I shucked my sweaty clothes, leaving my bra and panties on. There might have been six hundred acres of my grandma's posted forest land between me and the nearest person, but I wasn't *that* brave.

I stepped into the cool water. It felt unbelievably good, and I slipped under, blowing out all the stuffy humid air in my body. After a minute my lungs burned. I resurfaced, stood up in the waist-deep pool, and waited for the water to stop running down my face. Then I opened my eyes.

There in front of me, kneeling on the mossy bank and staring right at me, was a guy. A big blond guy, about my age.

I know him. No—wait—I don't know.

It didn't really matter because he shouldn't have been there. No one should've been there, but he was. *I'm basically naked and alone in the woods with a stranger. Not good.*

My chest was on fire. I wasn't breathing, and then I was breathing too much, too quickly. My mind spun and scrambled for anything like a rational thought. If I'd been watching myself in one of those stupid screamer movies, I'd have been shouting at the screen, "Move! Run! Do *something.*" But it was like that time when I was home alone and thought I heard an intruder. I just froze.

The guy looked almost as shocked as I felt, seeming unable to tear his wide-eyed stare away. Like me, he was frozen in place.

Then his face relaxed. And he smiled.

Sure. Alligators can smile, too. At least the sight ripped me out of my temporary paralysis. I finally moved, lunging toward the bank, intending to climb out and run, or at least get my clothes.

Oh. *My clothes.* I plunged myself back into the water up to my chin. I had no idea what to do. I was basically at this guy's mercy—miles from anyone who could hear me scream, ridiculously outsized and overpowered. He still hadn't said anything. No "I'm sorry," or "Hello there," or "Why no, I'm *not* a rapey stalker."

"Get out of here. You're trespassing." My attempt to be threatening came out sounding kind of pathetic, breathy and high-pitched.

The guy jerked back, lost his balance, and ended up on his rear. For a minute I was hopeful—maybe he was actually buying my bluff—but he got back up slowly to his haunches, and the corner of his mouth eased up along with one eyebrow.

"Trespassing? Well. There must be some law against public indecency, too. You shouldn't be out here like…" He gestured toward me. "…that."

His voice was deep, mature-sounding, though he wasn't more than eighteen, and his amused grin said he couldn't have been more pleased I *was* out here like this.

Who does he think he is? "No, you stupid ass—*you* shouldn't be out here. I own these woods, and You. Are. Trespassing. Now leave." That was it—I'd used the only cuss word I could pull off convincingly, and I sure did hope it worked, because if it didn't, I had nothin'.

My tough talk made me feel slightly less afraid. But I was still stuck in the shamefully clear pool, and he was still there grinning and looking at me like the kid who'd found the Halloween candy stash.

He stood, and I had to squint up at him. His dark blond hair was haloed by the rays of sun slipping through the leafy canopy above. Strands of lighter gold glinted through the loose curls. I was cornered by possibly the world's most angelic-looking peeping Tom. Or serial killer. Neither thought was comforting.

Our standoff continued for long moments. Then suddenly he was moving toward me. He reached down and grabbed my pile of clothes on the bank and extended them out over the water to me. "Sorry," he said, not exactly sounding full of remorse, "but I'm not leaving. I need to talk to you first."

I willed myself to breathe again. "*Talk* to me? No. Just leave. Go away or…" Or what? I'd scream, and all the forest creatures would rush to my rescue? I'd stay in there until I shriveled like a Craisin?

He looked at me, waiting for me to finish my empty threat, I guess. When it was clear I wasn't going to, he narrowed his eyes and twisted his lips in a calculating expression.

"Okay. Listen, if you don't *want* these clothes, I'll toss them over there, and go sit down awhile against that tree. My arm's getting kind of tired." He stretched it to demonstrate his point, grinning widely at me again. If I could've reached him, and done it without giving him another free peep show, I'd have slapped that perfect smile off his face. So… maybe I wasn't dealing with someone dangerous here, but he sure was annoying.

I had a choice—argue with the guy holding the only thing standing between me and full-frontal, or stay there wearing my arms for a shirt and hope he'd eventually get bored and leave on his own. Right. I snatched the clothes out of his hand and scowled at him.

"Could you at least turn around?"

He paused a second then turned his back, and I set a world speed record for underwater dressing. Then I crept up the bank, grabbed my shoes, and took off running. He might have been harmless, but why take chances? I managed a few yards and didn't hear him coming after me. Then the huge golden-haired guy dropped out of a tree right in front of me.

I let out a squeal as my wet body slammed hard into his. He grabbed my upper arms, steadying me. I started screaming and slapping at him with my sneakers, dropping them in the process.

He immediately let me go and raised his hands in surrender. His words came out in a hurry. "Hey, calm down. I know I scared you. But I'm not going to hurt you. I only want to talk to you. Please."

I stepped back and rubbed my arms where his fingers had been moments earlier. "I guess you're not going to give me a choice. All right then. You want to talk? You go first. What are you doing on my land, and why were you spying on me?"

"Your land. Right. Well, I wasn't spying. I was walking back from the library." He nodded toward a scattered pile of books on the other side of the pool. "I saw your clothes and shoes there—I was going to keep going so I wouldn't scare you, but then you didn't come up for so long. I was just checking to see if you were okay. I didn't mean for you to see me. And then there you were, and you were all..." He swept his hand up and down in my direction and blushed deeply.

"Exposed? Half-naked? Don't try to make me believe *you* were embarrassed. Sorry, but I've got the market cornered on humiliation today."

"I'm sorry. Really. It's not like I planned this."

I studied him. Though I had no rational reason to believe him, I did. Something in his voice told my self-preservation instinct to stand down.

"Okay then, assuming you're not a registered sex offender—you're not, are you?"

"No." He looked insulted.

"Unregistered?"

"No!" He gave a frustrated huff of a laugh.

"Okay. So you were walking back from the library... to where?" I thought of the few houses bordering my grandma's property. Most of the owners were old, like her. Maybe he was somebody's grandson, visiting for the weekend.

"I live... near here."

"Near here, like, off the county road, you mean?"

He glanced around. "Uh... yes."

Now that I was calm enough to care, I noticed he looked... different... not like any of the guys I'd ever seen in school. He was fresher somehow, healthier-looking, like no artificial color or flavor had ever crossed his lips. I couldn't decide if it was the skin or something else, but he looked like he'd never had a bad night's sleep. There were no freckles, no marks on him anywhere. His eyes were a pure, clear green, like sunlight shining through a leaf.

He wore ripped, faded jeans and an ancient plaid shirt with cut-off sleeves. It hung open to expose his smooth light brown chest and stomach. His feet were bare. It was like an Abercrombie ad gone wrong, because you didn't want to buy the clothes, just... him.

"You don't go to Deep River High. Did you just move here?" I had to ask—if I was going to have Spanish class next fall with a guy who'd seen me almost naked, I wanted to be forewarned. *Bonitas chichis, Senorita.*

"Oh, no, I uh... I'm home schooled."

"Good," I said quickly then slowed myself down. "I mean, all right. So what's your name?"

He hesitated but answered. "It's Lad."

"Okay then. Lad—I'm Ryann."

"I know."

Not what I was expecting to hear. I fired back at him, "How do you know my name?"

He looked away for a second then back at me. His eyes held a pleading I-know-I'm-busted look. He shook his head and opened his hands, palms-up to the sides. "I just... do?"

Wrong answer. I didn't care how cute he was, this was all too weird. I started backing away. "Well, um, Lad, now that we've *talked*, I have to get home. My mom and grandma are going to have the National Guard out here combing the woods soon."

He moved toward me and wrapped a large hand around my arm, the pressure not bruising, but firm. The heat of it sizzled on my wet skin.

"No. Not yet. Please, I have to show you something." He tilted his head down and stared directly into my eyes, lowering his voice. "You must come with me."

His gaze was so intense, almost like he was pushing me with his eyes, like he thought he could simply will me to agree with him. Right. My breath evaporated along with any feeling of comfort that had begun to develop. I leaned back, putting some space between us, and laughed nervously.

"You know what? The only thing I *must* do is get home. I'm not kidding about the National Guard. You've never met my mom or you wouldn't doubt it." I tried for flippant, but it came out sounding stressed.

"I can't let you go yet." He paused and then his tone turned up, like he'd just had a great idea. "I have something of yours. I want to give it back."

"What could *you* possibly have of *mine*? No thanks. I'm leaving." I wrenched my arm free, turned and stomped off, praying he didn't repeat that freaky dropping-from-the-branches move, and growing more nervous every second about this guy's inability to take no for an answer.

"I found your book."

His quiet words stopped me. I slowly turned to face him again, my stomach lined with ice. Finding the breath to respond was a challenge.

"What book?" But I already knew what he was going to say.

"The book you left out here… that night."

11

Ten years ago. "How do you know about that?"

"You can have it back. You want it, don't you?"

I did. More than that, I wanted to know how this stranger knew about my beloved childhood book. And what was he doing with it after all this time? There was really only one explanation.

"It's you, isn't it?"

He smiled and just looked at me, those scorching bright eyes like a magnifying glass over a dry leaf, burning a hole through everything I'd believed for the past ten years.

Chapter Two
Fireflies in January

Ten years earlier

We always had New Year's Day dinner at Grandma Neena's house—collard greens and black-eyed peas with ham hocks for good luck. Berry cobbler, my favorite, for dessert. As usual, there were plenty of old people and no young cousins to play with. I was the only child of two only-children.

The grownups stayed at the table for what seemed like hours, drinking coffee and talking about things I didn't remember. Bored, I sought out my favorite reading spot, a cozy chair by the picture window overlooking my grandma's backyard.

As the sun set, a spark in the gray winter landscape outside caught my attention. Fireflies. In January. Even at six years old I knew that was strange. Still clutching my book, I slipped out the door to get a closer look and maybe capture a few for a nightlight like I did every summer.

The mysterious lights multiplied, changing colors. Pretty. Fascinating. I followed them down the path then off it as they danced over the ground in the darkening woods. By the time they rose up into the trees and blinked out, it was completely dark. I looked around. I couldn't see the house, couldn't even see the smoke I smelled from the chimney.

I wandered for hours trying to get back, finally collapsing at the base of a big tree. It was way past my bedtime. Huddling against the trunk, I wished for Mommy, Daddy, my white canopy bed with the warm purple unicorn comforter.

I'd never forget the nighttime noises that filled those dark woods. I fell asleep with my hands tightly cupped over my ears. Once during the night I awoke to the faint sound of voices calling my name through the trees. No one heard the weak croak that came when I tried to answer. My throat was dry and raw.

The next time I awoke, I was in pain. I had wet my pink corduroy pants, and I couldn't stop shaking. My thin sweater was useless against the freezing temperature. My fingers and feet would no longer move. I squeezed my eyes shut and wished I could stop waking up, stop feeling anything, and sleep forever.

And then he was there.

I opened my eyes, my breath coming fast. Something very warm had touched my face. A boy, a little bigger than me, squatted in front of me, smiling. When I let out a surprised sound, my breath clouded the moonlit air between us. The boy jerked his hand back. We both jumped. Then his smile widened, and he laughed.

He had on even less than I did—no shirt at all and bare feet poking out from under his pant legs. He should have been freezing, too, but he didn't seem to notice the cold. I wasn't afraid of him. He looked friendly... and curious. He reached out again slowly and put both his warm hands against my cold cheeks, holding my face. It was the nicest thing I'd ever felt.

I smiled at the silent boy with wide eyes and messy blond curls. "What's your name?"

He didn't answer, but only stared at me, his eyebrows pulling together as he studied my mouth. I started to repeat the question, and he put his fingertips across my lips. Touching his own lips, he breathed out with a puff. I giggled at that. He laughed, too, but his smile went away when he saw my hard shudder.

The boy reached into his pocket and pulled out a tiny bottle made of metal. Holding it out to me, he tipped it toward my mouth. He wanted me to drink. I expected water, but it wasn't. It tasted like—I don't know—nothing I'd ever tasted before, sweet and sort of warm, bubbly almost.

I was so thirsty I didn't care what it was. I drank it all, and immediately heat filled my stomach, spreading quickly throughout my body, finally reaching my fingertips and toes. I felt… perfect.

The next thing I remember was the sound of boots crashing through the underbrush, a man's frantic shouting. "I found her. She's here." There was a lot of walkie-talkie noise.

It was just after dawn. Someone had spotted me on the shoulder of the county road that bordered one side of my grandma's land. I'd been missing for fourteen hours.

Chapter Three
Icing on the Cake

I looked at the grown-up version of the strangest, most magical memory of my life. All I could manage was a whisper as it truly hit me. "Is it you? Are you real?"

Lad reached out and gently cupped my face in his large hand, causing me to shiver. His mouth slowly spread into a wide smile. So beautiful. So familiar.

"All right," I breathed, my stomach quivering, "I'll go with you. Where is it?"

Lad wasted no time capitalizing on the moment, scooping my hand inside his and starting to pull. "I'll show you."

He stopped as we passed the pool and retrieved his books then led me deeper into the woods, much farther than I'd ever explored. It was like walking back into a simpler time in my life, a time when magical boys and enchanted forests and happily-ever-after families were entirely possible. As we walked, I was hyper-aware of his hand around mine. Warm. Strong. Rough-textured but gentle. It seemed silly I should even notice that stuff. I'd touched people and been touched my whole life, but this felt like a whole new thing.

And the fact that I was actually with him, that it was actually happening, was just… breathtaking.

None of the searchers had recalled seeing a boy when I was finally discovered the next morning. The ER doctor told my parents hypothermia was known to cause hallucinations, though they said I was in much better condition when they found me than anyone had dared to hope.

At first I'd been eager to tell everyone *why* I was okay, about the boy, fiercely insisting it was all true. But I'd quickly learned discussing that particular part of my adventure was "not okay." My story was initially met with sympathy and later with discomfort and disapproval. Even at that young age, I'd understood no one believed me or even wanted to. As time passed, the memories had grown hazy, mixing with my recurring dreams about that night, confusing me, and it had all started seeming less and less likely. Eventually I'd accepted the grownups were probably right.

Lad dropped my hand and moved ahead of me, finding the easiest path through the wildness of the late-spring undergrowth. His bare feet smoothly and unflinchingly navigated the rough ground. *How does that not hurt?* My mind skipped from wondering about that to wondering how angry my mother would be if she could see me—agreeing to go somewhere with a strange man—okay, a boy, but a man-sized boy.

Maybe I should have been afraid of him, but I just wasn't. He was the living answer to all the questions I'd been told to stop asking. I tried to get it through my head that maybe I *hadn't* imagined the whole thing, as everyone had insisted.

"They said it was hypothermia."

"What's that?" he said.

"It's when the body gets too cold and…"

"Oh—*Call of the Wild*!" Lad said with perplexing enthusiasm.

"What?"

"*Call of the Wild*. Jack London? I read about hypothermia in *Call of the Wild*. You don't have it."

"I know—I didn't mean now—never mind. How did you know it was me?"

Lad gave me a side glance as we walked. "I recognized you as soon as you came up from under the water."

"You did? But… you look so different. Don't I look different?"

"Well…" I could swear he darted his eyes at my chest as he searched for the right words. "In some ways. But I knew when I saw your hair."

"My hair?"

"Yes, I've never seen hair like yours. It's the color of wet maple leaves in the fall."

Wow. That was definitely the first time someone had spoken poetically of my hair. Or anything else about me. I felt myself flush.

We stopped at the base of an ancient tree with gnarled limbs starting close to the ground. Lad took both my hands inside his and pulled me to face him. An excited grin lit his face. "Do you know where we are?"

"Um… should I?"

"This is where we first met."

"Really?" I glanced around us. "How do you know? It looks the same as everywhere else out here in the sticks."

Lad laughed. "No it doesn't, Ryann. Besides, *this* is a special tree."

He patted the thick trunk next to us. Looking up into its impossible heights, I spotted something about halfway from the top. It resembled a large nest, resting on the thick branches. I glanced back at Lad. And then I understood.

I backed away with my hands in front of me, shaking my head violently. "Oh no. No. You don't think—I can't climb up there."

Laughing at me again, he said, "You'll be perfectly safe. I'll be right behind you the whole time. There's no reason to be afraid. I promise it'll be worth it."

I wanted to be brave. I really did. I wanted to keep talking with Lad, get some answers, get my book back. But my limbs were frozen, just thinking of climbing the enormous tree. It had always been like that—I couldn't even handle the top bunk at camp.

Lad's large, solid hands settled on my hips. He steered me toward the tree. At his murmured encouragement, I forced myself to lift one foot and place it on the bottom limb, only a couple feet off the ground. I reached up and grabbed a branch above my head. Trembling but trying, I climbed, the heat of Lad's body close behind me. I couldn't decide if it made me want to keep moving or slow down. With him shadowing my every painstaking move, I eventually managed to reach the bottom of the structure.

"Good job. Go ahead and climb in."

He didn't have to tell me twice. I got both my hands on the lip of the thing and pulled as Lad boosted me from below. I rolled into it. Lad followed. For a few minutes I rested, letting my wild heartbeat slow and my shaky arms recover.

Finally I took a look around. It *was* like a bird's nest, only for a terrifyingly large bird. Woven from strong vines and small, flexible branches and lined with an incredibly soft greenish-brown fabric, it was roomy and quite comfortable, actually.

Lad smiled at me triumphantly. "Well?"

"It's amazing. What is this?"

"It's sort of a hideaway—my special place. I built it when I was young. I still come here when I want to think or have some time alone. No one knows about it. Well, except for you. And… it's where I keep things I care about."

He pointed toward a wooden chest on the other side of the nest, weather-worn and old, with strange carvings covering its surface. "Go look inside."

I crawled over to the box, running my hands over its aged smoothness before opening it. The lid was surprisingly heavy. Inside, a haphazard collection of small objects surrounded a stack of books. A ragged hardcover picture book lay on top.

"Book of Virtues..." I spoke the title aloud, tracing the faded letters with one finger and swallowing back a lump in my throat. "I cried so much over this stupid book. I used to sleep with it every night before I lost it. They got me a new copy, but it wasn't the same. My dad came out here a couple days later and searched for this one, but he never could find it. I guess now I know why."

Lad gave me a sheepish look. "I was obsessed with it when I was younger... studying the words and pictures. I assigned magical powers to that book. I thought if I could read it and learn it by heart... it would someday bring you back to me."

"Really?" I wasn't breathing well anymore. "Looks like it worked," I said, hugging the book to my chest. "I'm taking this home with me, you know."

Lad's mouth relaxed into a lazy grin. "Well now... I might find it harder to let go of than I anticipated."

The look on his face made me unsure if he was still talking about the book or about me. He reclined against the side of the nest, watching me, his eyes glowing a bright green unrivaled by the backdrop of leaves framing his head.

Self-consciousness spread over me, raising gooseflesh everywhere his gaze touched. I knew I wasn't hideous or anything—I'd had dates. But I'd never been the girl in the room who everyone looked at, much less stared at for long uninterrupted minutes. I felt like I should say something but couldn't think of a thing. Tearing my eyes away, I reached back into the chest and pulled out another book. A library volume. Thoreau.

"Heaven is under our feet as well as over our heads," Lad said, quoting the author.

And right here in front of me. Lord help me if the boy didn't give me a smile so devastatingly beautiful I had to look down before I could think of a coherent response. "So... *Walden. Call of the Wild.*" I picked up another one. "*A Midsummer Night's Dream.* Shakespeare, huh? If they had fan pods for classic authors, you'd be first in line."

I laughed at my own joke.

Lad did not join me. Instead, his face got deadly serious. He leaned toward me. "Fan pods? You're not in one, are you?"

"Me? No. I never had any interest—"

"Good," he interrupted, seeming strangely relieved.

"Why?"

"Nothing. I just don't think they're... a good idea."

"O-kay." I dragged the word out, tilting my head as I waited for an explanation. When it didn't come, I dropped the topic—it wasn't my favorite one anyway, in spite of the fact that most of my friends talked of nothing else. I was kind of happy Lad shared my disinterest in celebrities and their rabidly devoted fan pods.

"So, you obviously read a lot of literature in home school." I lifted one of the books.

"Actually those are for fun," he said then blushed and looked away, as if embarrassed.

"What? That's a good thing."

He shook his head, still not meeting my eyes. "Not to my parents. They disapprove."

"Really? That's a first. I've never heard of parents who *don't* want their kids to read."

"It's…" Lad waved his hand in a dismissive gesture, apparently eager to change the subject. "… it's just not what we do. My father thinks it's a waste of time."

"Wow. That's so weird. What about your mother?"

"She's not as bad as he is, but she has to agree with him. After all, he—"

Lad checked his speech abruptly, and his eyes widened. After a moment, he continued. "He's the… the head of the family."

"Okay… that sounds pretty old-fashioned, you know."

Lad choked on a laugh. "Yes, you could definitely say my parents are 'old-fashioned.' Anyway, my mother agrees reading books makes me interested in things I shouldn't be… interested… in…" He trailed off slowly, his expression turning intense as he stared at me. He whispered, "I can't believe you're really here."

My stomach did a small flip.

Lad crawled slowly toward me. My breath caught in my throat as he stopped inches away. He reached out, but he didn't actually touch me. His palm ran lightly over the side of my head, barely skimming the outer layer of my hair, the heat from his hand radiating to my scalp. He took the end of one straight damp lock and softly rubbed it between his thumb and fingers as if he were fabric shopping and had found a swath of fine silk to be touched and tested.

Lad wrapped my hair once around his finger and then again, reeling me in. Heart pounding, I studied his face, trying to understand the fascination I saw there and trying to decide if he was about to do what I thought he was about to do.

Somewhere in my brain an alarm went off. It sounded a lot like my mother's voice.

Never want anyone more than he wants you. You can have a man in your life, Ryann, but never need someone. Just let him be icing on the cake.

I was at that moment in serious danger of violating every word of the manifesto I'd had drilled into me for the past year, since my parents had separated. I'd never felt so much wanting of anything in my whole life. I teetered on the edge. I could sense how good it would feel to close that last inch between us and give myself over to the pull I'd felt toward these woods and my shaky memory of Lad these past ten years. Instead, I popped the pretty bubble.

"It doesn't make sense," I blurted out.

"What?" he asked softly, drawing back a few inches.

"If your mom and dad don't want you to read, how do you do home schooling?"

Lad's face contracted in a grimace. He jumped up, stalked to the edge of the nest, and stopped, facing away from me. "I don't want to talk about that anymore."

Well then. Not only had I ruined a very interesting moment, my question had struck some kind of nerve. The silence between us stretched out and became awkward. I thought about the fact that Lad was barefoot and strangely dressed.

When I'd first seen his clothes, I'd pegged him as the indigenous redneck variety of local male. Now, I wondered. *Maybe his family is really poor.* I'd heard of backwoods people living in little more than dirt-floored plywood shacks without even what most would consider the basic necessities. It would explain how I'd seen him out here when I was lost as a child. He hadn't been a hallucination or even lost himself. His family must have lived somewhere out here in the woods. Maybe even on my grandma's property. He must have been ashamed for me to know.

I needed to change the subject, get him talking again. I hadn't even gotten any answers about that night yet. I stood and gingerly made my way across to him and touched him lightly on the arm.

"I'll tell you a secret about me," I offered.

Lad turned around, looking alert and interested. "What is it?"

"I'm completely, totally, and incurably afraid of heights."

He laughed with obvious relief. "Really? I would never have guessed."

I laughed, too, but in the next instant Lad clamped his hand over my mouth and dropped to his knees, pulling me down with him. His entire body was tense. I heard him hiss some kind of foreign-sounding curse under his breath. After a few moments he removed his hand from my mouth and let me go. "Sorry."

"What was that? What happened?"

"Nothing."

"Just body slamming me and cussing for fun?"

"No. Sorry. It's—I saw something. I should take you home now."

"You were so all-fired determined to get me up here, and now you want me to go home? Why? What did you see?"

"A deer. I saw a deer."

"A deer. Well, as far as I know, they don't climb trees or bite."

"I don't want... it to know this place is up here—never mind. It'll be dark soon. Let's get you back before those national guards start looking for you."

"National Guard. It's singular. You know, a group, a unit? How can you not know what that is?"

"Whatever it is, I don't want it out here. Let's go."

Once on the ground, Lad was all business. He scanned in all directions then charged into the thick of the woods. I had to practically jog to keep up. *Wow. He can't wait to get rid of me now.*

I, on the other hand, wanted to slow down, to postpone the end of our journey. My mind was still swimming with questions. I needed to know more about him. I couldn't exactly carry on a conversation with the back of his head, though, especially as winded as I was from trying to match his impossibly long stride.

As we passed the natural pool, Lad glanced back at me and kept going in the direction of Grandma's log house. *He knows how to get there already.* At the edge of the yard Lad stopped and turned to face me. He looked around then stepped close and spoke softly.

"I followed them when they came and took you that morning. I wasn't sure if it was all right for you to go with them, but there were so many men, and I was so small. I understood after they brought you here, it was where you belonged. I wasn't supposed to go close to the houses, but I came back in secret to try to see you again. I watched you in the yard with your family. I heard them call you Ryann."

I couldn't get over the way he said my name. He made it sound beautiful.

"Then one day you were gone and didn't come back. I thought I'd never see you again. And now I can't answer your questions. I'm not even supposed to be talking to you. I'm sorry. You should go in."

Lad took a step back, his jaw set. He nodded, as if having made an irreversible decision. His speech sounded like an ending.

Filled with a sudden sense of desperation, I stepped forward to re-close the distance between us and wrapped my fingers around his wrists. Lad drew in a sharp breath. I saw the light return to his eyes, and his jaw tightened, muscles flexing under the smooth, unblemished skin.

"Lad, don't go yet. That night—I don't know—"

He reached out and took my face in his hands as he'd done when those hands were so much smaller, when my tiny face was so cold. Now his hands were large and warm, and they were trembling.

I stopped breathing, my heart launching into a wild hammering rhythm that seemed to steal all the strength from my legs to power it.

Almost faster than I could process what was happening, Lad brushed his lips across mine in a hint of a kiss then crushed me to his body, his warm mouth grazing my ear.

"Good-bye Ryann." He released me and was gone.

I looked around me. My book was gone, too. I was left standing alone, shaking, and suddenly cold for the first time in months.

Chapter Four
So Much for the Pretty Face

I stumbled through the yard toward the back porch, lightheaded. I really couldn't explain to myself what had just happened. I wasn't even going to attempt to explain it to anyone else. If I told Mom or Grandma, they'd never let me set foot outside again. And I was definitely going back. Lad was at the center of the two strangest experiences of my life. I had to know more about him.

I stepped through the back door into the kitchen, and there was Grandma Neena, sharp blue eyes, wild white ringlets covering her head, and dirt on the knees of her too-short gardening pants. She had a plump fuzzy okra in one hand and a kitchen knife in the other.

"Hey, girl. I was wondering where you'd gotten to."

Grandma Neena had looked exactly the same my whole life. Or maybe it only seemed that way because of the hair. It had been white since I'd known her. Mom said Grandma's hair was once chestnut brown, like mine, but it had turned white when she was only in her twenties, around the time she was widowed. She was sixty and had hardly a wrinkle. Lord only knew how because there wasn't an ounce of fat to stretch out her skin. I hoped I'd inherited the good skin from her along with the freaky-tall-and-thin gene.

"Hey, Grandma. I was out exploring."

She spotted my damp hair and raised a brow. "Get caught in a rain shower?"

"No, I uh…" She knew it hadn't rained, and we both knew there were no lovely spring-fed pools along the *paths* on her land. "I found a natural spring and kind of splashed myself. I was pretty hot."

She looked me over, as if checking for… damage, maybe? Her squint broke and she grinned, turning back to the cooking. "You're just like me, you little wood sprite. I'd be out there myself, if I didn't have this oven going. You didn't see any signs of coyotes, did you?"

"No. Why?"

"I've been hearing them the past couple of nights. Just make sure and get back to the house before dark when you go out. And you should wear some brighter colors—don't want some fool with a gun mistaking you for a critter."

"But hunting season's over. And your land is posted."

"A few rusty old signs won't stop some of these boys. And spring turkey season just ended last week—not everybody obeys the rules. Just be careful, that's all."

"Okay. I'll try my best not to resemble a wild turkey." I laughed and peeked inside the old yellow porcelain bowl on the counter, smelling the savory cornbread mixture she'd been stirring. "Making chicken and dressing?"

"Mmm hmmm. Your momma should be back soon. She had to run by the lawyer's office after the interview—trying to take care of that IRS mess."

"Yeah, thanks, Dad," I muttered. I picked up a knife and started helping her slice vegetables, the blade chop-chopping against the wooden cutting board on the counter.

Grandma flashed a glance at me as she dropped batter-covered coins of okra into a cast iron skillet sizzling with butter.

"None of that, now, Ryann." Her tone was gently chiding. "Your momma's got enough bitter for the both of you. You don't know the whole story, and you need to remember your parents' problems are *theirs*, not yours." She looked back over her shoulder at my expression and turned back to the skillet, shaking her head. She'd always been able to read my face as if my thoughts were scrawled there in permanent black marker. "No, don't go getting all lemon-faced on me. You know I love her more than my own soul, but she's got so much poison inside right now about men—you don't want to let that leak into your life. Love can be good, honey."

After what my dad had pulled, I had my doubts, but what was I going to do—argue with my sweet grandma, who'd lost her husband basically right after the honeymoon ended? I wandered over to inhale the aroma of frying food and gave her a quick side-by-side hug. "Oh my God, that smells good. I swear—absolutely anything tastes good fried."

"You know what they say about Southern cooking— butter's the main course—everything else is just a side dish. Why don't you make us some of your sweet tea to go with supper, and then we can set the table. Maybe there'll be a new job to celebrate." She made a rah-rah gesture.

"Oh—I'm sorry. I can't tonight. I have to get in the shower. Emmy's coming by to pick me up in a little bit." Emmy Rooney had been my best friend since preschool. Our grandmas had been friends forever, too.

"That's good. Where you girls headed tonight?"

"The usual—ballpark, Sonic."

Living in a town of thirty-six hundred people had some advantages. Entertainment variety was not one of them. At least Emmy had a car. Under our new financial circumstances, if I wanted anything above room and board, especially a car, I was buying. That meant finding a job for the summer was my new priority.

An hour later, I heard the crunch and pop of tires winding down the tree-lined gravel driveway. Checking the window first, I went out to the porch. Her VW Bug came to a stop, and out popped Emmy, very little changed since we'd met. Same dark tan, straight, sandy-brown hair, and still wearing glasses, though she'd traded the Hello Kitty frames for some thin silver ones by middle school.

"So you ready for another exciting episode of 'Hicktown Nightlife?'" she said.

"Should I change into my Daisy Dukes and stilettos or am I okay like this?" I gestured to my usual warm-weather uniform of t-shirt, shorts, and flip-flops. We both laughed and got in the car.

Emmy drove us into town and all the way down Main Street, passing darkened storefronts, some small restaurants, the huge First Baptist Church, the Food Star, and the city park with its quaint white gazebo. We cruised slowly through the Sonic Drive-in to see who was there, and then made the loop through town again. Other cars full of teenagers leisurely traveled the same route, windows down, stereos up high. We waved at each one.

"So, I met this guy today..." I said.

Her hands gripped the steering wheel tighter, her interest instantly piqued. "Okay—every detail. Don't hold back. Where, when, and for God's sake, *how* did you meet someone new around here?"

"Apparently he lives out near my grandma. He's homeschooled."

"Hot?" she asked, without much hope.

"Very. In fact, weirdly hot."

"Okay, are we talking Jake-hot or *Nox*-hot?" Emmy put exaggerated lustful emphasis on the last part.

"Hard to say. He's... different." I gave Emmy an abbreviated version of the how-I-met-him story as we pulled into the cool side of the Sonic and parked. I did not mention the part about remembering him from my childhood *incident*. I still didn't know what it all meant, so I could hardly explain it to *her*.

"So you meet an amazing guy in the middle of the woods—why does this kind of thing never happen to me?"

"I guess you should go skinny-dipping more often," I teased.

"I am *totally* going to do it," she said. "And you know I will."

I laughed, not doubting it for a minute. If there were a Wikipedia entry for "boy crazy," Emmy's picture would appear beside it. Unfortunately, she had a chronic weakness for players—guys who were the high school equivalent of womanizers—what was the name for them? Girl-izers? Unlike me, she was always ready to open her heart one more time, to go with her gut and trust that *this* time it would work out.

We studied the menu, pushed the button and ordered. The subject changed to her latest epic crush while we waited for our food in the car, listening to the radio. Emmy loved jocks in particular, and lately it was Jake McKee, a senior with great biceps. She was giving me the play-by-play of their most recent school-hallway flirtation when a sultry-sounding female DJ teased us with promises of celebrity sleaze after the commercial break.

"Oooh—turn it up. I want to hear that," Emmy said.

"Why? You're already some kind of celebrity trivia savant."

"I know, I'm slightly obsessed, but I can't help it. I mean, they're so freakin' beautiful. Like Vallon Foster." She pulled out her phone and caressed the actor's famous face on the screen. Holding the phone up to me, she said, "Look at him. He's almost too gorgeous to live. I can't believe I didn't get into his fan pod—it sucks to be wait-listed."

"Don't feel bad—I heard they favor kids from big cities on those applications. But why do you even want to be in one of those pods? They're like… cults or something."

"No they're *not.*" She shot me a shaming look for suggesting something so blasphemous. "It's cool that A-list celebrities like Vallon give their biggest fans special access. If you think about it, it's not much different from an internship, just way more glam. And you get to go to cool parties, and meet other celebs—oh my God—I have to get in. And you're wrong. It's not only big city kids. Remember Allison Douglas?"

"No."

"Oh. She's like five years older than us. She went to my church. *She* got into a pod a few years ago. I bet she could help me, but nobody around here knows how to reach her anymore. Probably off having too much fun with the beautiful people to keep in touch with anybody back here in this podunk place." Emmy's mood made a lightning-fast swing from gleeful spokesperson to dejected kid.

"But don't you think it's kind of weird—how the pods are like, all the same? It's like some kind of government program or something," I said.

And back to gleeful. "That's totally on purpose. The celebs with fan pods all have the same agent—the *best* agent in Los Angeles—Alfred Frey. He represents all the top singers, and models, and actors. Even the really cute athletes. I read about it in *People*. *I* think it's brilliant. I bet his clients are the most popular *because* they're so connected with their fans. Or... maybe it's how ridiculously gorgeous they are. I mean, look at this girl, Serena Simmons." She picked up one of the magazines littering her car and thrust it under my nose.

I took it from her, studying the improbably perfect face and figure on the cover. "Okay, you're right. She *is* hard not to look at. This says she doesn't even wear any makeup for her close-up shots. How is that possible?"

"I have a theory that they're all part of some secret super-race, and the rest of us were born to worship them," Emmy said, holding her hands in front of her and bowing repeatedly.

I laughed. "Or maybe she's full of it. The guy who airbrushed this probably has his arm in a sling now."

We ate in the car before driving all of a minute and a half to the ballpark. It wasn't quite dark yet, but the stadium lights were already blazing.

"Ooooh, Jake's game has started," Emmy said. "I don't want to miss him batting." She pressed the gas pedal a little harder, leaning forward over the wheel to scope a good parking spot.

For a three-stoplight town, Deep River had a pretty decent ballpark. The complex had three baseball diamonds arranged around a common area with picnic tables and a snack hut. A tall announcers' booth stood behind the backstop of the largest field, the one with the expensive lighting. The smell of grilling hamburgers filled the air. A hint of popcorn, too. It was definitely the place to be on a late spring weeknight. Families and groups of teenagers walked around, and the stands were nearly full at all the fields.

Emmy and I made our way to the bleachers on the home team side of the largest diamond, where the older guys were in a play-off game. We found some space a few rows from the top and sat down so she could scout her number one crush.

"Look at him," she whispered to me in kind of a hushed squeal. She pointed to a big guy with a blond buzz cut—number eight. "Doesn't he look kind of like Thor?"

I followed her pointing finger and located the object of her desire, playing third base. Jake was attractive in an I-spend-hours-a-day-working-on-the-guns-in-the-weight-room kind of way.

"Yeah, he's cute," I said to please her.

Emmy nodded her head furiously and giggled.

"You should be careful with him, though," I warned. "He has a reputation for a reason."

She rolled her eyes at me with a groan. "'Be careful with him. Don't join a fan pod,'" She mocked my warnings in a goofy voice. "I swear, Ryann, you act older than your grandma. *Your* hair's gonna turn white if you don't relax and live a little. Are you honestly telling me you don't want a nibble of that man-candy?"

I shrugged, abashed, and looked away from her, out toward the players running in from the outfield. I certainly didn't mind muscles on a guy, but Jake wasn't my type. I really preferred the long and lean variety. Hard, rather than puffed-up. *More like Lad... or him...*

My gaze landed on a guy walking past our section of bleachers. Nox was lanky and tall with wavy hair so shiny dark brown it bordered on black. It looked like he'd showered just before coming here and let the air from the rolled-down car windows dry his hair on the way. He wore some well-aged jeans, a vintage AC/DC t-shirt, and western boots, in spite of the steamy night. He had a swaggering way of walking, lazily stretching out one long leg after the other, moving slowly past the stands with his eyes on the field.

Oh, and he was stunning. In fact, he would've looked quite natural in one of Emmy's magazines.

Emmy followed my stare. "Gorgeous jerk," she whispered with a conspiratorial grin. "*He* looks sort of like Vallon Foster, doesn't he? Too bad he totally knows it."

"Yeah," I agreed. Every female under the age of thirty in Deep River was aware of Nox Knight. He'd started at DRHS a few months ago. Anyone new in town would have made waves, but this guy had caused an estrogen tsunami.

He wasn't *just* good-looking—he'd moved here from California, had his own band and the bad-boy musician attitude to go with it. Like everyone else, I liked to look at him, but I'd known better than to dive in. Not that I'd ever been invited into the water.

I was still watching Nox when he glanced up in our direction. Sucking in a quick breath, I turned my head. When I peeked back again, he'd gone about his way. He hadn't noticed me—as usual.

"Oh, Shay's here. Come on," Emmy said, craning her neck toward the parking lot. She got up and started stepping over seats to get to the bleacher stairs. I followed.

Shay Cook was also a junior, with shiny dark curls and perfect skin. She'd won the Squash Blossom pageant the previous weekend. To make it even worse, she was a total brain and so sweet you couldn't hate her for being pretty and smart. We caught up with her near the snack bar.

"Hey, sorry I couldn't make it to the pageant. We were buried in moving boxes, and my mom was freaking out. Congratulations," I said.

"Thanks." She made the whoop-tee-doo signal with her hand. "Whichever contestant looks the most like a gourd wins." She performed a little curtsy.

"No, she was totally the best one." Emmy gave Shay's shoulder a playful poke.

"What was your onstage question? How to achieve world peace?" I teased.

Shay laughed. "No. They asked where I would take a tourist visiting Deep River if I wanted to impress them."

We all giggled at the thought of anyone being impressed by anything in Deep River. "I thought for sure she was gonna say the Sonic." Emmy laughed at her own joke.

"Right. No, I b-s'd something about the railroad museum and the historic library building. I don't remember exactly what I said—I was pretty nervous."

"You *should* have said you'd bring them here to check out the cute guys in their baseball uniforms." Emmy shot a dreamy glance over at the dugout where Jake now sat with his teammates.

"Yeah, or take them to drool over Nox, shirtless at the pool club," I added.

Just then, Emmy looked past me, high over my shoulder. "Hey Nox. What's up?"

I whipped my head around and stared right at the faded lightning symbol between the AC and DC on an ancient black t-shirt. I had to tilt my head back to see the face of its owner. This was the nearest I'd ever been to him. He was even better-looking at close range. Not goldenly perfect like Lad—Nox's hotness was messy around the edges—but everything about him made your eyes *very* happy.

He was a senior who looked old enough to be in college. Probably one of those guys who started shaving at thirteen out of actual necessity instead of wishful thinking. I'd never been close enough before to see his eye color, but they were a beautiful hazel, the light irises encircled by an outer ring of deeper color. He flashed me a wicked smile.

Oh God. How much did he overhear?

He addressed Emmy, but nodded in my direction. "So, what's up tonight with Emmy and the Amazon?"

So much for the pretty face. At five-foot-ten, I'd heard every tall joke in the book, "Amazon" the least funny of them all. He could've been a little more original. Besides, we'd never actually spoken before—it was awfully familiar of him to tease me when we didn't even know each other.

My irritation must've shown because he laughed and winked one of those mysterious greenish-brown eyes at me. I felt the blood rush to my face. He *was* actually looking down at me, though. That didn't happen every day. I guessed he was about six-foot-four. So *not* my type. I usually preferred shorter guys who were a little more... manageable.

"Nox, you know Ryann, right? And this is Shay Cook. I'm not sure if you've met," Emmy said.

Nox didn't even glance over at Shay or acknowledge he'd heard her name. Instead he continued staring at me like a starving cat perusing a tank of overfed goldfish. It was completely unnerving.

"Do you have plans tomorrow night?" Nox asked, his tone soft and low.

"What?" My voice sounded as confused as my face must have looked.

Nox seemed completely comfortable standing there, silent and studying me with those remarkable eyes. I, however, was anything but comfortable.

"I… we, uh… I think we might be busy." I looked over at Emmy and Shay for help, for all the good it did me. They offered nothing but silly grins.

He puffed out a laugh and started to respond when a baseball came out of nowhere and hit him solidly in the thigh. It fell at his feet with a thud. We all looked around to see where it had come from. Two little boys, around four or five years old, stood a few yards away staring wide-eyed at Nox. It wasn't hard to figure out what had happened.

Nox bent to pick up the baseball and walked over to the look-alike boys, who were still motionless, their small hands straight down by their sides. I felt bad for them. His size intimidated *me*—to them, he must have looked like Goliath.

He crouched right in front of them, getting down to their eye level, and held out the ball. "Who threw this?"

Neither boy opened his mouth. The smaller one looked like he might cry. I could almost feel their terror. Thinking I should intervene, I started in their direction but stopped in surprise when Nox cracked a smile.

"Well, *somebody's* got a pretty good arm. Wow. That was quite a throw." He rubbed his thigh with one hand.

Now both boys enthusiastically spoke up. "I did!" said the shorter one.

"I think it was me," argued the other.

"You're brothers, right? Hmm… I wonder who's stronger?"

AMY PATRICK

"Me!" The older boy said. He raised his skinny arm in a body-builder pump to show-off a non-existent bicep. The younger one copied him, eager to impress Nox as well.

"You both look pretty strong to me. Keep working on that fastball. Here you go—catch." He tossed the baseball gently to the smaller brother, and the little guys ran off together, obviously thrilled.

Okay, so he wasn't a jerk *every* minute of the day. Nox sauntered back over to our group, amusement still lifting his face. When he turned to me, the cocky grin reappeared.

"You should come check out my band." He pulled a rumpled flyer out of his back pocket, addressing all of us, but putting it in my hand and giving me the same intense stare from earlier. "We're playing in Oxford this weekend. Come. Really, I'd love to see you there. I've gotta go. Shay, Emmy, nice to see you. Ryann…"

Nox's gaze lingered on me then he gave us all a smile premeditated to dazzle before he turned and walked off. The three of us watched him stroll away.

"Wow-ow-ow," Shay said when he was out of hearing range, "What is the speed limit to Oxford so I can break it tomorrow night?"

"Did you see the way he was looking at you, Ryann? I think he's into you." Emmy said.

"He's never even talked to me before, and he invited all of us," I argued.

"Technically. But I bet he couldn't pick me and Shay out of a lineup. Sorry, girlfriend."

Shay shrugged. "It's okay. I could enjoy that one even vicariously. And anyway, our Saturday night just started looking a whole lot better. We're going, aren't we, y'all?"

"Will your mom let you go to Oxford?" Emmy asked me.

"I think so. It's only thirty minutes away, but I don't know if we should—"

"Good. 'Cause it's our last weekend as Juniors, and it has to rock!" Emmy threw a fist up in the air and punctuated her proclamation with a whoop.

"Sure, okay," I agreed, wondering what I was getting myself into as we left the park.

At home, I found Mom curled up on the couch with Grandma's dog Frisky, mesmerized by an entertainment news show. She didn't move as I entered the room.

"Mom?"

She finally turned to me, her eyes unfocused. She looked almost dazed—exhausted from a full day, no doubt. "Hey, how'd it go, babe?"

I sat down beside her, reaching over to give the elderly dachshund a gentle tummy rub. "Not bad. We watched a pretty good game. How was your interview at Channings?"

"Surprisingly painless. I *somehow* managed to convince them I'm employable."

"You got the job? That's great. When do you start?"

"Monday. I think I'm really going to like it."

"Really? So, you really wouldn't be creeped out working at a funeral home?"

She laughed. "Oh for Heaven's sake, Ryann, I won't be handling bodies—I'll be the receptionist and help the families with funeral planning, listen if they want to talk, host evening visitations, that kind of thing. I think I'll actually be pretty good at it."

I didn't doubt it. My mother had always been a people-magnet. She was a good listener and always ready to cry with anyone who needed accompaniment.

"Anyway, I need a paycheck," she continued, "and the classifieds section of the Deep River Herald isn't exactly expansive. I'm lucky to get any kind of job that doesn't involve scrubbing toilets or working a deep fryer."

"Now *I* need to find something," I said. Problem was, the only thing scarcer in Deep River than a full-time job opening was a part-time job opening.

"You will. We're going to be just fine, both of us." Mom patted my hand. She sounded like she was trying to convince herself more than me. "Of course things will still be tight—my salary isn't exactly huge. And the lawyer told me today I'm definitely on the hook for your dad's delinquent taxes, even though we're divorcing. I'm sure they'll garnish my wages."

I sank deeper into the couch, drawing my knees up and wrapping my arms around my bare legs, which were getting cold in the air-conditioning.

"But you weren't even working the whole time y'all were married."

"I know, honey, but we filed jointly, and that means I'm as much responsible for paying the IRS as Daddy is."

"Well, that sucks. Why doesn't he pay?"

"Don't say 'sucks.' It sounds rude. Daddy claims he has no savings, and now he has no income. They already took the house in town, but it didn't cover the whole debt. So, legally, I'm the next stop. Basically, the IRS doesn't care who pays them, as long as somebody does."

"How much is it?" I threw the question out there casually, as if she'd actually share that detail with me.

Mom looked up at me and hesitated then dropped her gaze to the sleepy dog in her lap, stroking the top of his tiny skull. "Don't worry about it, Ryann. It's not your problem. I'll figure it out." She was using her ultra-calm voice. The one she only used when things were seriously bad.

That must be some big number. "Well, when I find a job—"

"No. Absolutely not. When you find a job, you'll save your money for a car. I know you want one. This is not something you can fix, so don't try." She leaned over, wrapped her arm around me, and spoke into my hair. "Thanks, though, babe. You're a great kid, you know that?"

I flushed at her praise, but worry still plagued me. Drawing back to see her face, I asked, "Are we going to lose this house, too? And the land? Grandma told me she put it in your name years ago."

Mom's lips thinned as she pressed them together. She was obviously not pleased with her mother for letting that bit of info slip. "I won't let that happen. The lawyer says there's one more thing he can try legally. It's called an 'innocent spouse' petition. It says while we were married I was not the income earner and was not aware your father didn't pay taxes when he was supposed to. It's a long shot, but it's worth a try."

"And what if *that* doesn't work?"

"If it doesn't work… we'll find some other way to hang onto the house. Actually…" She stopped right there.

"Actually?"

"Well, there *is* a possibility I could raise a great deal of money very quickly to pay off the debt," she said, letting her gaze drift back to the television.

"How?" I couldn't begin to imagine. Was there some precious family heirloom we could sell on eBay?

She gave a quick head shake. "I'll let you know when and if it becomes necessary." Her tone made it clear the subject was closed for now. She pried her eyes from the screen to shoot me a sideways glance. "Your father left another message for you on the machine tonight. Apparently he's in *Miami* now."

I shrugged. "I know. He left one on my cell earlier, too."

That got her attention. She twisted back to face me. "Oh, did you already call him back?"

"No."

"Well, are you going to?"

"No."

Mom turned her head in an effort to conceal the smile creeping across her face. Some kids I knew from divorced families said their parents sheltered them from the whole thing, trying not to say anything bad about the other parent. Not my mom. She was old school—if I wanted to hate my father that was more than fine with her.

For an allegedly brilliant professor, Michael Carroll seemed to be sticking pretty close to the midlife crisis 101 textbook. Affair? Check. Experimental facial hair? Check. And now he was apparently a beach bum, too. Super. I didn't know what could have caused him to go off the deep end like this, but there was no excuse good enough in my book.

"Well, I hope he's calling to say he's done with his little 'sabbatical' from Ole Miss while he finds out if he still has a 'passion' for teaching," Mom said. "He needs to have more *passion* for sending the child support checks. *And* paying the IRS. Never need a man, Ryann. Don't make the same mistakes I made. You finish college, have your career, and then if you want a man in your life, let him be—"

"I know, I know. Icing on the cake." I sourly finished the prescription I knew so well. Thinking about my dad made me grumpy. And her never-ending warnings about love and dating made me even grumpier.

I turned away from the wounded expression on her face to the beautiful TV show hosts making happy talk with each other and gushing over some actress's new haircut. Why was everyone so into these crappy celebrity stalk-fests? Even my mom. It just didn't fascinate me like everyone else I knew.

After a moment of uncomfortable silence, Mom got up and left the room. Great.

Clicking off the TV remote, I headed for my own room. On the way, I peeked in on her and heard muffled sobs rising from the bed. I almost eased the door shut again and kept going.

Instead I climbed in next to Mom and stroked the back of her hair until she quieted down. We didn't talk. I still didn't know what to say to fix it all. I guess you get what you pay for when your divorce therapist is a sixteen year old who's never even had a real boyfriend.

CHAPTER FIVE
SILENCE

The next morning I got out of the house as early as I could and headed for the natural pool. I probably should have been beating the streets, looking for that job. Instead I spent my Saturday waiting in the woods. Well, not exactly the entire day—after wasting my morning hours waiting at the pool, I borrowed Grandma's car and went to the library, hoping to spot a tousled golden head bent over a desk in some corner. I left with a stack of books and disappointment.

Now I was back in the woods, sitting on a huge rock near the pool, hoping Lad would appear out of nowhere as he had before. That hope turned into several hours of nothing but squirrel chatter and mosquito bites. I pulled a clump of moss from the rock and threw it at a nearby tree trunk. It connected with a satisfying thunk. I blew away a piece of hair sticking to my face. *What am I doing?* I wasn't usually this pathetic when it came to guys. But I needed to see Lad again—had to. I would not give up so easily.

Sweaty, aggravated, and bored, I got up and moved to the bank of the pool to dunk my feet in. Just my feet. I wasn't going to swim out here without a bathing suit again. *Or maybe I should. Maybe that would—*

My eyes darted around, searching the bright woods. What had changed? Had I seen a flash of movement in the trees? Heard a noise that was out of place? No, it was actually very quiet. Maybe that's what it was, the absence of the usual woodsy murmur.

As the silence stretched on, the feeling of being watched, of another presence, grew stronger. I stood and looked up, turning in a circle, searching the branches overhead.

"Lad?"

No answer.

No Lad.

The busy forest noises resumed, and my excitement drained away. It was time to go home and get ready to go out with Emmy and Shay. Maybe Lad had come *here* earlier and was at the library *now*. It was possible we'd just missed each other. It was also possible he didn't want to see me again.

CHAPTER SIX
DROOLING GROUPIES

"The Hidden... what kind of a name is that for a band?" Emmy studied the flyer as we searched an alley off Oxford's town square for the club entrance.

"Oh, you know, it's one of those artsy musician things." Shay skipped a little on the sidewalk, bouncing to a stop. "I like it. It sounds mysterious. I think it fits him."

"Here it is," Emmy said. "Now, if we can get in it'll be a miracle. We don't even have fake I.D.'s."

"I bet Nox put our names on some kind of list. Or at least *one* of our names," Shay teased, bumping shoulders with me. We got to the door, and the guy working it predictably asked to see our driver's licenses.

"We all forgot them tonight. Can you believe it?" Emmy gave him a big smile and lied with impressive confidence. "I think we're on the list, though. Emmy, Shay, and Ryann?"

A guilty tremor shook my fingers. My heart pounded, echoing the drumbeat of the music spilling out of the club. I'd never even thought of attempting anything like this before. Was it arrest-worthy? My mom thought we were at the movies. She would K-I-L-L kill me if she ever found out I went to a bar.

"Yeah. I got Ryann here. Yeah, okay, Nox said to let you and your friends in," the bouncer said, shining a penlight on his clipboard. He looked up at us again, suspiciously checking out our baby faces, then stepped back and waved us in. "All right. But remember your I.D.'s next time, *ladies.*"

The music was reverberating through my internal organs before we'd even fully entered the building. It was a small club with brick walls and a thickly packed college crowd. The smell of beer filled the air. We moved past the entrance, and getting a clear view of the stage, I stopped dead.

Nox was there in the center. Bathed in the gold-colored stage lights, he'd looked like Lad for a second. The lights changed to red, the illusion dissolved, allowing my heart to re-start. But they did share a certain similarity. Their coloring was completely opposite, but something… I don't know, maybe it was like all those supermodels Emmy could name.

If you really looked at them, no matter what their hair color was, or what race they might have been, they almost all looked like the same person. Maybe it was the symmetry thing, or that gorgeous was gorgeous however you mixed and matched the colors and textures.

Or maybe I was becoming obsessed.

We stood watching the band playing a rock-jazz fusion instrumental with a hypnotic beat, and I involuntarily moved in place to the music. It was dark. I had no idea whether Nox saw me standing there—hopefully not. I wasn't even sure what I was doing here. He wasn't my type. In fact, he was exactly the type I was careful to avoid.

Still, it was fascinating to watch his fingers coax silky riffs out of that electric guitar. It was hard to miss how muscular his upper body and arms were, presumably from hours of practicing his aggressive playing technique. Nox's dark gray skin-tight t-shirt was soaked from his efforts. His inky hair was also drenched, and beads of perspiration glowed in the uplights shining on his face. I'd never appreciated before that performing music could be an athletic event. Or how sexy sweat could be.

When the song ended, the band took a break. To my dismay, Shalena called out to Nox, waving him over.

He jumped off the stage and came to us, smiling widely, towering over us. "Emmy, Shay—glad you could make it." He turned his forehead into his sleeve, wiping it quickly before facing me. His gaze traveled from my face slowly down my body and up again. "Ryann," the word came out in a purr. "You look nice tonight."

In an attempt to look older, I'd upped my usually non-existent fashion game for the evening. My typical shorts-and-t-shirt combo had been replaced by a short black sundress. It wasn't clingy, but it was strapless and showed my figure more than my usual attire—a fact I regretted as Nox's attention lingered on my shape.

"Um, thanks," I mumbled, tearing my gaze away from his too-interested eyes and dropping it to his feet instead. They moved closer, and I got a hint of citrus and cedarwood from his warmed skin.

"I trust you had no trouble getting in?" he asked in a low voice close to my ear.

I fell back a step and flared my eyes at my friends, willing them to enter the conversation. Nothing. My words were rushed and impatient as I finally answered him. "No, it was fine. The bouncer had our names."

An amused grin sneaked across his face. "That's interesting, considering I only gave him *yours*... Rye."

My eyes widened as my heart gave a hard thump. His grin spread. He was *trying* to make me uncomfortable, with the suggestive look, the new nickname, the disturbing closeness.

I hated guys who played mind games. I didn't get the chance to protest though because Nox was pulled away from us by another group of patrons, all female. Looked like he had a good start on his own little fan pod. For the next few minutes, he held court, laughing, posing for pictures, and playing the rock star. I was suddenly embarrassed to have come. I definitely did *not* want to be counted among his groupies.

Nox darted his eyes over at me, probably to confirm that I saw him surrounded by adoring women, before he jumped back on stage to start the next set.

I was way past ready to go by the time the drums started up. It was so loud I had trouble communicating that to Emmy and Shay. Besides, they were smiling and having a great time, so I decided to go outside alone and wait for them. I was almost to the exit when Nox's amplified voice echoed through the club.

"Hold on," he sang, drawing out both words.

Though I didn't want to, I stopped and turned back around. It seemed I had lost control of my own body.

"I'd like to dedicate this song to the most beautiful girl in the room."

There were screams as every star-struck girl there reacted, each clearly hoping the song was for her. But Nox stared past the crowd and the lights directly at me. I was pinned in place as he began to sing.

Suddenly, I was willing to cut the drooling groupies some slack. I didn't know how to describe Nox's voice, except to say I'd never heard anything like it. It was beyond beautiful. It was like sex for your eardrums. At least how I imagined sex would be. I was immobilized, mesmerized, transported. Tears welled up in my eyes, which was weird because I never cried.

"Pretty awesome, aren't they?"

The bouncer. I hadn't realized he was standing right beside me.

"They've only been playing here a few weeks," he continued, "and we're getting swarmed—even had some record label scouts. It's great for business. I told my boss I should get a raise because I'm the one who put them on You Tube."

He was clearly enjoying the music, but he wasn't affected by it in the same way as all the girls in the bar. Every last one of them, Emmy and Shay included, were focused on the stage as if the Pied Piper had come to life and poured himself into a pair of size thirty-four extra-long boot cut jeans.

I nodded mutely in response to the bouncer. Something deep inside was trying to pull me toward the stage—where I'd do what—scream like those other girls? Worship at the altar of Nox? *No thank you.* I fought the strange allure of the music until the song segued into a spooky guitar solo. Finally managing to gain enough control over my lower limbs, I backed toward the door, even more anxious to get out of there than before. Because Nox was no longer just arrogant.

Now he was terrifying.

CHAPTER SEVEN
CATCH AND RELEASE

The next day after church Mom went to a baby shower, and I headed out to look for Lad again. After being in Nox's strangely disturbing presence last night, I was craving the inviting warmth of Lad even more.

"Home before dark, remember?" Grandma Neena called out to me as I left the house. Unlike Mom, she never argued with me about hiking. She got it—she was an outdoors girl, too. Of course, she had no idea my enthusiasm for the woods these days had nothing to do with the flora and fauna.

"I will. Don't worry," I called back.

This time I took a different approach, trying first to find Lad's nest hideaway. No luck. I walked the paths calling his name, feeling more than a little foolish. Finally, not knowing what else to do, I went back to the spring-fed pool where I sat in the soft ferns, plucking the fronds apart leaf by leaf, listening, watching, waiting. Same pointless activities as yesterday. It was official—I *was* pathetic.

And I was done. I got up and brushed myself off, picking through the low brush back toward the path.

Maybe his parents had found out about all the reading and grounded him. Maybe he was too busy with home schooling. Maybe he just didn't care if he ever saw me again. I had no way of knowing why he didn't show up. It was only after I started hiking home that I got my answer.

Frustrated and uninterested in nature by this point, I took the main footpath toward the house instead of venturing off it and exploring, as I'd done on the way to the pool. It was getting late, the afternoon sun quickly sinking into the treetops. I picked up my pace. Sure, I was confident in the woods—*before* dark.

About halfway home, I spotted something out of place through the pines and dogwoods and sweet gum trunks. I couldn't tell what it was—large, brown, motionless. Slowing down, I moved cautiously toward the mysterious shape.

The loud buzz of flies made my skin crawl. My brain finally registered what my eyes were seeing right as the smell hit me. A deer carcass—a doe. Oh, my stomach did not feel good. Holding my arm over my face, I pressed my nose deep into my shirtsleeve as I circled her lifeless body.

Seeing the gunshot wound in her neck shocked me. Deer season had ended months ago, and no one was supposed to hunt on our land ever. It looked like she'd been killed no more than a day ago. I hadn't heard any rifle fire. *Must have happened last night while we were all away from home.*

I stood there debating what to do next. Call the Sheriff's office? Tell Mom?

I immediately decided against both options, knowing either would be the absolute death of any future hikes. Mom would ban me forever from the woods if she ever thought illegal "hunters" had been on our property.

The sound of movement behind me broke my deliberation. My stomach went watery as I heard a low rumbling growl. I whirled around. A coyote. My legs locked as another growl, equally as menacing, joined the first.

The second coyote appeared from the underbrush, flanking its mate. Both of them had teeth bared, hackles up, and were staring directly at me. With my back to the slain doe, I had no doubt what had drawn the coyotes there. I was standing between them and their feast. My scent must've been overpowered by the smell of decomposing flesh until they got close.

I'd heard coyotes rarely attacked people, and in fact, would cower in the presence of a human. Someone forgot to tell these two.

I saw no sign of cowering. The small part of my brain still capable of it searched my memory for the appropriate action. Was I supposed to play dead or make loud noises? I couldn't remember which, and I really didn't want to make the wrong choice.

What I wanted was to step out of the way, or more accurately, *run* as far and as fast as possible out of the way, and let them have at the dead deer. I took an experimental half-step backward with one foot. The coyotes snarled louder and stepped forward several paces.

A few more steps in my direction by the pair, another step in retreat by me, and my feet stumbled on the doe's legs. My back scraped a thick tree trunk. There was no escape for me now.

My pulse rocketing through my veins, I scanned the ground immediately around me for a stick or anything I could use to at least make killing me more inconvenient. The beasts broke their stalking pattern and charged toward me. With a scream, I squeezed my eyes shut tight.

There was a sudden and deafening guttural cry close to my ear, and my heart flew into my throat as something grabbed me hard around the waist. I was hauled upward. The crushing tension around my middle now pressed up painfully into my rib cage. It wasn't the excruciating sensation I'd been bracing myself for—teeth tearing into my skin—but it was no less frightening than a coyote attack. Wind and small branches whipped my face as I was pulled higher, higher. The motion stopped with an abrupt thump, and I sat hard against a solid but pliable surface. I began to shiver. Somehow I was still alive, not in pain, and sixty feet off the ground. I turned my head, looking for the explanation.

And saw his face.

"Lad." I blinked several times as my brain tried to process it.

Lad tightened his hold around my waist with one arm, and with the other hand stroked my hair. "You're safe now. It's okay. They can't get you up here."

They. I peered down at the feeding frenzy far below. The coyotes ripped at the deer carcass, snarling and snapping at each other in their greed for the dead flesh. The sound was nauseating. I couldn't help picturing my own body in place of the doe's.

Awareness of my surroundings began to return as the near-death panic subsided. Lad was holding me securely on his lap, my back to his chest, and my thighs supported by his own steely legs. The scent of him was all around me, too, fresh like the woods and a little salty. I inhaled deeply. It was the fragrance of safety.

Lad was really here, and I was wrapped in his arms, cradled by his body. I twisted again to see him. Impossibly-green eyes glinted with what looked like worry.

"Are you injured?" he asked.

I wasn't hurt, but I was breathless. Probably in shock. Also, hearing his voice again, so much more beautiful than I'd remembered, and seeing his flawless face so close after days of searching and finding nothing was disorienting. I started considering the hallucination theory again.

"Are you real?"

His eyes crinkled slightly at the corners as the edges of his mouth pulled upward. "You're always asking me that."

"I've spent most of my life doubting my memories of you. It's a habit. But here you are—you saved me." I looked at the ground again, shaking my head in wonder. "How…"

"Yes, well, I couldn't sit and watch as you became coyote chow."

"Right. Thank you. That was… close."

Another full body shudder rocked me, and Lad gently tightened his hold. I peeked down at the ground again. Mistake. Turning my head back, I pressed my cheek for a moment against Lad's solid chest to let the vertigo pass.

He was wearing leather pants that nearly reached his knees, and like the last time I'd seen him, his feet were bare. But today he wore a collarless shirt with a wide open neck. It was soft and thin, of a strange, almost sheer material. The heat of his skin passed through it to my face. He hugged me close and rested his chin on the top of my head. The vibration of his deep voice hummed through my cheek as he spoke.

"You didn't answer my question, Ryann. Are you hurt? I was worried I might have been too late."

I shook my head. "I'm fine. You were just in time. I thought it was all over. Where did you come from?"

"I was… nearby. Unfortunately, I was so busy watching you, I didn't notice the coyotes until too late. If I'd seen them sooner, I would've scared them away before they ever got close. You must have been terrified."

I raised my head to look at him. "You were watching me? Why didn't you say something, let me know you were there?"

Lad sighed heavily. "There are strict rules about contact with...outsiders. Rules I've broken three times now." He shook his head side-to-side in a gesture of dismay.

"Really? You couldn't even talk to me? Not once? I've been looking for you," I said.

After a long moment he answered, "I know. I saw you, heard you. I stayed out of your sight, up in the treetops. I... followed you." He hesitated, looking embarrassed. "I wanted to talk to you again, to see you. But it didn't— doesn't matter what *I* want." He brushed the thought away with an irritated hand gesture.

"Why? What do you mean?"

"The last time we were together, Ryann... someone saw us. That's not good—for me. For you... it's dangerous." He stroked a long finger lightly across my cheekbone and something in his eyes looked pained. His words were a whisper. "You are so beautiful up close."

My belly went crazy with a sudden release of butterflies. I could hardly believe what I was hearing—Lad saying something like that about me—it was too close to the fantasies I'd been having about him. And some of the other stuff he'd said was just... weird.

"I can't stop shaking. I don't think my fear of heights has improved. Can we get down?" "Well, we can't go down the way we came up, at least until they're finished." He nodded to the pack below us. "If you want to get to the ground, you're going to have to trust me. It'll get a bit worse before it can get better, okay?"

I reconsidered staying right where we were until the coyotes had moved on. But I really did want the earth under my feet again, so I could focus on what Lad was telling me. I'd finally found him again, and I was too frazzled to focus.

Also, I needed to put some distance between our bodies so I could think straight. The warm pressure of his skin against mine was *not* helping my confusion.

"Turn toward me," he instructed.

"What are you going to do?" My voice rose with my intensifying acrophobia. "You'll have to hold on to me. I'll need a free hand."

I obeyed and shifted my body, so Lad and I were chest to chest. He was sitting on a wide branch with his back against the trunk, and me sideways on his lap. The hard bands of his arms were still wrapped protectively around me, letting me maneuver without fear of falling. Well, *much* fear.

"Good, now put your arms around my waist," he said.

I reached around Lad's back. Powerful muscles flexed under my palms. So much for relieving my frazzled state, but I assumed we were getting there.

"Great. Now, move one leg to the other side of my lap."

"What?" I blinked in instant embarrassment.

"It's okay. You're going to straddle my legs for a minute, so I can move to lift us up." At this rate the frazzled state would last the rest of my life. My arms and legs trembled. I wasn't sure if it was from fear or the discomforting intimacy of our position. Lacking a better plan though, I followed his instructions.

Raising my body so one knee pressed into his thigh, I raised my other leg up and over his lap. That accomplished, I ungracefully plopped back down, now sitting astride him, clinging desperately.

"Okay, now slide your arms up around my neck."

I complied, and then we were up. I instinctively wrapped my legs around his waist as he lifted me. "You're going to drop me. I'm too heavy."

Lad laughed out loud and held me against him with one arm while grabbing an overhead branch with another. "Do I look like I'm struggling?"

"No… you seem to be doing pretty well, actually, but I'm not exactly dainty."

The side of his mouth quirked in bemusement and one eyebrow went up. "I would argue, but this is probably not the best moment for me to detail exactly what I think of your body, so we're going to move now. Don't be afraid, Ryann. There's no way you can fall. I have you, and I'm not letting go. Ready?"

I nodded, but internally, I was in a deep panic. Lad kept one arm wrapped around me, extending the other out to the side for balance. He began walking along the large branch. I looked down at his bare feet gripping the bark, moving steadily and swiftly along toward the branch's end.

It was amazing, but I also saw the ground spinning impossibly far below us. I buried my face in his neck.

He jumped, and I glanced up long enough to tell we were in a different tree, its soft green leaves brushing my face. It occurred to me I might be choking Lad with my death grip around his neck. I tried to loosen it.

Lad dipped his chin and nuzzled my cheek, murmuring, "Let go of your fear, Ryann. Trust me and try to enjoy the ride."

I looked up to meet his gaze. I was trying. Then he leapt to the next branch, and I buried my face and squeezed again for all I was worth. Sometimes he made a small jump down, sometimes to a slightly higher branch, steadily taking us west, further away from the coyote pack. We finally stopped in a tree near a clearing, perched on its lowest branch, about twenty feet from the ground.

"Okay, it's all over. Not so bad, right?" Lad leaned back against the trunk, attempting to loosen my petrified fingers.

At first, I clung tighter, but eventually let him pry my grip from his neck and torso and attempted to cut off the circulation to his fingers instead. "How on Earth did you do that?" I asked when I could finally manage speech.

He shrugged. "It's not hard. I've been doing it since I was a toddler."

Bending his knees to level his eyes with mine, Lad searched my face. I'm not sure what he saw, but even a county fair fortune teller should have been able to tell I wasn't doing all that well. He broke into a grin, his eyebrows rising in apparent amusement.

"Don't you dare laugh at me, Tarzan," I snarled.

"Who's Tarzan?"

"You've got to be kidding me."

"Listen, will you be okay to stay here for a minute? It's a secure spot. Hold on here." He took one of my hands and placed it on a y-shaped offshoot near my shoulder. "And here." He placed the other hand on a branch about the diameter of my forearm. I gripped it greedily. "I'll be right back," he said.

"Where are you going?" I demanded, my panic level rising again.

"Don't worry. You're coming with me in a moment."

That had me more worried, actually, because I realized he was about to jump to the ground.

"Oh no," I started to protest, but it was too late. He'd stepped off the branch and dropped, in the way a normal person might have done on the side of a swimming pool, with water waiting inches below. Nothing waited for Lad but a twenty-foot plunge to the ground.

He slipped below the branch and landed lightly on the earth as if he'd hopscotched to the spot instead of falling out of a tree. He looked up at me and smiled.

My breath left me in a whoosh. It might have been the surprise of seeing him jump and execute the landing. Or maybe it was the sheer beauty of his smile that left me breathless once again.

"I guess you've been doing that since you were a toddler, too?" I yelled down.

"Of course not. That would be suicide. I was at least seven before I made a jump from such a height." Lad held his arms up to me. "Okay, now you."

"Now me, what?"

"Drop, and I'll catch you," he said as if it was obvious.

It might have been—to him. To me, it was out of the question. "No. No thanks. I can't do that. When I was seven, I was still riding with training wheels. I'll stay here." I looked around for something, a staircase or an elevator to appear, I guess.

"Really, Ryann. It's going to be all right. I will catch you. There's no chance you'll get hurt."

"If I jump down, there's every chance I'll die."

He laughed again out loud. "You won't die. I promise. I rescue terrified girls from trees all the time. It's much easier than saving them from coyotes, and look how well *that* turned out." Knowing I had no choice, I girded myself for my first and what I vowed would be my last leap from a tree. Nudging my way to the edge of the limb, I offered up a silent prayer and stepped off the bough. My body hurtled through the air. My eyelids squeezed tight, tensing for impact. It never came.

Lad's hands and arms materialized gently under me as if I'd simply rolled out of bed instead of falling from such a height. I opened my eyes again to his very pleased expression. He held me high against his chest, his muscled arms pressing into me, supporting me like I weighed nothing.

"I'm alive," I said with a little laugh.

Lad grinned. "See what happens when you trust me?"

I couldn't answer. Now that I was no longer in mortal fear of plummeting to my death, I was acutely aware of how close his face was to mine. Impossibly, his eyes were even brighter than before, the delicious fresh-green color of growing things.

Part of me knew I should stop staring at him, but I couldn't seem to. *He's really here.* The living breathing reality of him was so much better than any memory could ever be. He set me down, keeping his hands on my waist.

"Ryann, can you stand?" He released me. "There you go. Safe and sound on solid ground."

He was right. I looked down at the green grass beneath my feet then up at our surroundings. The daylight was almost gone. The red and gold of sunset had faded into gray streaks low in the sky. A shiver worked its way through my body.

"Are you all right?" Lad pulled me close again. Heat radiated through his paper-thin shirt, bathing me in warmth everywhere he touched me.

"Yes. Wow. You're really, really warm."

He held me away from him at arm's length. "Sorry. Am I making you hot?"

An involuntary giggle slipped past my lips. *Yes.* "It feels good. I like warm. Thank you," I said. "And thank you for saving my life. I don't even care that you were following me. You showed up when it mattered. But… you've *got* to tell me what's going on. I mean, this is not normal stuff here."

Now that we were safe, I wasn't giving up until I got the answers to the questions I'd carried around for the past few days… for years actually. And now I had some new ones—why he had kept his distance and *how* he could do the things he'd done today.

Lad's face contorted, making him look tortured, like he wanted to speak but couldn't find the right words.

How could I get him to open up to me? I was so afraid he'd disappear into the woods again, leaving me with more questions than answers. "You said you *wanted* to talk to me, to see me again, too?" I prodded.

He let out a breath. "I did, I do. I'm not happy you were in danger today, but in a way I'm relieved something happened to force my hand. I didn't know how much longer I could go on just watching without going to you… being near you…" His voice drifted as his fingers brushed the outside of mine.

I took his hand in both of mine and ran my fingertips lightly across his palm. He shivered. Tilting my head back to look up into his face, I said, "I'm really, *really* happy to see you. I have so much to ask you."

Lad's breathing changed. It was getting quicker, shallower. He withdrew his hand and turned away, gazing back toward the tree line. He swallowed hard then turned and met my eyes again.

"I know you have questions. I don't blame you. I missed you, too, Ryann, but this—" He gestured back and forth between us. "—isn't possible. I come from a very private... group. You can't understand how serious they are about that. All contact with outsiders is forbidden. In fact, you're the only one I've ever really spoken to."

Chapter Eight
Alien Girls from the Planet Blind and Stupid

"I don't understand," I said.

He exhaled a harsh breath that was almost a laugh. "I'm sure you don't. I've basically just admitted to being a stalker from a *very* strange family."

"No. I mean, how is it possible that you've never spoken to anyone but me outside of your own family?"

"Well, not only my family. There's a whole... community I live with. The simple answer is—we don't talk to outsiders."

I narrowed my eyes, shaking my head in confusion. "But that can't be true. You go into town sometimes—to the library."

"Yes. Not a lot of chatter there. The librarian gave up trying to talk to me years ago. The fact I even go into town at all would cause more trouble than you can imagine if my father found out. Especially now. He's even worse than usual about it."

"So why do you risk going?"

"Well, I've got to have books." His tone suggested the slowest of the slow should already understand that. "I told you—after I met you all those years ago, I went back and watched you in the yard of that house. I was working up the courage to approach you, trying to figure out how to somehow lure you back into the woods, so I could... I don't know, get to know you, see you up close again. Then, I didn't see you for a long time."

I thought back to the weeks following my rescue from the woods. "I was always trying to find you again—every time we came over to Grandma Neena's house, I tried to sneak away to the woods, but someone would stop me. They kept telling me you weren't real. My dad put deadbolt locks near the top of Grandma's doors. After I figured out to pull a chair over and stand on it to get them unlocked, we stopped visiting Grandma here. She came over to our house in town instead for... I don't know... years, I guess."

"Ah, I see. After a few weeks, I feared you weren't coming back here. That's when I went into town for the first time, but I had no real plan, no idea how to actually find you. And there were so many other people. I was amazed. I watched people. One day I spotted a mother and two children pulling books in a wagon on the sidewalk. I followed them into a building, and it was wonderful inside—so many books. I started going every few days to read. And to listen. I listened all the time. Listening to conversations there, together with what I'd read, I gradually learned to speak... the way you do."

Lad glanced over at me and then away again with a shaky laugh, like he couldn't quite believe he'd told me all that.

"You mean your family speaks a different language?"

He pressed his lips together, darting his eyes down and to the side, apparently thinking of how to explain. "We communicate... differently. I learned to speak the way you do for the same reason I learned to read the books and newspapers and magazines at the library. I wanted to understand your people... so I could someday talk to *you*." He gave me a tentative smile.

A hot wave passed through me, a feeling of rightness, of something being completed. I was supposed to be here—to be with him. Our meeting again hadn't been an accident. "If I'd known you were actually looking for me, waiting for me—wow—I probably would've ridden out here on my little bike, with or without the training wheels. So then... what happened? Where have you been the past few days?"

"I've told you. I *couldn't* see you again. I'm not seven years old anymore, Ryann. I understand now it doesn't work. You ask questions I can't answer."

"Why not? Why can't you? Lad, try me. It's okay—I won't be mad or anything," I said.

A bemused expression lifted his face. "Mad about what?"

"Whatever you tell me. I mean, I won't be mad if you and your people are... you know..."

"What? If my people are what?" The amusement was gone. He was tense, his eyes widening. This wasn't going well. He was supposed to be getting more comfortable about opening up to me, not feeling more threatened. Lad stared at me, waiting.

"If your people are... squatters." I rushed through the last word, squinting, waiting for his reaction.

"Squatters?" He laughed, and all traces of concern left his face. "What are squatters?"

"You know, people who live on someone else's land without permission. It doesn't matter. I don't care. I won't tell my grandma, and I'm sure she wouldn't mind, even if she knew—she's very generous."

His head fell back, and his laughter rang through the woods. "We're not..." His voice strained with unfinished laughter. "...squatters."

"Well, what? Some kind of survivalists? A cult?"

"No, Ryann. We're not a cult." Tears leaked out of the corners of his eyes now from the exertion of his laughter.

I was growing impatient and starting to feel very silly. Clearly I had grossly misread the situation. "What then? What?"

He stopped laughing, but he still seemed entertained. Lad took my hands again and rubbed the pads of his thumbs gently over my knuckles, making my skin tingle with pleasure. He pulled me closer to him, and I was bathed in the heat of his body and his enticing scent. He could've told me he was Darth Vader at this point, and I wouldn't have cared.

"It's nothing bad, and it's nothing illegal. We're just different. Think of it as… another culture. You wouldn't understand, even if I were allowed to tell you. Can we still be friends if I don't explain?"

I paused as his words sank in. "I guess so." That's what I *said*. My thoughts weren't so agreeable. *Super. No answers.* And he wanted to be *friends.*

I'd always been the girl hot guys were "just friends" with. Normally that was what I wanted—it made me comfortable. When a really cute guy would show any interest in more, I'd make a point of saying something like, "I'm so glad we're *friends*. You're such a great buddy." But this time—I actually *wanted* to be with the guy, to get closer, to move forward.

"Good." Lad dropped my hands. "I need to get you back home. The sun's almost down, and you are apparently too tempting for the local predators to resist. We don't want to give them another shot after dark."

"Take me to your house first," I blurted. "I don't have to meet your family. I just want to see where you live." *So I can find you in case you disappear on me again.*

"No. Ryann, did you not listen to anything I said?" He looked skyward and made an irritated noise. "Never mind. Come here." Lad put his hands on my shoulders and looked down into my eyes, staring hard. I saw his exasperation shift into something else, a very intense concentration.

After a few seconds, I said, "What *is* that?"

"What?" He broke his stare and glanced away, blinking.

"When you look at me all weird like that. You gave me the same 'pushy' look the other day at the pool."

Lad blinked a few more times, opening and closing his mouth without any sound coming out.

"Another secret, hmm?" I asked. I moved closer, leaving only inches between us. I placed my palms against his chest and looked up into his face. "Believe it or not, you can trust me. I haven't told a soul about you. Well— not since I was six years old—but everyone thought I made you up then anyway. And I literally owe you my life. I would never do anything to cause you problems."

"I know. I'm sorry. I wish I *could* show you where I live." Lad spoke softly, barely above a whisper, focusing on me so intensely, I felt like he could see inside my thoughts. "I want to tell you things… but I can't. Besides, you would never believe me."

"Yes I would. Of course I would. Why would you say that?" I couldn't control the urge to reach up to his troubled face. I wanted him to know he was safe with me. And I felt safe with him—weird—maybe it was our childhood connection or the fact that he'd saved me twice now, but I trusted him. I wanted him to trust me, too.

I pressed my palm gently against Lad's cheek. His sharp intake of breath was audible. His hands gripped my waist. Starting to set me away from him, he stopped mid-motion. His forearms were tightly tensed, corded with muscle. He was trembling.

With indecision? With excitement? The thought excited me, and I pressed closer to him.

"Ryann, please... don't." He closed his eyes and went silent as my fingertips slipped up to his temple.

His obvious response to me coupled with his restraint only made me braver. My heart beat harder. I stroked the worry lines on his warm forehead, smoothing a curling golden lock of hair back away from his face. One of my fingertips skated lightly over his lips.

When Lad opened his eyes again, they were bright, blazing like green sea glass reflecting a beach bonfire.

Hearing his harsh breathing and absorbing his quickening pulse under the hot skin of his face with my fingertips, my own breathing changed. My head felt funny. I closed my eyes and drew a deep breath, trying to regain control of my wild heart palpitations.

And suddenly I knew he was going to kiss me. I sensed it coming. I didn't need my vision to tell me his mouth was only millimeters away from my lips. I could feel the heat of his breath, smell the inviting warm scent of his skin. And I wanted it.

I'd been kissed a few times before—hesitant, clumsy kisses involving mouth metal or abundant saliva, and wondering how long was an acceptable length of time before pulling away and ending it. This was nothing like that. I waited, face upturned toward his, for the moment of contact, for the kind of first kiss I'd always dreamed of.

Lad's lips slid gently across mine at first. My skin went hot all over, and I was dazed by the warmth and softness of his mouth. I stood on my toes and stretched to get closer to the source of all that maddening heat and sweetness. His arms closed tighter around my waist, and my hands slid to grip his shoulders.

The kiss was perfect, firm but not too aggressive, gently exploring and inviting me to do the same. An involuntary sound came from my mouth, embarrassing me, but it seemed to excite Lad. He caught and muffled it, fitting his burning lips perfectly to mine. He brought a large hand up to cradle the back of my head, so tenderly, and I could feel the coiled tension of his arms and shoulders. Under the luxurious, patient pressure of his lips, mine began to part, opening up to him.

With a rough gasp, Lad pulled away from my mouth and cupped the back of my head in his hand, pressing my cheek tightly against his chest. It rose and fell in a dangerous rhythm. His breathing was audibly fast and harsh.

I was a little worried for him. And for me. Because I wanted to put my hand behind his strong neck and pull his mouth back down to mine, to beg or force him to kiss me again and again until… I didn't know what, but I didn't want it to end. Most of all, I didn't want to let Lad out of my grasp. I was too afraid he'd disappear again.

"Lad…" I whispered, unsure of what I wanted to say. He held my upper arms and moved me away, putting a tiny bit of distance between us. His eyes flared with excitement as he looked at me.

"I've never done that before." He continued to breathe abnormally fast. "Did I do it right?"

Are you kidding me? He'd practically incinerated me with his kiss, and he asked if he'd done it right. As if I was some kind of authority on the subject. Lad looked into my eyes with such hopeful sincerity. He wasn't kidding.

I tried to compose myself enough to give a coherent answer. "It definitely felt right." He looked relieved. And happy. His words finally registered fully. "What do you mean, you've never done that before?" Surely he couldn't have meant he'd never kissed *anyone*. Not with that face, that body.

"That was my first time… kissing," he confirmed.

"You've never had a girlfriend?" I was starting to become irrationally hopeful I'd somehow met the only boy alive less experienced than myself, and he was gorgeous to boot. Miracles happened, right?

"There are girls among my people with whom I have… spent time… but I've never kissed a girl before. I never wanted to kiss any of them, and they wouldn't have wanted me to." *Yeah, right. Alien girls from the planet Blind and Stupid maybe.* I gave him a look that expressed my

82

disbelief, and he responded by taking my hands in his. His grip was warm and intimate. His smile was just as warm.

"Whether you believe it or not, Ryann, that's the truth. It was my first kiss." A long pause. "I liked it."

"I… liked it, too." Straight from the understatement-of-the-year file.

Lad rewarded my reply with a breathtaking smile.

"Lad… if you've never… kissed anyone before, why did you start with me?"

"I couldn't resist," he whispered.

I felt crimson heat creep across my cheekbones, and my heart leapt. For the first time in my life, did someone really find me irresistible? Did Lad truly see something different and special in *me*?

"And one can only read about something so many times before wanting to experience it," Lad continued. "Kissing's actually even better than it sounds in books," he said.

And there was the real story. I was like an air mattress with the plug pulled out. Deflating, but not surprised—I'd happened to be in the right place at the right time. Lad was curious and experimenting. Nothing personal. The kiss had meant much more to me than it had to him. Of course.

Icing on the cake, Ryann, remember?

Something inside of me started to close. He *wasn't* safe. Yes, he pre-dated all the bad things that had happened in my life this past year, and *clearly* he was not like other guys, but Lad was more dangerous to me than a player like Nox could ever be.

Still, staring into the clear green of his eyes, I found myself powerfully drawn to him. His warmth and sweetness pulled me in—no one had ever made me feel like this. I didn't want to think—just to be kissed like that again, no matter what his motivation was, no matter the risk.

I fought the urge, summoning every last reserve of inner strength and stepping back. "You know what? You're right. I do have to get home. It's almost dark."

"I wish you *could* stay with me." Lad pulled me close to him again, stepping his feet apart so I was sort of caged by his body, surrounded by him. And he sounded so sincere. *Maybe I'm* not *just an experiment to him?* My heart resumed its pounding. *Icing icing icing.* I needed to get out of there fast.

I pulled away. "My mom and grandma will be worried." It was truthful, if not the full truth about my urgent need to escape this too-tempting closeness. "And I have to make the sweet tea for supper."

"Sweet tea?"

"Yeah, you know, the drink?" I forced a lightness I didn't feel into my voice, trying to re-establish a sensible distance with him. "What—never kissed a girl and never tasted sweet tea? Where've you been, living under a rock?"

"No, under a tree." He laughed at his own puzzling joke. "I would like to taste this sweet tea."

"Oh. Okay… well, I guess I could bring you some sometime."

"When?"

Tilting my head to the side, I evaluated him through squinted eyes. "I thought you weren't going to see me. I thought it was *forbidden*," I challenged.

He smiled back at me, moving closer once again. His voice lowered to a soft, graveled tone. "Yes, well, maybe I don't care about that anymore. How about tomorrow? After school?"

A thrill went through me at his eagerness. At the same time, it frightened me that I was having such a hard time controlling my attraction to him. Tomorrow seemed too soon to be alone with him again. *Way too soon.*

"Okay," I said. "Tomorrow."

We agreed to meet at the pool an hour before sunset. When Lad had walked me home, it took all my shaky willpower not to slow my pace at the clearing line and give him the chance to kiss me again. I uttered a quick goodbye and stepped into the open yard. *Don't look back. Don't look back.*

I looked back. But Lad had disappeared into the woods.

Chapter Nine
A Real Appetite-Killer

Emmy gave me a ride downtown after school Monday so I could put in some job applications before going home to meet Lad.

When I slid into her car, she was practically wiggling with excitement. "So, I saw Nox before sixth period. He was asking about you." Emmy's raised-eyebrow delivery told me she considered this some kind of great news.

"So?"

"So… it's *Nox.* I mean, you were there at his show the other night—you saw him—he is like, *way* hotter than I even realized."

Of course she'd be crazy for him. He fit her M.O. perfectly. "Why don't *you* go out with him?" I said.

"I'd love to, believe me, but he's not asking about *me.*" At my lack of enthusiastic response, she added, "You are unbelievable. What, is he too good-looking for you? Too sexy, too tall and gorgeous? I'm right, aren't I? You know what your problem is?"

"I can't wait to find out."

"You'd rather waste your time on go-nowhere dates with guys like Gary Pratt, or what is that little guy's name who looks like he's still in ninth grade?"

"Peter."

"Right. You'd rather waste your time going out with guys you have *zero interest in* than take a chance on a hot guy you might actually like."

"I like Peter and Gary. They're nice."

"Nice. You need to put on your big-girl panties and take some risks, Ryann, or you're going to *nice* yourself into spending your life with the world's most boring guy. I've never seen anyone less excited than you are after you go on dates with these guys. That's not what you really want."

"What I *want*… is a job," I said, switching the subject. "You took all of them. I only need one."

"You know I'd give you one of mine if I could," she said, laughing. Emmy was the girl of a hundred and one jobs. In addition to babysitting, she also helped out at her family's business, a flower and gift shop called Rooney's Garden. She sewed purses, which she sold on Etsy, and worked waitressing shifts at a diner in town called The Skillet.

"Actually, you should go by The Skillet—I could put in a good word for you with my boss," she said.

"I've already called there. They said they weren't hiring." I would've loved to work at The Skillet. It seemed like a fun job, and Emmy made good money in tips. I'd even take something in the kitchen. Of course that would mean learning to cook. The only thing I could really make well was sweet tea. Pure liquid calories and worth every one of 'em.

In the South, sweet tea was more than a beverage—it was an art form. There was so much more to it than tea bags, water, and sugar. There were heated arguments over which was the superior brewing method. Everyone agreed the tea had to be sweetened while it was still hot. Some people insisted the brand of tea bag was crucial. Others said the key was boiling a sugar syrup to add to it, while some argued the only way to make proper sweet tea was to pour the still-steaming brew directly over a pile of pure cane sugar in the bottom of a glass pitcher.

I had my own secret recipe, which naturally, I was keeping secret. But it was no spoiler to say properly-made sweet tea was diet homicide. Artificial sweetener was just sacrilege. Actually, it was the one thing that made me feel lucky to be built like a string bean. I never counted calories, and I never drank tea without sugar. My tea was always in demand at our church picnics and family reunions. Last summer I'd even had a sweet tea booth at the Squash Blossom Festival in the town square park. I'd sold completely out in two hours and had to go home and brew some more.

Emmy dropped me off on Main Street, where I stopped into shop after shop, asking about job openings. After getting many sorry-but-no's, I started walking back toward Channings—Mom had told me I could take her car home when I was done. She had to stay at work late for her first visitation and said Grandma would pick her up tonight after her Bunko game at the church.

On my way to the funeral home, I passed The Skillet. *Breakfast All Day* was painted on the glass door, and underneath, *Real Pit Barbeque*. Maybe it was worth one more try? I reached for the door handle, but a large hand came from behind me and beat me to it.

"Allow me."

I looked back over my shoulder. It was Nox, towering over me again and smiling like he knew something no one else did.

"Getting an after-school snack? Some real pit barbeque, perhaps?"

It took me a moment to respond. It was sort of a shock to see him again in the light of day, acting so normal, after the strange experience in the club Friday night. But there was nothing scary about him now—no sex-merizing hypnotic rays shooting out of his eyes as he waited for my answer.

"Um… no. A job. Hopefully."

His smile widened. "Well, in that case, come on. The owner's a friend of mine. I'll introduce you if you don't know her already."

He opened the door for me, and the tinkling of a bell accompanied us inside. Several pairs of eyes, most of them encased in wrinkles, glanced up in curiosity. Some of them I recognized from church or just around town. The Skillet was a small place with red leather booths along one wall and pedestal tables sprinkled around the center of the room, and in back, a counter lined with barstools. About half the seats in the place were filled.

It wasn't what I'd call cute, but it looked clean, and each table was covered with a neat red and white checked vinyl tablecloth. The walls displayed framed black and white photos of Deep River's landmarks through the years.

"Hey there, Nox. Come on in, honey." The greeting came from a friendly-faced middle-aged woman in a generous pair of mom jeans and a large green t-shirt that read *I brake for grits*. "Who's this lovely lady you've brought us?"

"This is Ryann Carroll."

I'd eaten at The Skillet many times but had never met the owner. I heard she'd moved back to town recently from Oregon when her mother had gotten sick and was no longer able to run the place.

"Ryann, it's nice to meet you. I'm Dory. I know your Grandma Neena. She and my mom were good friends. Your momma was a few years behind me in school, too. " She had a pen stuck behind her ear, partially concealed by her choppy salt and pepper haircut. She grabbed a couple of paper menus and walked toward a booth, inquiring loudly about Nox's band, and obviously intending to seat us together.

I hated to interrupt her steady stream of chatter and seem rude, but I definitely didn't want to end up sitting down for a cozy one-on-one meal with Nox. I opened my mouth to say so, but he stopped me with a shiver-inducing whisper in my ear.

"Just sit down. It'll make her happy. We'll order something then see about getting you that job. Trust me."

I answered his wicked grin with an irritated glare but did as he suggested.

Dory put down the menus in front of us. "Don't look now, but there's a dangerous man headed your way," she said with a laugh and walked away.

An elderly man shuffled toward our booth. "I don't want to bother you young people, but I overheard Dory's big mouth."

"I can hear *you*, Dan," Dory yelled from behind the counter.

The old man chuckled before continuing. "So you're Neena Spears' granddaughter. You look just like her."

"Yes sir. We're living with her now in the log house."

"My name is Daniel French. I remember Neena when she was a young thing like you, right after she married your Grandpa Ben."

Several of The Skillet's other senior patrons were listening now and began chiming in. Old people loved nothing better than to talk about whom they used to know and how all of them were related. Six degrees of separation was around long before Will Smith or Kevin Bacon.

"She was a fine-looking girl, Neena," said a thin old man with a Skoal cap and a sagging anchor tattoo on his arm. He must have been a Navy man back when that tattoo was new. "She weren't your ordinary girl. Looked like a princess from Europe or somewheres. Real quiet, but she sure was nice to look at," he reminisced.

It was strange to hear someone talk about Grandma like that. A heavyset man with a red face he'd forgotten to shave in a few spots offered his take as well.

"Yep. Fact o' business, we all used to wonder where Ben found such a beautiful girl. All that shiny hair and pretty skin and those big eyes. She didn't even seem real. He never would say anything about it, though, 'cept to josh with us. Said he found her out in the woods, brought her home and taught her everything she knew... like pretty girls grow on trees. If I'da believed him for a second, I woulda been out there myself, chopping down hickories and lookin' for another one." He let out a big bellowing laugh, joined by appreciative guffaws from the other old men.

"Now I know where you get it from," Nox whispered, leaning across the table, stretching his hand out so it landed near mine. I felt my face color with heat. He was *really* good at flustering me.

"That was a real shame about your grandpa, dying so young," Mr. French said. "And Neena, well, I guess it was the shock or the grief, maybe some of both. Her hair went pure white after he died. She was only a young girl still, no more than twenty-five or so. Like I said, a shame. But she's done a'right for herself, I guess, even with all that. Got herself a purty little granddaughter, too. Tell her we said hello. I'll get out of your way now. Nice to meet you, young lady. You take care, son." He punctuated the last by tousling Nox's hair, making Nox duck and blush like a little boy.

The man slowly made his way back to his table, where a checkerboard waited, surrounded by drained coffee cups. For a few moments, I was lost in thought about Grandma's former life, before I was born or Mom was born, back when she'd been a young, beautiful girl.

"They're funny, aren't they?" Nox nodded toward the aged checkers players.

"Yeah, they're great," I said, coming back to the present. "So, I guess you're a regular here?"

"You could say that." He shrugged. "I eat pretty much every meal here, unless I have a gig. Then I eat at whatever bar we're playing."

I blinked in surprise. "You go out for every meal? That's so expensive."

"Well, I have to eat," he said, almost apologetically.

"Your mom and dad don't ever cook?"

"Oh… they're dead. I live with some relatives, but I don't really like to hang around their place."

"Oh, I'm sorry." I looked down and fiddled with my napkin. I'd been feeling sorry for Grandma Neena, who was so young when her husband died, leaving her to raise my mom all alone. And here was a teenager with no parents, and apparently no one else who really cared for him—that was even worse.

"How long ago?" I asked softly.

Nox looked at me a few moments before speaking. For the first time since we'd met, I saw emotion swimming in his eyes. He opened his mouth, closed it again, inhaled deeply. "You know what? Dead parents are a real appetite-killer. Do we really want to talk about this right now?"

He clearly wanted to change the subject, and I wasn't going to push it. "Not at all. So what do you like here? I'm a fan of the country ham and cheese omelet."

"Yeah, that's good—you can't really go wrong. Dory's biscuits are fantastic. She makes a pretty mean BLT. The cheese grits are my favorite though."

"Really? Cheese grits are like, the ultimate Southern food—you don't sound like you're from the South. You moved here from California, right?"

He nodded. "Los Angeles. The South's growing on me, though. It's different from what I expected."

"You mean *everyone* here doesn't live in a trailer and have only four teeth?"

He laughed, a guilty expression crossing his face. "Right. Well, a *few* people I've met kind of fit the description. Like Casey Culpepper—you know him?"

"Of course—he's worn head-to-toe camo every day since the second grade."

"Right. So, he noticed I don't have a Southern accent. He said, 'You're not from around here, are ya?' I said,

'No,' and he said, 'You're from out West, ain't cha?' I said, 'Yes,' and then he thought a while and said, 'Arkansas?' I guess it was as far west as his mind could stretch."

Nox shook his head side-to-side, tickled. I couldn't stop myself from noticing how attractive his face was, all lit up with humor. Intensified by his amusement, his eyes looked several shades of green and brown blended together, and his teeth flashed brightly.

I buried my face behind my menu, relieved to see Dory heading our way in the periphery.

"Can I get y'all some drinks?"

"I'll have a Coke," I said.

"Sweet tea for me."

"Oh Nox honey, you sure? You know all we have is that instant stuff." Dory waved her hand in a dismissive gesture. "I can't brew it good to save my life. My momma's sweet tea was always fine, but it must skip a generation—either that, or I was away too long. What I need is to get someone in here who can make it right."

I felt a sudden stab of excitement. "Really?"

"Yeah." She looked at me with one eyebrow raised. "You know somebody?"

"Me. I make sweet tea from my own recipe, and people always say it's addictive, and I really need a job—"

Nox interrupted my ramble, grabbing Dory's attention with one of his patented killer smiles. "I hear it's unbelievable."

She smiled back at him then at me. "Hired. When can you start?"

"Next week? When school's out?" I couldn't believe after all my searching it was going to be this easy.

Dory pulled the pen from behind her ear and scribbled on her pad. "Here's my direct number. I'm making out the schedule tomorrow—give me a call and we'll get you down for some hours. Nox—thank you for bringing her in, honey. Check's on me today."

Dory handed me the paper and left to place our drink orders. I looked over at Nox silently taking credit for "bringing me in." He tilted his head back, surveying me with half-closed eyes, his arms folded across his chest.

"What did I tell you? One job, made to order." A slow grin spread across his face. "You're welcome."

"Thank you." I rolled my eyes and exaggerated the words. Actually, he had been awfully nice, considering we hardly knew each other. In a more serious tone I said, "Really—thank you—I appreciate it."

"I'm sure you'll think of *some* way to repay me." He raised one dark brow.

Okay, I wasn't *that* thankful. I lifted my chin and sassed him back. "I already have. You're getting a free meal out of this. Enjoy."

He grinned as if it was exactly the kind of comeback he'd been hoping for.

A waitress arrived to take our food orders. I went with the turkey sausage biscuit sliders. Nox ordered, and ordered, and ordered.

"What?" he said, noticing my stunned expression. "I'm a growing boy."

I shook my head and took a sip of the coke our waitress had delivered. How much more growing could he possibly do?

"So… you left early the other night. You missed the best part of the show," Nox said.

Fun and games over. I pushed the salt and pepper shakers back and forth on the table in front of me then straightened the sugar packets in their clear plastic holder, unable to meet his eyes. "Yeah, I had to get home. We weren't even supposed to be there. I'm sure you didn't end up lonely."

A long pause. "Well, after I played a song just for you, the least you could have done was stick around a little while."

My gaze flew to his face. *Oh help.* What did he want with me? I'd seen his type before. A guy like him would devour me like a T-Rex snacking on one of those little chicken dinosaurs.

I took a second to think of a response that would show him I wasn't affected by him the way other girls so obviously were. When he saw I wasn't buying his whole smooth-player thing, he'd get bored and move on to the next victim. God knew there was a line of hopefuls a mile long.

"Maybe I'm not much of a music lover." I shrugged. "Maybe I'm into jocks instead of musicians."

He shook his head with a knowing grin. "You liked it. I could tell that from across the room. And—if you actually *were* a jock-worshipper, you'd already be hooked up with one of those meatheads dragging their knuckles down the hallways at school."

A laugh burst from my throat. "That's not a very nice thing to say about our student athletes. Where's your team spirit?" And where was I getting all this sassiness? It must've been a reaction to his unparalleled cockiness. I was starting to enjoy myself. "Maybe I'm discreet. Maybe I'm meeting Mr. Jock when I leave here." I arched one brow and gave him my best "so-there" look.

"Touche." Nox laughed. He put his elbows on the tabletop, leaning toward me. "Listen, we should do this again sometime—go out to eat in Oxford or do something else—whatever you want."

What? My heart performed a complete somersault. Once again Nox had surprised me. Even if I hadn't met Lad, my first thought would have been *No freaking way*. Considering what just hearing Nox's voice had done to me in a crowded nightclub, I didn't want to find out how I'd react to him in private. I was way out of my depth with this guy. And he knew it.

"Oh, I… I don't know about that."

"Why not? Has anyone ever told you—you should take more chances? You might be happy you did." He gave me possibly the most charming smile I'd ever seen. And those *eyes*.

I hesitated before answering. Back to sugar-packet-stacking. *Think straight, Ryann.* "The last time I saw you, you were hypnotizing an entire roomful of college women. What could you possibly want with me?"

Nox didn't answer for a minute, and I didn't necessarily like the way he was looking at me. Then his whole demeanor changed. He actually reached across the table and closed one of my hands inside his.

His tone was soft and… humble. "Ryann, I think you've read me all wrong. Maybe I've come across as sort of a player—"

I pulled my hand back. "You think?"

"Okay, now I *know* you've gotten the wrong impression of me—if you only knew—" He paused, seeming to search for words on the diner's ceiling. His gaze dropped back to me. "Tell you what—let's start over. You haven't even seen the real me yet. All I want is to get to know you better—be friends."

I didn't know what was going on, but after what I'd seen of Nox's arsenal, I wasn't about to fall for the harmless-little-me act. *Time for emergency avoidance maneuvers.*

I pulled out my cell phone and checked the time. "You know what? I have to go."

"Ryann," he groaned, lifting a hand and letting it fall to the tabletop. "Come on—"

"Really. I didn't think I'd be here so long, and I actually do have somewhere else to be."

"What about your biscuits?"

"You eat them. Growing boy—right?" I slid out of the booth and pulled my purse with me. My phone fell in the process, clattering loudly to the floor. Feeling my face heat, I picked it up. "Thanks again for the help with the job thing. See you at school, okay?"

I was speaking unnaturally fast, backing toward the door, and bumped into the coat rack near our booth. Mortified, I turned and kept going.

As I speed-walked away, Nox called out, "That's okay. I'll take a rain check. I have some local housewives to hypnotize this afternoon, anyway." His smoky laugh followed me out onto Main Street.

Chapter Ten
Best Buds

Take more chances. Twice in one day I'd gotten the same advice from two very different sources. And I was actually thinking of following it. Not with Nox. With Lad.

As I approached the natural pool, I spotted him sitting on a boulder waiting. He looked up and broke into a bone-liquifying smile. It took every milliliter of self-control I had not to run to him. This was getting out of hand. I seriously needed to practice some self-talk. *Icing on the cake...*

I forced myself to slow down, but Lad jumped up and quickly closed the distance between us. He swept me up in a full-body hug, wrapping me completely in his strong arms. He radiated warmth, his body hard muscle everywhere we touched.

"Ow—my ribs—you're crushing the Thermos up under them." I'd made a fresh batch of sweet tea before going out to meet him. And yes, I did put in extra sugar.

Lad pulled away immediately and reached to cover my ribcage gently with his large hand.

Oh… Icing… It took me a few moments to think clearly. "Um, here." I managed to fumble the bottle to him.

We sat down together on the rock. Lad's face glowed with anticipation. He took an enormous swallow, and his look of rapture that followed actually made me blush.

"This is wonderful." He took another healthy drink. "It reminds me—" Lad hopped to his feet. "I want to give *you* something, too." He pulled a small vial out of his waistband and held it up.

I recognized it in a flash of distant memory. "This is the drink you gave me… when we first met?" I reached out to take it, suffused in a dreamy blend of joy and relief. It really *had* all happened, exactly the way I remembered it. It had not been hypothermia. Not imagination.

"Taste it." Lad sounded eager, impatient. "Not a big drink—a tiny bit."

I carefully removed a small cork from the top of the thin metallic tube and pressed it lightly to my lips, directing a trickle of the liquid into my mouth. The sensation was immediate and exquisite. The delicious sweetness spread across my tongue and into my cheeks, down my throat and through my stomach, carrying a pleasurable heat with it. Exactly as I remembered from long ago, the warmth bloomed throughout my body, tingling and melting through every part of me. I realized then why Lad's mouth had tasted so good when we'd kissed.

"What *is* this?"

"Saol water. It's a staple of our diet. Your language doesn't really have a direct translation, but it would be something like 'water of life.' What do you think?"

"I think it's incredible. Where does it come from?"

I recognized his guarded look. It meant no answer would be forthcoming. I nodded my head side to side like a bobble-head doll. "I know, I know, you can't tell me."

"Sorry." He smiled at my silliness and held up the Thermos. "I drank all the tea. Will you bring more for me?"

He looked so eager and sincere, and God help me, so gorgeous. I couldn't help but forgive him his maddening secrecy, at least for now. But I saw an opportunity to negotiate at least a little information out of him.

"I'll be happy to bring you some more... on one condition."

Lad's eyes narrowed with wariness. "What condition?"

"You have to answer a question." He started to shake his head, and I held up a finger in warning. "No answers, no sweet tea."

"You are cruel," he accused, smiling, then paused. "All right. One."

"Show me where you live." It was worth a shot.

"That is *not* a question, and if it were, the answer would be 'absolutely no.' Try again."

"*When* will you show me where you live?"

"You're impossible. You've actually been there already. Next question." He grinned in a *gotch*a kind of way.

Shock left me silent for a few moments. "What? You mean your tree house?"

"You really don't remember, do you? I guess it worked."

"What worked? What are you talking about?"

"Next question." His tone made it clear I'd get nowhere by asking again, so I moved on... for the moment.

"Okay, how were you able to walk through the trees like you did when you saved me from the coyotes? I've never seen anything like it. And don't tell me you've been doing it since you were a toddler. I want a real answer. *How?*"

He brushed his fingers over tiny cracks in the rock, delaying his answer, no doubt editing his response in his mind. "All of us can do it," he said finally. "We start learning at a very young age to climb and maneuver through the trees. It's a matter of practice and also, I think, a hereditary natural ability."

He stopped and gave me a half-smile before continuing. "It's an efficient way to travel, and it helps us to remain undetected. Most of us never go where we'll encounter other people, but sometimes they come here where we live. It's easy for us to hear you coming and conceal ourselves among the branches and leaves. Not that your kind would even think of looking up to find us." His expression was a tiny bit superior.

"Are you really telling me there are young children climbing around up in those monster trees like you did? That's unbelievable. I didn't know people could do things like that outside of Cirque Du Soleil."

"Well, they can't. Your people anyway."

Then something occurred to me. "So your people are not just reclusive, they're really... different."

I expected more hedging from him, but what I got was the most revealing thing he'd told me about himself yet.

"I think we could safely say we would be classified as another... race... one that has not been considered by your Census Bureau."

He said the words slowly, studying me as he spoke. My heart darted around inside my chest, though I tried to project outward calm. I was finally getting somewhere, and it was miles away from where I'd expected to go.

I pushed my luck one more time. "What about the girls you dated?"

His eyebrows drew together in a slight frown. "I believe I've already earned my sweet tea now."

"What are they like?" I persisted.

Lad exhaled. "Different."

"From me?"

"From all females of your kind."

"How?" I tried to imagine these amazing tree-walking girls who'd spent time with Lad but supposedly never wanted to kiss him, who were not at all like me.

"Well, they look somewhat different. They *are* tall and slender like you are. They're strong, athletic." He paused then reached over to stroke my hair as he continued. "But they all have very curly hair."

"All of them? I hate them already." I flipped my own stick straight hair in disgust.

"No—I love your hair. Before I met you when I was little, I'd never seen anyone like you. Afterward, I thought all girls should look like you."

Oh my. Icing. "What else?"

"Hmm... well, they're intelligent, practical, very controlled."

"You're right. Nothing like me."

I laughed at his unintentional insult, but Lad shook his head, frowning for real now. "I'm doing a poor job of explaining it. You're not like them, but that's what makes you so special. They're all alike. Predictable." He took my hands inside his, looked down at them, then back up at my face. His gaze pleaded with me. "But you... you're warm and surprising. After I discovered you, the girls where I live held no interest for me. It's been a source of tremendous frustration for my parents, but I can't help it. It's actually been driving me sort of crazy."

Oh God... icing on the cake, icing... oh hang it all. I was going to do it—take Emmy's and Nox's advice and take a chance. This time, *I* was going to kiss *him*.

106

I leaned toward Lad, lifting my face to him. He couldn't have had any doubt about what I wanted. He responded immediately, leaning in to meet me. I deliberately kept my eyes open as he brought his face close to mine. His clear green eyes glowed with intense emotion. He was more beautiful than I'd thought a male could possibly look.

Still, when his warm lips touched mine, my eyelids shut anyway. Maybe trying to hold in all the wonderful feeling threatening to flood out of every pore in my body. There was sweetness again, like the drink he gave me, but even better combined with the unique flavor of *him*.

I opened my lips, hungry for the melting sugar taste of his mouth. He responded with a gasp and clenched his large hand around my upper arm, roughly pulling me even closer. The kiss went on and on, deepening and pulling me further into a dangerous unknown place that was exactly where I wanted to go.

I was vaguely aware of a self-protective instinct struggling to be heard. The one that had never allowed me to go beyond friendship or hand-holding and lukewarm kisses with anyone before. The one that had kept me at a distance from any boy who'd ever seemed capable of inspiring interest in anything more. I pushed it back down, shutting it temporarily away, while I plunged recklessly down this new path with Lad.

His arms came around me, nearly crushing in his intensity, and I pressed against him, trying even harder to erase every last breath of air between us. I truly don't know where it would've ever stopped had he not abruptly ended the kiss and pulled away—just like the first time when he'd halted our kiss much too soon.

"Ryann, we have to stop." Lad still gripped my shoulders firmly in his hands, his face and upper body turned away from me. He looked and sounded like someone in agony.

"What's wrong? Why do we have to stop? We just started," I whispered with a pout, sounding like the pitiful kiss-drunk fool I was. I'd decided to go for it, and now *he* was being cautious?

Lad's breathing calmed little by little, until finally, he turned his face back to me. He spoke softly, seriously. "You're right. We have started something. I shouldn't have let that happen, but I couldn't stop myself. I don't know if I can stop where this is going now. I like it too much. I like *you* too much."

He let out an anguished groan, pulling his hands away and clenching them into fists, burying his face in them. He stared at the ground and spoke into his knuckles. His voice was rough. "This is terrible. You're everything I've wanted for so long, and now you're here, and it's as good—no, better than I always imagined. And I can't have you. It's killing me."

I had no idea what he meant, but my mind raced, charged by his extraordinary words. He was so distraught. I stretched my hand out and brushed it through the soft curls on the back of his down-turned head.

At my touch, Lad went completely still, sucking in his breath through clenched teeth. His fingertips dug into his hard thighs as he sat rigid on the rock beside me. I slid my fingers through the golden locks, soothing and stroking his scalp and the tense muscles of his neck, feeling him gradually relax minute by minute. Eventually, he looked up at me.

"I'm sorry," he said in a low voice.

"It's all right. Why did you say you can't have me? I'm right here. I want to be with you." I continued with a bashful grin. "And, in case you didn't notice, you were well on your way to having me."

"That's the problem. It's too easy to get carried away with you. It feels so good, so right. I've wanted this more than you can imagine. But it's not that easy. Even if you think you want me, too, we can't simply have what we want."

I practically climbed into his lap in my quest to get close, comfort him, and understand his distress. "Why not? Tell me. I'll try to understand."

He gently traced my cheekbone with one fingertip. "For my people, the choosing of a mate is a serious, and... lasting decision. We couple for life. If one mate is lost, the other remains alone and goes through a mourning process so severe... they're never the same again." His tone sent a chill through me.

"What do you mean?"

"The one who's left behind transforms. The mark of mourning remains for the rest of their lives."

I was bewildered by his ominous explanation, but I was also starting to get a sense of what was troubling Lad about me. "So... you're afraid of making the wrong choice. That if you get involved with me, it'll be a mistake you can never take back?"

"No." He laughed softly. "Not exactly. It's... complicated. Besides, it would certainly be a mistake—for you."

I was hopelessly confused. What he was describing was impossible, wasn't it? A permanent mark due to... a broken heart? And even more puzzling, Lad seemed to be declaring deep feelings for me, for *me*, as if that made perfect sense. Sure, why not?

Beautiful Adonis-like male, stunning green eyes, wavy golden hair, flawless teeth. Athletic, outdoors-type, well-read and velvet-voiced, seeks: Average-looking, dating-challenged girl for irrevocable lifetime commitment.

Again, I had to fight the suspicion I'd dreamed up the whole thing. I was struggling to comprehend how being with Lad, the most amazing person I'd ever met, could possibly be a mistake.

"Why don't you let me decide what is and isn't a mistake for me. Can't we just spend time together and see where it goes?" I asked.

He shook his head, sadness filling his pretty green eyes. "Sweet Ryann. It's not that simple. You don't know."

I balled my hands in frustration. "Because you won't explain anything."

"Yes. And it's impossible for you to decide what's right for yourself without knowing the truth. And yet, I'm not allowed to reveal it. So... I've made a decision for us both."

I didn't like where *this* was going.

Lad searched the ground and then the trees around us, talking to the woods instead of looking at me. "I've tried keeping my distance from you and failed. As long as we live so near to each other, I'm sure I'll continue to be unsuccessful at staying away from you. So there's only one solution." He set his jaw, finally looking at me, and resumed his pronouncement. "We can see each other, but we can never kiss again, or do anything beyond the realm of friendship."

Wonderful. I was back to being the just-friends girl. Best Buds with the most appealing male on the planet. Not my idea of a great solution. However, I *had* thought Lad was going to say we could never see each other again at all. I decided to feign agreement while I regrouped and figured out how to deal with this.

"Okay."

He seemed surprised at my lack of argument. "Okay?"

"Okay," I repeated. "We'll start over—no kissing. Just friends." I kept my voice light, pleasant, determined to hide my dismay.

"All right... friends then." Lad's wary expression gave way to belief and then resignation. He nodded and stood, offering me a hand down from the big rock. He thought his powers of reason had persuaded me.

Now I had to come up with some way to show him how wrong he was.

Chapter Eleven
Smooth Ride

When Mom got home from work that night, I was in the kitchen, brewing tea for my first delivery to The Skillet and stewing over the way my meeting with Lad had ended. Her bright chatter was a pleasant distraction. She told me all about her first day on the job, and I roped her into being my taste-tester.

She took a swallow from one of the glasses lined up before her on the table. "Ryann, this is so good, but my hips and thighs are begging for mercy. I already have ten extra pounds of un-tanned cellulite. I don't need any more."

"Please. Don't give me that." I shot her a look. "And don't let any of your friends hear you talk like that, or they'll want to slap you silly. You look about ten years younger and twenty pounds lighter than any of the other moms." It was true, though she'd been dying her hair for at least a decade, thanks to the hereditary premature grays.

"Well, I have to admit, the Divorce Diet is pretty damned effective. Maybe I'll write a book." She gave me a grim smile.

"Mom? Grandma grew up out here, right?"

"Yep. This place was a small hunting cabin when Momma and Daddy got married. He offered to buy her a house in town, but she loved these woods so much, he added on to this house. Why?"

"Well, I met some old guys today at The Skillet. They were telling me about Grandma when she was young. They said my grandfather told them he found her in the woods and brought her home... like a wildflower."

Grandma Neena walked into the kitchen, her white curls floating even more wildly around her face than usual. "Oh, Benjamin used to say outrageous things like that— drove everybody crazy."

I jumped in guilty surprise. "Hi Grandma. I thought you were asleep already. Were we too loud?"

"No ma'am," she said. "I was thirsty, that's all. What's going on in here?"

"Producing a few thousand gallons of sweet tea. I'm starting working at The Skillet next week, and Dory wants me to make tea deliveries even on the days I'm not there. Want some?"

"I'd better not, or I'll be up for the rest of the night." She poured a glass of milk and sat down with Mom and me.

I really wanted to ask her about the things I'd heard today, but I hated to bring up painful memories for her. She never spoke of her life with my grandfather.

"Grandma, where was your house when you grew up? I know you lived around here, but where exactly?"

"Oh, way out in the woods. I don't even know if the old place is there anymore. It's been so long, I can barely remember life before I met your grandfather and had your momma. Don't get old, darlin'. This is what you're in for," she joked.

Grandma reached over and took my hand on the tabletop and squeezed it. Then she stood quickly—well, quickly for her—and carried her glass to the sink. "Guess I'd better put these old bones back to bed, or I won't be able to get up and do my chores in the morning. Looks like my top helper's going to have her hands full tomorrow." She nodded meaningfully at the gallon jugs lined up on the counter.

"They said you were quite a beauty," I called out as she padded out of the room.

Grandma stopped for a moment and looked back. "Benjamin thought so, and that was good enough for me," she said with a wistful smile then continued down the hall.

What was that like, a love so strong the memory of it was enough to sustain her all these years? I'd never be able to deal with such loss. And I had never allowed myself to be in a position to lose anything before.

But now, with Lad—thinking of our conversation today, our kiss—it kind of scared me to realize how afraid

I was of losing him. Even scarier—the prospect of being with him, even as "just friends," was way more appealing than the idea of dating anyone else.

Emmy called early the next morning to tell me she was sick and wouldn't be going to school, so our usual carpool was off. Mom drove me to school before she went to work. I promised her if I couldn't get a ride home, I'd walk to Channing's and study for finals there until she got off. There was certainly no shortage of quiet study space at the funeral home.

As it ended up, I decided not to even ask anyone for a ride. Channing's was only a mile and a half from the school. I was young and healthy, right? But after about ten minutes on the blistering sidewalk with a full backpack, I started to regret my decision. It must have been ninety-five degrees out with one hundred percent humidity.

I slogged along, sweating and cursing Mr. Allen for assigning a massive year-end U.S. History paper, necessitating the transport of my massive U.S. History book.

A car pulled up beside me, rolling to a stop. It was a huge chunk of metal, an old Cadillac. Mud brown. Glancing over at the driver, I did a double take. Nox was behind the wheel.

I'd never seen him driving before, and *this* was the last vehicle I would've expected him to drive. A sleek black

AMY PATRICK

sports coupe, sure—even one of those souped-up muscle cars. I was tempted to check the back window of this thing for an afghan and a box of tissues.

"Jump in my lady, your royal chariot awaits," Nox said through the rolled-down passenger-side window without a hint of automotive shame.

I hesitated for a moment. *Should I?* Then a cool wave of air-conditioning floated past my face. I climbed in. The air inside was blasting at a gas-guzzling, absolutely heavenly sixty-five degrees. I directed the vents at my face and melted into the oversized leather seat. "Royal chariot, huh? I guess that makes someone in this scenario a handsome prince?"

"Shhhh." He ducked dramatically, one finger over his full lips. "I'm hiding from the stalkerrazzi, and I don't want them to find out my true identity."

"Oh, sorry, your Highness," I whispered with a bow. "So… is this your grandpa's car?"

He raised an eyebrow at me, grinning, putting the car into gear and pulling away from the curb. "You dare disparage the chariot?"

"No, no." I giggled. "It's very… spacious, and I'm sure it was quite hot in its day… whenever that was."

"1979, as a matter of fact. And I assure you, this car was never, ever hot. But I bought it from an old lady in town who put about forty-eight miles on it total. You can't argue with the pillow-y ride. Best of all, it was five hundred bucks and it runs." He shrugged.

"No, I mean, it's great. It's just… uh… not what I pictured a Rock God driving."

Nox frowned. "I told you, Ryann. That's not the real me. It's a front."

"And the real you drives a 1979 brown Coupe De Ville?"

"Exactly."

I giggled. "Okay then."

Now he was smiling. "So… where to?"

"Route sixteen? Then I'll have to tell you the turns—there aren't any street signs out in the sticks." I sighed with pleasure, starting to cool down. "Thanks for stopping. I was dying."

"No problem. I didn't know you lived out there in the county."

"Yeah. We lived in town until recently, but after my parents… well, my mom and I live with my grandma now. If it's too far, don't worry about it, I can—"

"No—it's no problem," Nox interrupted. "I just didn't know."

As he drove, I pushed buttons until I found something good on the radio. Adam Levine begged me for one more night, and I relaxed, soaking up the artificial climate perfection.

Sometime after we'd left the bypass and turned onto the county road, Nox pulled over abruptly and slammed on the brakes. Jumping out of the car, he dashed over to the shoulder of the road on my side.

I rolled down my window, alarmed. "What is it? What happened? Did you run over something? Are you going to throw up?"

In answer, Nox beamed at me and bent down to gather large handfuls of Oxeye daisies growing wild along the roadside. He strolled up to my window and presented me a bouquet.

"Flower emergency," he explained with a nonchalant shrug.

"You are insane," I told him, but I couldn't stop smiling.

My smile faded when it occurred to me that this might mean something. Nox got behind the wheel again and resumed the drive home, but I was suddenly at a loss for conversational topics. The last few minutes of the ride were mainly silent.

There was an awkward moment when we reached the log house. I felt like I should invite him in or something. *That would probably be a mistake.* I decided to go with my gut—if I read him right yesterday at The Skillet, Nox was interested in being more than friends, which was a nice balm to my bruised ego. But in spite of his frustrating hot-then-cold behavior, Lad was the one I wanted to be with. I was supposed to meet him in about an hour. Just friends, of course, but I was still eager to see him.

"So… thanks again for the ride." I opened the door and started sliding out of the front seat.

Nox caught my wrist and stopped me before I got all the way out. "Ryann?"

My heart tripped over a few extra beats. I looked at him a bit wide-eyed. "Yeah?"

"Are we friends now?"

I exhaled and smiled at him. "Absolutely."

"Give me your phone then." He let go of me and turned up his palm.

"Why? You need to make a call? Is yours dead or something?" I pulled it from my purse.

"Just give it to me." He took my phone and put in some numbers then placed it back in my hand. "There. Now if you ever need a ride again, you can call me—anytime."

"Oh. Okay." Emmy would die if she knew Nox had given me his number. I wasn't sure how to feel about it. Friends did that kind of thing, right? "Well… thanks. I'll see you tomorrow." I slid out and started to shut the door, but his voice stopped me mid-slam.

"Hey, don't forget your flowers." He held them out to me.

I took them and headed for the back door. My phone rang as I opened it and let myself in. Was Nox calling me? I looked at the screen, relieved to see it was Mom.

Nox was nice—a lot nicer than I'd given him credit for—but he wasn't the guy I wanted to call me. Not that Lad had ever asked for my number.

"Hi, sweetie. Did you find a ride?"

"Yes. I just got home."

"Good. Listen, I wanted to let you know, I'm going to be a little late tonight."

"Another visitation?"

"No. I'm going to have dinner in Oxford with someone. Phil Melvin, actually." Her tone was defensive, as it should have been.

"*Why?*"

"Ryann! Because he asked, and because he's a nice man. He's responsible, well-thought-of…" She left off *deadly boring.*

Phil Melvin went to our church and owned Deep River's only furniture store, which was appropriate because he had the personality of a piece of wood and strongly resembled a soft, overstuffed sofa.

"But he's so—"

"I don't expect you to understand at your age. But trust me—a man like him is the best thing for me. And *you* should be looking for someone solid and dependable, too."

When I failed to respond, she said, "Well, I'll see you when I get home. Are you studying?"

"About to. Have fun, I guess." My tone made it clear I doubted it was possible.

CHAPTER TWELVE
COOL FRONT

Thursday was the last day of school, and just in time. There was no air-conditioning and the classrooms were roasting. A cool front was predicted to come in overnight, bringing long overdue rain, but when I met Lad in the woods after school, it was still blazing hot.

"Want to swim?" he asked.

"Sure. At the spring-fed pool?" I wore a tank top and some nylon shorts, which would dry quickly, so I wasn't worried about needing a suit.

"No, there's another place I know. It's a bit of a walk, but I think you'll like it."

The walk *was* long but worth it when we reached our destination—a two-part waterfall, a stunning, secret place deep in the woods. We came to a stop at the basin of it and looked up at clear water streaming from a high rocky bluff, the tendrils of it fanned out evenly like a comb.

Because of the recent dry spell, the water wasn't gushing—the streams feeding the falls must have been low, but it was still a beautiful sight. Several feet below the bluff, the water landed and ran in sheets down a large sloping rock into the basin. It looked cool and inviting.

"We used to come here when I was little," Lad said, starting toward the smooth sliding rock, pulling off his shirt and throwing it to the side. He looked back over his shoulder. "You slide down—it's fun."

I followed him, nodding and trying to keep my mind on the waterfall instead of his muscled back. Right. It took everything in me not to reach out and run my hand over the perfect sun-browned skin. I took a few deep breaths and folded my fingers into my palms.

We hadn't so much as held hands since Lad's just-friends edict a few days earlier. It wasn't easy. After the kisses we'd shared, I couldn't manage to sink back into the platonic coma I'd been living in before. I was so ready for something more, but this was the most I could have of him for now. It frustrated me that Lad wasn't struggling with it.

"I had no idea anything like this existed out here. How is it you know more about my family's land than I do?" I said.

"Oh, I know everything about these woods." He waded onto the flat top of the rock and sat in the water, the falls overhead providing an ideal backdrop. He turned to me with a mischievous gleam in his eye. "My people have been here a very long time, Ryann. Actually, my family was here long before your family was, so you could say that *you* are the squatters, not us."

He grinned at me, his eyebrows raised in a what-do-you-think-of-that-one expression, and pushed off, propelling himself down the natural waterslide, whooping and yelling. "Now let's get wet!"

I joined him, and we splashed and played like children. At one point I jumped onto his back, wrapping my arms around his neck, attempting to pull him under. He shrugged me off, laughing, and twisted out of my grip. We ended up face to face. His hands went around my waist, apparently without his planning it, because he snatched them back and held them up in front of him as if I had a gun on him.

I looked up into his wide-eyes. *Oh—it's not so easy for him after all.* My heart began crashing like the waterfall hitting the rocks around us. Never taking my gaze from Lad's, I placed my palms on his firm abdomen, relishing the feel of his hot, wet skin. His muscles contracted, forming a *Men's Health* cover six-pack.

His breathing stopped.

I waited for something to happen—this would be the perfect moment for him to cave and admit he saw me as more than a friend.

Lad shuddered and stepped back, turning and diving under the water. He swam a few feet away and climbed out to make his way to the top of the rock slide again.

He's just going to ignore it.

Excitement converted to liquid frustration in my veins. Suddenly I'd had enough swimming. I waded over to the side. My red tank top was sopping, stretched, and saggy. If I'd been wearing a bikini underneath, I would've stripped the shirt off without a second thought and let it dry on some branches. All I had on underneath today was a pink and red striped bra with lace trim and a tiny pink bow in the front center. Not something a just-friend should see.

But as I climbed the rocky bank I had a wicked idea. It had gotten his attention before. *Can I really do it?* I didn't know if I had it in me. Then I thought about my mom settling for comfy-couch Phil and made my decision. Let's see Mr. Unmovable Platonic Friend stay indifferent to *this*.

With my back turned to Lad, I slowly peeled the wet tank up over my head and arms and hung it from a low branch. I shimmied out of my shorts, exposing the matching panties. I had no idea if he was even looking, but I sure hoped so.

I turned back around, purposely not noticing Lad, searching for a spot on the warm rock to stretch out and sun-dry. As I got settled, I finally allowed myself to glance up.

Lad stood stock-still in the water, staring at me, his arms hanging at his sides, his fingers closed tightly into fists. His face was severe, and his green eyes glowed with intensity. I hadn't really seen it in person before, but I recognized the feeling behind the look anyway. It was lust.

Now my heart didn't thump, it was more like the rapid tapping of a sudden spring storm on the tin roof of

Grandma's cabin. *It's working.* I forced myself to hold Lad's gaze.

When he finally spoke, his voice was a low growl. "What are you doing?"

I made my voice as nonchalant as I could manage. "Drying off. I'm through swimming."

"You took off your *clothes*." He sounded like he was in pain. *Goody.*

"Yeah, they were soaked." I gave a little shrug. "That's not a problem, is it?"

He stayed silent a few seconds, his jaw working tensely. "You shouldn't do that around me."

"Why not? You took off your shirt. And I'd do the same thing if I were swimming with any other *friend*."

"Ryann." He spoke through his teeth, barely moving his lips.

"La-ad." I dragged the word out into two syllables, my tone adopting a bratty note.

That's when he realized I was tormenting him on purpose. He strode through the water, marched up onto the rocks, grabbed his own dry shirt, and threw it over me. "Put it on," he ordered.

"Say 'please.'" I smiled up at him sweetly.

He only scowled and turned his back. "Let me know when you're decent, and we'll get going."

Oh, so now he was mad? Not nearly as angry as I was. Didn't he know he was torturing me, too? Every time we were together it was a physical strain to keep myself from reaching out for his hand or sifting my fingers through his hair. I'd had about enough.

"Fine." I stood and pulled the shirt on roughly. *Dang it*. It smelled just like him. More torture.

I snatched up my wet clothes, and he followed me to the path, talking to my back. "I'm sorry, Ryann. You know the situation."

"Yes. You've made it *very* clear. We're just friends. So I'm not sure what your problem is with seeing a little skin." I stopped walking and turned to face him. "Do you not want to do this anymore?"

He blinked several times, looking taken aback. "Of course I do. I just want to spend time with you without—" He took a short breath and blew it out. "Yes, I still want to see you."

"Why?" My tone was defiant.

Lad stayed silent, regarding me with a helpless expression. I turned and started down the path again, my heels digging into the dirt. I really needed to ask myself the same question—*why?* I wasn't sure there was much of a point to this. I couldn't stand much more, and now that the show-him-what-he's-missing trick hadn't worked, I was out of ideas.

We trudged along, the clouds of silence between us becoming as ominous as the dark ones forming in the sky overhead. By the time we reached the wooded edge of my yard, it had started to rain and the temperature had dropped at least twenty degrees. Maybe it only seemed that way because of the chill between us.

I turned to face him before going in. "Lad?" It was the first word I'd spoken in a half hour.

"Yes?" He stepped close to me and took one of my hands in his, folding it up against his chest, dipping his forehead down to meet mine. *Dang*, he was making this hard.

"You need to think about something, and be honest with yourself. What do you really want? Because I know what I want. And I'm not sure you can give it to me."

Actually, he *could*. He just wouldn't.

It took all my strength to pull my hand away and walk into the house without looking back. I was almost glad I wouldn't be seeing him again for several days.

Chapter Thirteen
Too Hot to Handle

We'd been planning a family road trip to Atlanta for the long Memorial Day holiday. Starting a new job at the beginning of summer was kind of crummy, but at least my mom's new boss had encouraged her to go on and take the pre-planned vacation. It would be her last time off for a long time. Since I'd just started at The Skillet, Dory didn't have me down for many hours anyway.

Our plan was to set out Friday and drop off Grandma at her sister-in-law Daisy's house in Birmingham on the way. Mom and I would stay with her closest friend, Shelly, who'd moved from Deep River to an Atlanta suburb fifteen years ago. They were like sisters, and Mom couldn't wait.

Though all my friends had planned school's-out trips to Florida or would spend time at the lake, skiing and swimming, Mom thought I'd appreciate the chance to get away and explore a big city. It was guaranteed to be better than sitting around here, moping over my lack of a love life. I was doing enough of *that* tonight. The rain and plunging temperature outside didn't help.

Mom was at another visitation, and Grandma was at her Thursday night quilting club meeting. I was supposed to be packing, but feeling mopey, I'd put on my coziest sweatshirt and yoga pants and curled up on the couch instead with a bowl of microwave popcorn and all the romantic comedies basic cable had to offer. I was channel-surfing, hoping for something with Sandra Bullock or Julia Roberts at the very least when the doorbell rang.

I peeked out through the sidelight window and opened the front door. Nox's dark hair glistened with raindrops. He grinned at me and shook his head like a Labrador, purposely giving me a cold shower.

"Ew!" I squealed, scooting away from him. "What are you doing here, goofball?"

"Providing a public service—boredom relief. We got a call about an emergency situation at this address."

I laughed. "Actually, you're just in time. We're about to lose the patient, I think."

Nox stood outside the doorway, looking down at me, an expression on his face that I couldn't quite read.

"So, really… do you mind if I come in? You're not busy?" He looked past me into my house, scanning for—what—a guy? I should *be* so lucky. "I mean is it okay I came by?" he said.

Was it okay? I thought about it for a second.

Why the hell not? It wasn't like I had a *boyfriend*, right? I flashed back to Lad's rejection today at the waterfall and stepped back, opening the door wide. "Sure. Come in. It's pretty gross out there, huh?"

Nox nodded and stepped into the foyer, handing me the basket he was carrying so he could remove his dripping jacket and hang it up.

I lifted the lid to look inside. "So what did Red Riding Hood bring us?"

Nox laughed, taking the basket back. "No peeking there, nosy. It's a surprise."

He walked into the living room, looking around. I was amazed at the way he filled it up. Other than my father, I'd never actually seen a man in the room before. It had never been feminine and frilly—it was a rustic house—but Nox gave the place a cologne-ad-ski-lodge air. Weird. The house I'd known since birth had been changed somehow by his being here.

He set the basket on the floor and pulled out a quilt, spreading it in front of the stone fireplace. Then he scattered a few throw pillows from my sofa over it. He straightened and looked at me expectantly. "Okay, get comfy." He gestured to the pallet he'd made.

I sat down on the edge of one sofa cushion instead. "That's okay. I'll just sit up here. Want to watch TV?"

I reached for the remote, but Nox grabbed it first and set it on the mantel behind him.

"No. Come on now—play along. Please?"

I felt kind of funny about it, but I crawled to the floor and sat cross-legged on the quilt, dragging a pillow into my lap.

Nox lit the fireplace, and when it got going, he joined me on the quilt, reached into the basket, and pulled out a paperback copy of *The Princess Bride*.

"*What* are you doing?"

Ignoring my question, he started reading aloud. I shook my head and smiled in wonder. *Who does this?* Just when I thought I couldn't be any more dumbfounded, Nox reached back into the basket and pulled out a bunch of big red grapes.

"Lie down," he instructed.

"What?"

"Lie down, *please*. I brought snacks, and they can only be properly enjoyed while reclining. Rainy Day Entertainment 101."

I narrowed my eyes at him. "You—are nutty. What are you going to do? Feed me?"

"Only one way to find out." He plumped up a pillow on the blanket and waited.

Finally, I rolled my eyes and shifted positions, lying back with my head on the pillow. Nox pulled a plump grape from its stem and held it over my mouth until I laughed and opened up.

"Ready?" He waited for my nod and dropped the grape onto my tongue.

When I finally stopped giggling, I chewed and swallowed it. He gave me another, this time letting his fingertip linger on my lower lip after inserting the grape. I was no longer giggling. The place where he'd touched my mouth felt very warm. The fruit was sweet and juicy, and the whole situation was... it was weird. But also fun. And it felt decadent... and sexy.

I didn't know exactly what Nox was up to—two days ago, he'd asked if we were "friends" now, and I'd agreed.

But looking up at his strong beautiful profile in the firelight, with his shiny dark hair falling in his face and a smile curving his lips as he read... well... let's just say if he ever *did* actually want to seduce someone, it wouldn't have been a bad approach.

Nox stopped reading abruptly and looked up from the page to focus directly on my eyes.

Oh my goodness. What must my expression look like to him with those *thoughts going through my mind?* Thank God he couldn't hear them.

I darted my eyes away and focused on the fireplace. "Keep going. That was a good—"

Nox's mouth covered mine before I could finish the sentence. And then the weight of his body was pressing me into the quilt-covered floor. He was so big, so warm, so... everywhere. He felt amazing. And it felt amazing to be *wanted*. The pleasure of it all paralyzed me for a second.

These were not like the gentle, innocent kisses Lad had given me, that he'd never give me again if he got his way.

Nox's kiss told me he *knew* what he wanted and exactly how to get it. It was aggressive, skillful, and the sheer knowledge behind it was shockingly exciting.

Finally, a shred of sanity pushed through my hormone-muddled brain. I had to stop this—now.

Yes, I was sick of the platonic-everybody thing. But a guy like Nox could easily take me from first kiss to first *time* within a few short, hot minutes. And I definitely wasn't sure my first time should be with *him*. I wasn't sure of anything where he was concerned.

I bucked and pushed Nox off me then scrambled away on my hands and knees and got to my feet. "What was that?" My voice was high and breathy.

He rolled to his knees and sat back on his haunches, raking a hand through his hair. He was breathing hard. Head tilted back, he grinned up at me and raised an eyebrow in an *isn't-it-obvious?* way. "Do I really have to explain it? You can't be *that* innocent."

"No, I… I'm just confused," I stammered. "You said you wanted to be friends."

"I lied."

The blunt admission made me blink. "Oh. Well… I didn't know—I'm not used to—I'm sure the girls you've been with usually… uh…" I blushed and looked down, unable to continue.

As Nox got to his feet, I crossed the room to the foyer and jerked the front door open. Chilly night air rushed in, cooling my fevered skin. He followed and stopped right in front of me.

"You'd better go. I have to pack for tomorrow," I spluttered, staring at the floor. I glanced up again when there was no response.

Nox gently pushed the door shut with one hand as the other came to my chin, urging me to turn my face up to him. "Ryann. I'm sorry if I pushed too hard," he said softly. "I only meant to kiss you. I think you wanted me to… still do. Let me?" His mouth moved slowly toward mine.

I scooted out of his reach and opened the door again. "My mom will be home in a few minutes, so… I'll talk to you later, okay?" My heart was thrashing around like a fish on the bank of a pond. My teeth pressed hard into my lip as I watched him.

He stood staring at me as if he couldn't quite believe what he'd heard. Finally, he exhaled loudly and walked out without another word.

I shut the door behind him and pressed my back against it, breathing hard. Through the thick wood I heard a soft curse. He was still standing on the other side.

After a few moments there was the sound of his boots descending the stairs and crunching across the gravel drive. I stayed where I was, staring at the twisted quilt and spilled grapes on the floor until I heard his engine start and slowly fade into silence as he drove away.

Suddenly feeling weak, I sank down, my back sliding against the cold door to the hard wood floor. *Oh my God.* What the heck had just happened? *He* obviously wanted to be more than friends. Something was wrong with me— who wouldn't be excited to have Nox want her?

I was obviously way more into Lad than I should be. And Nox—yes he was hot, but he seemed like—*wow*—

too much for me to handle. I mean, how many seventeen year olds had their own groupies? And kissed like *that*?

I couldn't go back to watching TV. I used the unspent nervous energy cleaning up the aftermath of our living room picnic and packing for my trip, which I should have done already anyway. As I folded clothes, I considered the events of the day.

Now I had two problems—Lad was determined to avoid anything resembling physical contact while Nox was apparently training on a steady diet of romance novels. And it seemed like I had to decide... something. Or whatever. Anyway, things were different.

I'd never be able to look at Nox the same way again, that was for sure. At least I wouldn't have to face *him* for a few days, either. I needed some space and time to think. This road trip was turning into the best idea of all time.

Mom and Grandma returned from their activities, and after we chatted a bit, went to their respective rooms to get ready for bed. It wasn't actually that late, and I wasn't even close to sleepy.

I read in bed for a while, but my attention kept drifting to the darkened window of my room, which looked out at the back yard and the woods. Where was Lad right now? How would he feel about not seeing me for four days? *How would he feel if he could have seen me with Nox?*

Thinking of that and the way Lad and I had parted today caused a hollow ache in my stomach.

A firefly landed on the window, its greenish-yellow flash catching my eye. As I watched, two more fireflies landed, followed by several others. Within a few minutes, nearly all the glass was covered with the insects, flashing intermittently like some kind of off-season Christmas display gone haywire. I breathed out a short laugh. I'd never seen anything like it.

Fascinated, I walked over to the window and put my palm against the glass. The fireflies lifted off at once and flew away in a scatter of tiny twinkling lanterns across the backyard.

And there was Lad.

He stood at the edge of the lawn, clearly visible in the light of a nearly-full moon. He lifted his hand in a silent hello. I did the same. Suddenly I wanted, no, *needed* to see him up close.

I peeked out my bedroom door at the dark, empty living room then tiptoed across the wood floor into the kitchen and slipped out the back door onto the porch. Lad was already there waiting for me.

I stepped closer to him and looked up into his face. The temper I'd felt with him earlier today evaporated into the cool night air. "Hi."

"Hi." He gazed down at me, touching my hair softly, letting his hand brush my cheek before withdrawing it. Heat shimmered in his extraordinary green eyes. His smile melted me.

Just friends? Really? Somebody just shoot me.

"Did you see that? With the fireflies?" I asked.

The smile deepened. "Did you like it?"

I gasped. "Did *you* make that happen?"

"I had to get your attention." He lifted his shoulders and let them fall, wearing a mischievous look. "It worked when you were six."

He'd stolen my breath once again. "Who *are* you?" I whispered.

Lad laughed softly and looked down at the porch then back at me, raising his brows and twisting his lips into a rueful expression. "I'm the guy who acted like a jerk today. I came here tonight because I need to apologize. I didn't like the way we left things."

Warmth rushed through me. I wanted to kiss him, but that was nothing new. And it was not allowed. Instead I smoothed a raindrop from his nose. "You're all wet." The rain had let up to a light sprinkle, but he was still soaked.

Grabbing my hand, he enclosed it in his. "And I came to ask if I can see you tomorrow."

"I can't. I'm leaving town tomorrow with Mom and Grandma."

His happy expression dropped. "You are? How long will you be gone?"

The forlorn look he wore irritated me as much as it thrilled me. *Make up your mind, boy.* "Four days," I said.

"Can't you stay here?"

"Alone? And do what?"

"You wouldn't be alone. You could spend time with me." Lad tugged gently on my fingers.

"Hmm... as friends?" I smiled up at him.

He didn't answer my question, but said, "We need to talk about some things."

Ooh. He had no idea how tempting that sounded. Seeing him there, so sad and sweet, the thought of spending several days alone with him held way more appeal than the prospect of tagging along on my mom's girls weekend. And it sounded like he might finally be willing to open up to me. Could I pull the difficult-teenager-card and get out of the Atlanta trip? Say I wanted to stay home and hang out with my friends at the lake instead?

"I don't know. My mom was planning on us leaving around noon tomorrow. Come by then, and if I'm gone, I'm gone. But if not..." I grinned at him.

I should probably get out of town and leave both *of these troublesome guys behind.* But the pleading eyes gave me in return tempted me to stay.

My mom's bedroom light flicked on, casting a rectangular glow on the grass beneath it. Lad leaned toward me, and for a moment I thought he might—

"See you tomorrow," he whispered before slipping away into the dark.

Chapter Fourteen
Enjoy the Show

"Ryann, you will lock every window and door and text me every hour on the hour."

It wasn't easy to pull off, but after much pleading and arguing, Mom had relented to my I'm-not-a-baby-and-I-need-my-own-life ploy. I'd convinced her it was *critical* to my social life to be here for Memorial Day weekend and sort of suggested I'd be spending a couple nights at Emmy's or Shalena's. And I did intend to call Emmy and tell her about my change of plans. Maybe I'd spend days with Lad and go out to her family's lake house at night. She'd already invited me, so I knew she wouldn't mind.

"You're growing up too fast on me, Ryann. Before I know it you'll be moving out and starting your career, and it'll be Grandma and me, turning into two old prunes here together."

"Speak for yourself, Maria." Grandma laughed and slapped softly at her daughter's leg as Mom joined her in the front of the SUV.

"I don't see much shriveling going on here," I teased, leaning in the window. "Where was it y'all were heading? Old Maids Convention—oh no, wait—to see your cool friends in the big city—that's right."

Mom laughed and reminded me one more time to be safe. There were hugs and kisses all around, and I wished the two of them safe driving and a fun trip.

I practically skipped back into the house to get ready to meet Lad. I still wasn't sure how to do it, but I was determined to find a way to convince him our being together was not a mistake. This was my chance—now or never. I had four days to spend time with him and figure it out. I called Emmy, told her I was staying in town, and asked her to cover for me with my mom if necessary. Naturally she was eaten up with curiosity. I promised to explain everything—later. Then I took extra care doing my hair and makeup, trying to make myself as tempting as possible before meeting Lad.

I was nearly ready to go when I heard someone pulling into the driveway. I looked out the front window. Nox's car. *Great.*

Nox parked and got out then bent over to pick up a few pieces of gravel. He pulled a Sharpie from his pocket and wrote on the stones. Baffled, I stepped back from the window and walked toward the front door, taking deep breaths. Seconds later, he knocked.

"Hey Nox. What's up?" I smiled nervously in the doorway.

He held his hand out to me and opened it to reveal three pieces of gravel. He'd written an "o" on each tan rock. "I came to grovel."

It took me a minute to get it—gravel, grovel. I laughed. "For what?"

"Your forgiveness."

He looked so adorably miserable, my heart couldn't help but soften. And Nox hadn't exactly been alone here on the quilt last night. I had known the situation was ripe for romance, and in my self-pitying, nobody-loves-me mood, I'd gone right along with it. If I was being honest— for a minute or two there, I had participated in that kiss. Now he thought I blamed him entirely.

"No groveling necessary. We're fine," I assured him.

He shook his head, lines bracketing his downturned mouth. "I don't think so. I think I really screwed up. It's pretty obvious you were mad at me... or maybe you were scared?"

"I wasn't scared."

Busted. That's what I was. I would have to fess up. I decided to go ahead and rip the Band Aid off. "Okay, well maybe you scared me a tiny bit. I wasn't expecting...what happened. And it's just—you and I are so different. You're obviously used to... a lot. And I'm not. At all. I'm a—" I stopped for a fortifying deep breath. *God, this is harder to say than I expected.* Finally, I spit it out. "I'm a virgin."

I buried my burning face in my hands then peeked at him from between my parted fingers, waiting for the derisive laughter I was sure was coming.

But Nox only teased me. "How do you know I'm not?" At my *yeah right* expression, he laughed. "It's all right, Ryann. I figured it out… *after* I cooled off a bit. You're right, we are different, but that's one of the things I like about you. I don't want you to be anything other than what you are. I didn't mean to push you. I'm really, truly sorry. I got carried away, but I'm not a monster. And I'm still your friend. I'm fine with slowing it way down. I think we can get back to where we were, if you want to try."

It sort of sounded like he was saying what he thought I wanted to hear. But truthfully, it was *exactly* what I wanted to hear. I was happy to take it at face value and not ask questions.

"Good. 'Cause I'd probably miss you." I gave him a big smile, and in my relief, reached out to hug him.

Nox pulled me close with unexpected intensity. He buried his face in my hair, crushing me in his arms. He whispered, "I'd miss you, too."

Okay… I pulled away as casually as possible and led the way into the kitchen. We sat at the table drinking tea while Nox told me about the latest recording contract offer his agent had fielded for him, news he'd meant to share last night before things had gotten all crazy. His band had been playing bigger gigs in cooler venues.

"You should come to another show."

"Sure," I said. But I had no intention of going. It was safer for me that way.

I was about to politely excuse myself—it was already past time to meet Lad—when an idea grabbed me. The sun was back today. Smiling an invitation to Nox, I said, "Why don't we go outside and talk? It's too nice to stay in."

He accepted so happily, I felt a little guilty but shoved the feeling back down. I was on a mission. Lad had told me that in the past, he'd hidden in the woods bordering the house and watched, waiting for me to go out on my walks. I was hoping that today he'd grow tired of waiting and come looking for me.

Nox and I headed for the bench swing hanging from the limb of a large tree in the back yard. It was my favorite reading spot—I'd made it cozy with a quilt and several canvas-covered pillows.

As we swung lazily, I smiled like a toothpaste commercial and laughed more loudly than usual at whatever Nox said. He seemed thrilled we'd made up and responded by regaling me with funny stories and his usual flirting. Guilt prickled around the edges of my conscience.

Then I imagined Lad watching, seething with jealousy and regret over his just-friends rule. And I went a step further. As Nox talked, I reached over and gently brushed back a lock of silky dark hair that had fallen onto his forehead. I let my hand come to rest on his arm, where he had stretched it along the back of the swing. I expected him to stop any moment and accuse me of being a tease, or at least of being wishy-washy, but he seemed nothing but pleased.

At one point, without interrupting the flow of conversation, he reached down and lifted my legs up onto the swing, slipping off my sport sandals and pulling my feet into his lap.

"You have the softest feet I've ever felt on anyone over the age of five," he commented as he rubbed them, looking up at me with a certain increase in intensity.

"Um, I guess I never really walk around barefoot." I faked ticklishness and pulled my feet back to the ground. It was too much. I'd gone too far. I stood up. "Okay, well, I guess I'd better…"

Nox took his cue and stood, too. "Yeah, I've gotta take off—get to rehearsal before our show in Memphis tonight. And you have to get going to Atlanta pretty soon, too, right?"

I nodded.

"So… we're okay then?" he said, dipping his chin and raising his brows.

"Yes. We're great."

"Promise you're not going to avoid me and treat me like I smell bad next week at the ballpark?"

I laughed and held up one hand. "I promise."

He gave me a bear hug good-bye, lifting me up onto my tiptoes, and sneaked in a soft kiss on the cheek before setting me down and leaving. *Shoot.* I'd have to worry about it later. Right now I was eager to get to Lad and find out whether he'd seen my performance.

I didn't have to wait long.

CHAPTER FIFTEEN
POINT OF NO RETURN

As soon as I entered the woods, Lad was standing there in my path. He seemed somehow larger and more imposing than before. He was bare from the waist up, wearing only his leather breeches, a necklace made of a leather cord and some carved stones... and a very perturbed expression. The heat in his gaze should've evaporated me into a puff of steam.

"You're late." His voice was deep and menacing.

My heart lurched, but I managed to maintain my outer composure. "Sorry. A friend of mine stopped by to visit. Were you waiting long?"

"A friend?" he demanded.

I'd never seen him like this. It was a little frightening, but also thrilling. Because he'd obviously witnessed the scene I so carefully constructed for him in the yard, and it seemed to be having the exact effect I'd hoped for.

"Yes, my good friend, Nox."

"Your *friend*... Nox." he repeated. His lip curled in revulsion as if the name tasted filthy on his tongue.

"Yes. I do have other friends you know. He popped in for a visit. I couldn't be rude."

Lad was clearly struggling to master his breathing. His clenched fists betrayed his shaky grip on control. "He touched you," Lad accused.

"How do you know he touched me?" I snapped back, pretending to be offended. "Were you spying on me again? Is that your definition of friendship? Can't I expect any privacy in my own yard? I guess Nox and I will have to stay inside next time."

Lad looked like he'd been slapped. "Next time." His lips pressed into a trembling grimace. I could almost feel the waves of heat rolling off him.

Seeing him like this, I started to feel remorseful about my deception, but I was still desperate to convince him we were not meant to be just-friends. I delivered one final provocation. "You said you and I would never be more than friends. That's fine, but you can't expect there won't ever be anyone *else* who'll want me like that. For instance, Nox—"

A tortured sound erupted from Lad's throat as he grabbed my upper arms and dragged me against him. "Stop. Please Ryann... don't say anymore. I can't stand it." Lad dropped his forehead to my shoulder as if he were exhausted. Breathing raggedly, he lifted his face to look into my eyes again.

I was paralyzed with self-loathing as he continued.

"I'm going crazy. I've never felt like this before. You don't know... when I saw you with him... I wanted to *hurt* him. I had to stop myself from rushing out into your yard and hurling him away from you. If I'd been sure your mother and grandmother were already gone, I would have." He finished, looking broken.

I was a terrible person. I had to confess. "Lad, he and I..." I started to explain, but Lad pulled me tighter against his body and stared down at me fiercely as he interrupted.

"No... I don't want to hear about *him*. And I don't want there to be a next time—with him or anyone else."

I tried again to tell him my trumped-up display of affection for Nox had been a terrible mistake. A lie. "But you don't understand. I—"

"Ryann—I've changed my mind."

And here it was. He was going to tell me we couldn't be together at all now, not even as friends. I'd blown it. My plan had backfired completely. I was mean and deceitful, and I was going to get exactly what I deserved. I waited for Lad to deliver my sentence.

"I was wrong," he continued. "I can't be just friends with you. I don't know how this is going to work, but it has to. I have to be with you... if that's what you still want. But I need to ask something of you."

I could hardly believe my ears. I was weak with relief and remorse, and ready to say "yes" to anything. I nodded my encouragement for him to continue.

"Don't let anyone else kiss you. Please. If you do… don't let me know about it. I can't take it." He ended with a shaking exhalation.

Slipping my hands up between our bodies, I held his distraught, beautiful face between my palms. I made sure he was looking straight into my eyes.

"I don't *want* to kiss anyone else. Only you."

"Good. That's…" He let out a huge weary-sounding breath. "…good."

There was a long silence as we held each other. Finally, he breathed in deeply and spoke again. "So, it's just us now? You won't see him again?"

"Just us," I agreed.

"Do you still want to spend today with me?"

"Yes," I answered quickly, feeling lucky he miraculously still wanted to spend any time with *me*.

"I planned out the day for us, since we've never had a whole one together." He took my hand and led me into the woods.

I followed along, dazedly oblivious to my surroundings as my mind sifted through the morning's tumultuous events and the incredible things Lad had said to me. *He wants me. We're together now.* The walk was long, but I was glad because both of us needed time to emotionally recover and settle into this new reality.

Finally, Lad stopped and gestured for me to look around. We had come to a high bluff, which dropped steeply off into a gorge. Spread out below us, a landscape of woodland and meadows was tinted various shades of green and gold with patches of purple and white and yellow wildflowers.

"It's beautiful."

"This is one of my favorite spots," he said. "I knew you'd like it."

We sat together on a wide rocky ledge jutting out over the gorge, enjoying the view and a nice breeze. After a while, Lad climbed a nearby tree and came down with a woven sack.

"Hungry?" He brought it over and started pulling out food—bread, nuts, apples.

When we finished eating, Lad jumped up and offered me his hand. I followed him a short distance to the tree line where he ducked under a low-hanging branch and disappeared from sight momentarily. I ducked under after him, stopping short at the sight of him stretched out in a hammock strung between two thick tree trunks.

"Oh, am I keeping you awake?" I laughed.

He held his arms out to me in an invitation I didn't even try to resist. I crawled in next to him and snuggled close to his right side, resting my face on his smooth warm chest. His solid arm and shoulder supported my head. I immediately relaxed, so much so I let out a surprising yawn. Lad lifted his head and strained to look down at my blushing face.

"I thought you might be tired after our hike. Guess I was right."

"Well, I didn't exactly get a lot of sleep last night, knowing I'd be spending today with you, and I guess the walk did take a lot out of me. Besides, it's your fault for making me too comfortable. Mmmm. You feel so good." I wrapped my arm around his waist and squeezed, pulling myself tightly against his side.

"If you keep that up, I'm not going to be able to *let* you rest." He gave me a suggestive grin. My face burned with embarrassment, and I tensed, not sure what to say. Lad laughed softly and smoothed my hair with his free hand.

"Only kidding. Actually, I do want you to rest. This feels nice. Besides, we don't have a schedule to keep today. Why don't you close your eyes and nap for a while? Let me hold you while you sleep."

I was sure sleep was out of the question, considering the way my pulse was racing, but somehow I did manage to doze and slipped into the most pleasant dream. It was filled with images of drifting leaves, raindrops falling onto dusty paths, and an exquisite hummingbird, hovering and sipping nectar from an array of beautiful flowers. I could actually taste the delicious sweetness of the nectar on my own tongue, and the intense flavor roused me from my sleep.

My eyelids fluttered open to discover Lad's face only millimeters away. His lips were pressed gently against mine, their heated softness melding with my mouth again and again. *Who needs to dream?* I returned his kisses but was distracted by a sound.

"What is that?" I whispered.

"You've forgotten already? It's called kissing. I am waking Sleeping Beauty in the traditional way."

"No, believe me, I remember your kisses," I assured him. "I mean the noise—what is that?" I looked around, trying to locate its source.

Lad laughed softly at my persistence. "Is it the rain? It started sprinkling while you were sleeping."

"No. It sounds like a hummingbird. I was dreaming of one, but I still hear it."

Lad looked down at me, wearing a strange apprehensive expression. He guided my head gently across his chest until my cheek rested right over his heart. The sound was much more distinct. I sat up in alarm.

"Why does your heart sound like that? Are you okay?"

"I'm fine. Actually, you're partially to blame for how it sounds. My heart always beats rapidly, but it seems your nearness exacerbates the condition."

I raised up onto one elbow and stared down at him, flattered, but not too sure about the state of his health. I studied him for sweating or discoloration or any other sign of cardiac distress I'd seen on the news, but he looked perfectly healthy, as usual.

"Are you sure you feel all right? I've never heard of a person having a heartbeat so fast."

Lad reached up and sifted my hair with a big hand. "I promise. I feel perfectly normal."

"No. You're not normal, Lad. You're... I don't know what to call it... special, I guess," I argued, trying to work it out in my own mind.

"Not special…" He shook his head. "You're the special one."

His crystal green eyes roamed over my face, making me feel more beautiful, more *seen* than I'd ever felt in my life. And I saw him, too, for the kind, amazing person he was. Even if I didn't have all the answers about him—I had *him* now. The answers would come in time. I hoped.

"Look at you," he whispered. "I wish you could see the way you look at me. I wish—"

I silenced him with my lips, making my own wish come true. Lad responded immediately to my kiss, one of his hands slipping beneath my hair to grasp my nape gently. With his other arm he pulled me on top of him and even closer against him, though lying together in the hammock as we were, our bodies were already tightly aligned. *This* was the intimacy I wanted. And Lad obviously craved it too. As he kissed me again and again, his arms crushed me to him—it felt like he would have absorbed me if he could have.

Within minutes our kisses had grown deeper, harder, and I was lost to the sensation. I was fully clothed, but heat and electricity flowed back and forth between us like there was no barrier, making it impossible for me to stay still. It seemed all the nerves in my body were strung tight. I'd never felt this alive, and yet my body was also heavy and weak, completely under the power of Lad's mouth and hands. I squirmed on top of him, driven to seek a more perfect fit, a more satisfying closeness with him.

His hand gripped my hip and held me still. "Ryann. Stop. We have to stop." He sounded winded, his breaths heavy and fast, matching his heartbeat against my chest.

"No we don't," I whispered, going in for another kiss. "It's okay. We're together now."

His grip grew tighter, more desperate. "Please—don't try to talk me into anything." His soft laugh was a sound on the edge of pain. "You have no idea how close I am to agreeing to *whatever* you suggest."

"Good," I said with a grin, arching into him. "I like getting my way."

Our lips met again briefly, but Lad broke the contact and leapt out of the hammock, leaving me swinging there alone.

"I'm sorry," he said. "I guess I should tell you a little more about... how it is where I come from regarding... coupling."

I sat up, letting my feet touch the ground to steady the hammock. "Okay."

He paced slowly around the small clearing. "Well, you know how I told you about there being a point of no return?"

"Right. It's a permanent decision—once you get married, you can't be separated or you'll transform and have a permanent mark."

He nodded. "You've got it mostly right. But... it doesn't become permanent at the point of marriage." He stopped moving. "Ryann... if we were to ever keep going with what we started today," he gestured toward the hammock. "… take things to their natural conclusion… that's when it would happen. We can't have sex unless you're really, really sure you want to be with me… for a lifetime. Because that's it for me. If you were to change your mind at any point…"

"Oh," I said, finally understanding why Lad always cut off our making out just when things were getting good. I was actually relieved. "So then, it's not only me—it isn't easy for *you* to stop, either."

He barked a short laugh, though his face looked more pained than amused. "No. It is definitely *not* easy. It gets more and more difficult all the time, in fact."

I got up from the hammock and took Lad's hand. "Because you like me?"

He gave me an adoring smile and laced his fingers with mine. "*Yes*, because I like you, among other reasons. Come on—it's getting late—I should take you home."

I knew from his tone I wouldn't be finding out what those *other reasons* were—not today. We walked together hand-in-hand toward my house. I was already feeling a sense of let-down at the thought of being apart from him tonight.

"Hey, why don't you come in when we get to my house? There's no one there. You could stay for awhile. We could watch some TV, or listen to music, or…" I was babbling now as we walked because my mind was racing through all the exciting and frightening possibilities of being alone in my house with Lad. It might put a strain on the no-sex-before-lifetime-commitment-policy, but—

He stopped abruptly and held up his palm, a warning to be quiet. I looked around. There was nothing out of the ordinary. He closed his eyes, listening to something.

"Someone's coming. Several people. Be very still. Maybe they'll change direction and not even see us," he whispered. After a few seconds he shook his head. "No. They're coming right this way. They'll be in sight within minutes."

"It's probably some neighbors. Our property's posted against trespassing, but they know *they're* welcome to come walking out here anytime."

I studied Lad in his strange attire. To me he was magnificent, but any casual onlooker would instantly realize he wasn't just some country boy out for a nature hike. It would be simpler for him to stay out of sight.

"You go climb a tree or something," I suggested glibly. "If they do come this way, I'll say a quick hello, they'll be on their way, and so will we."

Lad's expression tightened. He started backing away, holding out one hand to me. "Come with me," he urged.

"No. No way. It's one thing to climb a tree like a drugged caterpillar and another to have you yank me up like a parachutist who's just pulled the ripcord. No thank you. I'll stay right here on terra firma."

He was still standing there.

"I'll be fine. Go!" I shooed him away with my hands. Lad finally turned and disappeared into the thick timberland. I watched him go, and when I turned back around, I saw the group approaching. They were not neighbors.

CHAPTER SIXTEEN
HIS PEOPLE

Uneasiness rippled through my stomach when I realized who they were—Casey Culpepper, the camouflage-obsessed boy from school, and two other men. I recognized Casey by his unusual haircut, buzzed short all over except for one long piece hanging in the back like a tail, a style my mom said was popular a few decades ago. Somehow it was a perfect fit for him.

He hung out with kind of a rowdy crowd and was on the principal's short list whenever the boys' bathroom smoke detector went off at school. With him was his cousin, Jared. I'd seen him a few times at one of the town's two gas stations, working in the garage. The other guy I'd never seen before. He looked closer to Jared's age than Casey's. Maybe older. He broke into a wide leering grin and spoke first as they approached.

"Well, hey sweet thing. What's a little bit like you doing way out here all alone?" Another sickening wave hit my middle at his tone, and I noticed then that all three of them carried hunting rifles. And bottles.

It was too late to reconsider my decision not to go with Lad. A fast trip up a tree was looking pretty darned good right now. But, that being out of the question, I decided the best strategy was to walk directly toward the guys, pass confidently by, and go on my way as quickly as possible. They'd have no interest in stopping to chat with a girl they barely knew. I headed toward them, and before our paths crossed, veered into the underbrush to give them a wide berth, ignoring the thorns grabbing at my bare legs as I tromped through the wiry vines there.

"Hello." I raised my arm in a stiff wave and tried to seem nonchalant.

Casey sidestepped into my intended path. I had to stop or run right into his chest. "Hey... I know you. Ryann, right? Hey, Jared, Andy, this is Ryann. She's a *good* girl," he added with a boozy laugh.

"Ooh hoo—a good girl? I haven't seen one of them in so long, I forgot what they look like," Jared said, laughing more loudly than was called for.

Andy appraised me slowly. "Well, I have, but when I get done with them, they ain't such good girls no more." He sneered, grabbing his crotch. They all roared with laughter.

I'd made a critical mistake not going with Lad. Couldn't he see or hear what was going on? Maybe he

157

hadn't spent enough time around guys like these to realize the amount of trouble I was in—they weren't exactly a library crowd.

Maybe Lad was so reluctant to expose himself and his people to discovery he *couldn't* intervene. If he didn't make a move soon, I'd have to. I planned to make a break for it, hoping my sobriety and adrenaline level would give me some chance of outrunning the three of them.

But as they stood staring at me, snickering and taking swigs from their bottles, a new emotion started replacing my fear. Who did these idiots think they were, threatening me on my own family's land?

I raised my voice. "All right now. You all just move on. This land is clearly posted, and you're trespassing."

The guys looked at each other and erupted in drunken laughter. Casey actually snorted.

"Awwww, come on now, Ryann. We were trying to be friendly." His insincere tone and the resulting amusement from the other two only increased my anger and my inadvisable bravado.

"I mean it, you drunk fools. From the looks of things I wouldn't be surprised if y'all were the ones who shot that deer on my land and left it to rot. You get out of here right now, and *maybe* I won't call the sheriff and tell him I saw you here."

I knew my last words were a stupid mistake as soon as they left my hot-headed mouth. The laughter was gone. The guys gave each other sideways glances, and Casey started to move around agitatedly.

"What are we gonna do now?" He directed his whining question at Jared, but Andy was the one who answered.

"I'll tell you what we're gonna do," he snarled. He moved slowly toward me, and the other two nervously followed his lead, shifting their positions to form a loose triangle around me. "We're gonna teach this good little girl some manners. She's kinda short on Southern hospitality."

The other two tittered with nervous giggles. Casey's eyes darted from one to the other of his friends and then back to me.

"You just back off!" I yelled. Then, lowering my voice, I said, "Look, if you'll go right now—I promise not to tell anyone about any of this. We'll all go on our way."

Ignoring my words, Andy continued to advance. He didn't believe me or he didn't care. He had no intention of going anywhere.

Time's up.

My toes bit into the earth, I made my move, breaking to the side to dash away, but he sprang into motion as well, darting his hand out to lock around my wrist. I felt his filthy blunt fingernails digging into my skin as he jerked me back to him.

"Gotcha!" He laughed maniacally, having fun.

The smell of his liquor-soaked breath in my face made me gag. "Please…" I sobbed.

Anarchy erupted then with an otherworldly roar. Something big slammed into Jared and Casey, knocking them into one another with a crash of skulls. Andy reacted with a startled shout, shoving me away from him with such force I landed hard on my back and lost my breath in a painful rush. In one motion he raised his rifle and fired.

The gunshot rang through the woods, hurting my ears, leaving total silence in its wake. I lay on the ground stunned and struggling to breathe.

"Oh hell," Andy muttered. He stood frozen, looking at the target he'd taken down. He seemed to have forgotten all about me. A minute later, he turned and ran into the woods, leaving me alone with his companions. I lifted my head cautiously, looking for them. I spotted them sprawled in a moaning heap about fifteen yards away.

A few feet to the right of them another crumpled form lay motionless in the bramble. Every cell of my body went cold in an instant.

"No! No, no, no, please no… oh sweet Jesus, no, no, no." I got to my feet and stumbled toward the nightmare vision. When I reached Lad, I fell sobbing to my knees beside his still body.

"Oh my God… no, please, Lad… Lad," I begged.

The amount of blood covering his torso was staggering. The sight was more terrifying than anything I could've ever imagined. I didn't know how a person could lose that amount of blood and still be alive, but I had to hope beyond desperate hope that he was.

I had no first aid knowledge whatsoever. Aping every medical drama I'd ever seen on television, I felt Lad's neck for a pulse and drew my hand away in shaking frustration, unable to locate one. I had to get help for him. Knowing I couldn't lift him, I tried anyway, planning I guess to miraculously carry him through the woods. He groaned in agony when I moved him, and I was almost delirious with relief to hear some evidence of life. I lowered his shoulders back to the ground.

"Lad... I'm here. You're going to be all right. Don't worry. I'm going to help you."

I pressed a quick kiss to his damp forehead and leapt to my feet, turning one way and then another. I screamed in the direction Andy had fled, though he was most likely past earshot already.

"Help! Come back! He's dying—you have to help me. You coward—you come back here right now!" I screamed it so loudly my throat was seared. It was pointless. He wouldn't help me, even if he could hear my voice.

Using my phone to call 911 was hopeless. I had little to no coverage out here. Worse, Deep River had only one ambulance, and it would've taken the paramedics at least thirty minutes to cross town from the county hospital and make their way down the winding back roads out to Grandma Neena's house.

Even if they could've defied the laws of physics and made it there sooner, I had no hope of describing my location in the woods. I'd simply followed Lad, not really knowing where he was leading me, and we'd covered a lot of ground today. The ambulance crew would be lucky to find us by morning, if ever.

Morning would be far too late for Lad. He needed help right now. Desperate, I ran to the unconscious men on the ground, yelling, "Wake up! Wake up! You idiots!" I dropped beside them, shaking and pushing and pummeling their bodies as I sobbed and shouted in their faces. They didn't move. Casey moaned feebly as I pounded him with both my fists.

"Get up and help me. Help meeeeeeee!"

I turned my face to the sky, letting out a scream of impotent frustration. The desperate keening sound of my own voice stunned me into silence for a moment.

I was on my knees, head tipped back, listening to my own breathing and the noises of the woods. In the absence of my screams, everything was so calm. So normal. Dark blue sky, a faint early moon, treetops.

And then I knew what I had to do.

I ran back to Lad, kneeled beside him and put my ear over his heart. I was overjoyed to hear something. His heart had slowed nearly to the pace of an average person's, but it was still beating. How much longer could it continue?

"I'm going to get help for you," I promised. "I'm going to find your people and bring them back. They'll know what to do, and you'll be fine. Fine. Do you hear me?" Gently lifting his head, I slipped off his necklace, wrapping the leather cord around my hand. "I'll be right back. Hold on Lad. Don't leave me."

I tore myself away from him and stood up, surveying the woods. Every direction looked exactly the same to me. I had no idea which way to go to find his mysterious people, could only trust in what Lad had told me about them—that they could see and hear us when we could not see or hear them. I picked a direction and started running, waving his necklace, raising my voice as high and loud as possible.

"Help. Help. Lad is injured and needs help. You have to come right now. Lad is dying. He needs you. Please help him!"

Blinded by tears, I ran, falling again and again, barely registering the pain as sticks and rocks tore my knees and hands. Thorns ripped my clothes and skin as I flew deeper and deeper into the rapidly darkening woods.

"Please—help Lad. He doesn't have much time. He's dying, and you have to help him. Please God, help him… someone."

I didn't know how I'd ever find my way out of the woods again, and I didn't care. All that mattered were the deadly minutes ticking by as I ran and screamed, screamed and ran, my voice growing hoarse and rough.

I skidded to a stop and fell on my backside as two huge men stepped into my path. They were tall and muscular like Lad, with chiseled faces and wavy hair. They were dressed like him as well, one of them bare-chested and the other wearing a gauzy light-colored tunic with leather breeches. Each of them held a handful of glowing colored stones. I'd found his people.

The men glowered at me, their stances tense and aggressive. Both carried gleaming knives. At the moment I wouldn't have cared if they filleted me on the spot, as long as they allowed me to tell them how to get to Lad first.

"Oh thank God!" I blubbered. They probably didn't understand my words, but I gave them Lad's necklace. That got their attention.

"There isn't much time. Lad is bleeding to death and needs help immediately. Follow me." I turned and ran, hearing the two exotic men following close behind me.

I had no idea how to find my way back—only that I had to somehow. As I ran, I begged God to show me the way, to save Lad, and promised anything He wanted, if He'd only help me get to Lad in time. Someone must have been listening because we seemed to reach Lad's location in a fraction of the time it had taken me to find his kinsmen. I ran to him, collapsing at his side, weeping.

"Lad, I'm back. You're going to be okay." I kissed his face and whispered reassurances.

Looking up at the two men, I caught them in a strange furtive glance at each other. The exchange passed immediately, and they moved to Lad's side to assess his injuries. They worked together to lift Lad between them.

He made a small muffled noise of pain, and again, I was relieved. But my hope turned to near-hysteria when I realized the men were beginning to carry him away, clearly intending to leave me there.

"Let me come, please!" I called after them, my voice rising in an anxious whine.

They looked back at me in unison then at each other and turned to continue undeterred on their way. Lad let out a heart-wrenching moan, causing the men to stop. His eyes fluttered open. His kinsmen stared at his agonized face for a few moments, then turned back to me and indicated with hand gestures that I should follow them. They looked less than pleased about it, but my entire body flooded with relief. Somehow Lad had let them know he wanted me to stay with him.

The men moved amazingly fast, considering they were carrying the dead weight of Lad's long, solid body. I forced myself to keep up, huffing and sweating. The adrenaline-infused energy was wearing off. I managed to continue only through sheer will. My legs screeched at me, feeling more like stone than flesh as I lifted them.

Before that day, I would've bet any amount of money I couldn't have run that fast for that long. But I knew if I ever lost sight of them, I might never see Lad again, or even find out whether he'd lived. He had probably sacrificed his life to save me, and if he wanted me by his side for whatever remained of it, I was determined not to fail him.

After a painfully long time, the men slowed their pace and finally stopped in front of the largest magnolia tree I'd ever seen. I couldn't imagine the age of the old giant. It must've been seeded when the world began. The trunk was enormous. Its root system scoffed at the confinement of the earth and surfaced at will, spreading its knotty tendrils out for hundreds of feet in every direction. Nothing but the most self-sufficient scrub brush and foolhardy seedlings grew in the cool shadows of its branches.

I slumped to the ground, grateful for the break in our marathon, and sucked in a great lung full of air before clambering quickly to my feet again when I saw Lad's rescuers carry him around to the back side of the immense tree. I made my own way around it.

They were gone. *Dang it.* They'd decided to lose me after all. The panic began to simmer again.

Something touched my foot, and I looked down. The sober face of one of the men peered at me from an opening in the ground, under a thick root near the base of the tree. He motioned for me to follow him then turned and disappeared into the darkness.

I sank immediately to the ground and slid my feet into the hole, wondering in my delirious exhaustion when I'd be making the acquaintance of the Cheshire Cat.

CHAPTER SEVENTEEN
INTO THE DEEP

A few years ago, my family took a summer trip to Dahlonega, Georgia, the site of the first U.S. Gold Rush. I'd always wanted to pan for gold, which turned out to be hokey but fun, and yielded a few pretty, if worthless, gold flakes to bring home in a tiny glass souvenir vial.

The most memorable part of our visit was a tour of the inactive gold mine there. I felt transported to another world as we descended the damp, sloping stone walkway deep into the heart of the earth. The guide explained to us the constant trickling sound we heard came from aquifers flowing through the mine, the water running down the walls and bubbling up from beneath its floor. I'd shivered when I heard the only thing keeping the inky dark man-made cavern from filling up with water were electric pumps, operating twenty-four hours a day.

The journey down into Lad's world was infinitely more thrilling... and terrifying. There was no charming guide to reassure me with corny jokes and historical tidbits. I could only follow the two uncommunicative mystery men as they carried Lad down a winding earthen ramp, deeper and deeper toward his eventual cure or death.

The walls of the passageway appeared to be made of packed earth, marked liberally by large rocks and twisted tree roots. It was neither narrow nor wide, and the ceiling was high enough to give the roughly six foot tall men barely enough room to pass without stooping. They continued to move fast but walked now instead of running.

After a few moments it occurred to me I could easily see where I was going, though we were deep underground. I looked around for lights or torches, but there were none. Scattered about, half-buried in the walls and floor, were glowing rocks that emitted various colors of muted light. They looked like the rocks Lad's rescuers had been holding. I'd heard of florescent minerals before, but I'd never actually seen any in action. The effect was beautiful and strange. By this time, I was beginning to expect strange.

We finally reached the bottom of the decline, and I trailed the men out of the tunnel. The fictile ceiling gave way to vast openness. When the one in front of me changed direction and moved out of my line of sight, I gasped. My feet stopped moving without my permission.

I know this place. Was that possible?

The space was cavernous, the solid earthen walls rising high as skyscrapers, dotted with openings, which I guessed were entrances to other halls and rooms. High above us, the ceiling, also made of soil, was interwoven with intricate patterns of tree roots, some thin and wiry, some thick as logs. Staggered throughout the open space were massive columns of intertwined roots coming down from the ceiling, plunging into the floor.

A magnificent, wide crystalline river ran through the center of it all. If my secret pool was a natural wonder, this was a natural miracle. The water was as clear as Caribbean seas, and in its center, the river gave the impression of stillness. But near the edges, I saw evidence of a swift current, and the sound of running water filled the environment, making me realize how thirsty I was after the endurance run.

People were everywhere, people amazingly like Lad, tall, graceful, beautiful. The ones at a distance moved busily about their way, resembling worker ants inside an overgrown colony. Those closer to us stopped and stared, first at Lad's limp body being carried between the two men, and then at me. I returned their gazes, fascinated by this longed-for glimpse at Lad's people.

In all my imaginings about his mysterious family and home, I'd never gotten anywhere close to this.

The looks on most of the faces were closer to shock than interest. I might have been the first outsider some of them had ever seen. Grappling with a sense of disbelief, I fought the desire to simply dismiss what my eyes were telling me. How many times had I questioned my own sanity since meeting Lad?

There was no time for questions at the moment. I stayed right at the heels of Lad's rescuers, determined not to come this far only to be separated from him now. We entered another tunnel, a much shorter one, which opened into a room about the size of a hotel ballroom.

My eyes briefly took in objects hanging on the walls, heavy wooden furniture, more multi-colored light, and then we were inside another smaller tunnel. This one had a lower ceiling and openings every few feet on either side. I assumed they led to rooms, but ornately carved heavy doors prevented me from seeing into any of them.

Finally, the man holding Lad's legs pushed open a door, and the two carried Lad into the room. I slipped in behind the one in back, as close to him as I could get without tripping over his heels.

The room was modestly sized, dimly lit, and contained a bed, a large chest, a few small tables, and what appeared to be someone's personal belongings. In one corner, an unusual stringed instrument lay across the seat of a beautiful wooden chair. Like the rest of this underground universe, the walls and ceilings were made of tightly packed dirt and rock that resembled stucco more than loose soil. I stood with my back pressed against the cool earthen wall opposite the bed, trying to stay out of the way and give the impression I wouldn't be any trouble.

Considering what Lad had told me about his people though, I was sure *trouble* wouldn't begin to cover it. No doubt they considered my being here more of a catastrophe than a nuisance.

The men placed Lad gently on the bed and left the room. I hoped they were getting medical help. As soon as they were gone, I darted to Lad's bedside, wanting to touch him, but I held back, my hands floating above his chest and head.

I was desperate to help him and powerless to do so. My gaze ran down the length of his body, taking in the bloody mess of him. I still couldn't tell where he'd been shot, but it wasn't the neck or head, so that's where I allowed myself to touch him. He felt cool for the first time since I'd known him. It scared me.

I whispered to him as I stroked his hair and face. Lad responded to my voice and touch, moving his lips and turning his head side-to-side weakly. A heartbreaking groan came from deep inside him as if he might be trying to speak. I shushed him and reassured him I was all right, that he'd be all right.

"You're home now. They're going to take care of you. You're going to be… fine." My voice broke over the last word. Now that I'd done all I could to get help for Lad, the emotions I'd been holding in check began to surface, threatening to brim over. My throat felt thick and hot as I choked out the words I needed to say to him.

"Thank you for being strong and holding on. I'm so proud of you, and I… I need you to be okay and to stay with me. You're not leaving me. I won't leave you either.

I'll be here as long as you want me to be." I leaned over him, speaking the words close to his ear.

Someone entered the room. I bolted upright like a child caught in a naughty act. A man strode to the bedside, regarding me with unconcealed hostility, and I stepped back quickly, retreating to my position against the wall.

He looked as foreign to me as all the other men I'd seen here. Tall and lithe like the rest of them, he had loose chocolate-brown curls cut closer to his head than Lad's. He wore a longer version of the leather breeches I'd come to expect and a form-fitting shirt made of natural-looking fibers. He appeared to be middle-aged, but well-preserved and unrealistically handsome, like the actors you see in those Viagra ads or smiling and holding tennis rackets in commercials for *active adult* communities.

The man exuded competence. I assumed he was some sort of a doctor. He examined Lad, and I knew when he located the gunshot wound. Lad cried out and lurched in the bed. The doctor stilled him quickly. He reached into the woven fabric bag strapped across his body and drew out a long cylindrical metal flask. Extracting a cork from one end of the tube, he put it to Lad's lips, parting them. Lad sputtered but swallowed.

It must have been a pain reliever because after a few minutes the anguish on Lad's face dissipated, replaced by a peaceful expression. Watching the color wash back into his skin, my legs went weak and shaky as I realized how comparatively gray it had been before. *This was close. I almost lost him.*

I was so grateful to see his agony eased, my eyes teared up again. He was so helpless there. The desire to go to him was almost overwhelming.

The two men who had come to Lad's rescue re-entered the room. They carried cloths and earthenware bowls of water. Lad lay tranquilly as they efficiently washed the blood from his body, only wincing briefly when one of them ran a cloth over his wound. When they finished, they gathered the cloths and bowls and moved to leave the room, but paused. They both looked back at the doctor, who stared expressionless at their faces. Then all three men looked at me.

I was suddenly hot and nervous. I couldn't explain how, but they seemed to be having some sort of... *discussion* about me, for lack of a better word. The doctor's face contorted in a disapproving scowl, he shrugged and turned back to Lad. The other men left the room without another glance in my direction. It seemed whatever had transpired, I wouldn't be forced to leave, at least for now.

Lad yelled out.

I jumped, shocked and pained by the sound of it. Just as abruptly, he was quiet again. The doctor poured some of the liquid from his bottle over the wound and bandaged the area. After looking Lad over one more time, he brushed by me and out of the door. When he passed, I saw a bloody lump in his hand. The bullet.

I stayed in place, breathless for a few moments before stealing over to the bedside. I needed to feel Lad's skin and hear his breathing for myself.

Carefully, I stroked his golden hair, his tanned brow, his eyelids as he lay sleeping and motionless. Inches away from him, I ran my fingertip lightly over the bridge of his elegant nose, across his perfectly formed lips. I felt his breath, warm and reassuring. My fingers gently explored the strong lines of his cheekbones and the hollows beneath them. My palm opened to glide over his neck then moved to his chest.

His skin was warm again, the heartbeat beneath it unnaturally fast. That was good. I didn't understand why, but I knew for Lad, the racing rhythm was a good sign.

My hand still resting over his heart, I sat on the edge of the bed and watched Lad's face. There was so much I didn't understand about him. Not just his nature-defying pulse, or the things I'd learned about him before today. But now, this place, these people. I couldn't begin to make sense of it all.

Whatever the explanation, whoever he was, I had to see that he recovered. He'd risked everything for me. It was my fault he was in this condition—if I'd only listened to him and climbed the damn tree—those drunken hunters would've passed us right by. Lad and I would probably have been cuddling on my couch watching a movie right now, or better yet, *not* watching the movie.

As if he could hear my thoughts, Lad smiled in his unconsciousness. My own heart sped up and fluttered a few extra beats. And then we were no longer alone.

A man burst through the door, followed closely by a woman. Her eyes were wide and feverish as her gaze darted around the room. The man's face was tight, his hands clenched into fists as if he was ready for battle. From the familial resemblance and the distress on their faces, I knew I was looking at Lad's parents.

I fell back a few steps from the bed, staring at them. They paid no attention to me. The woman's face crumpled when she spotted Lad stretched out on the bed. She ran across the room on bare feet to reach him. Her hands fluttered across his body, his face, finally settling on the curls crowning his head. She didn't cry but looked like she might at any moment.

Her hair was the same golden shade as Lad's, spiraling in hundreds of ringlets pulled back from her face and falling around her shoulders. Her hands were smooth and delicate. She was fair-skinned and just... lovely. I couldn't guess her age, but she seemed too young to be Lad's mother. She gazed at his face as she petted his hair, then she turned and looked up at the man staring down at her and his unconscious son.

Lad's father stayed unmoving at the side of the bed, not touching Lad, but standing controlled and staunchly upright, holding his wife's gaze. With his square jaw lifted high, he reminded me of movie depictions of Julius Cesar, only dressed in leather and natural tones instead of Roman armor and a rich red cape.

His close-cropped hair was dark blond, and like his wife, he looked young to have a teenaged son. But he also gave an impression of maturity. His face was strong and handsome, bearing a resemblance to Lad, but more austere. He looked... forbidding. I had no trouble seeing this man as the demanding patriarch Lad had described.

His parents turned their attention back to his sleeping form. His father still didn't touch Lad in any way, but as I watched his face, I saw the evidence of worry. Deep lines strained across his brow. The corners of his eyes pinched.

Then he glared intensely at Lad. I could have sworn he was silently shouting at him. Lad began to stir, dazedly moving his head side to side. His mother straightened and stood over him, joining her husband in a careful study of their son.

My heart vaulted when his eyelids eventually parted and blinked. Lad regarded his parents' faces with confusion. He blinked a few more times, and his expression changed from disorientation to recognition. His mother's face melted into a tearful smile, and even his father's softened a bit. The three of them shared a probing, intimate look for long minutes as I watched, transfixed, afraid to breathe.

And then Lad darted his eyes around, tried to sit up, and grimaced. He immediately collapsed back, grunting and breathing hard. He tried again, this time lifting only his head, moving it in a scan of the room. When his searching gaze reached me, my heart stopped momentarily. It restarted in a new, restless rhythm.

Lad's developing smile was weak, not the brilliant flash of sunshine that had knocked me out so many times before, but it was without a doubt the most beautiful thing I'd ever seen. He was looking for *me*. He was happy I was there. I wanted to run to him, but I stayed back and silently returned his smile. I had to blink forcefully to stem the tears burning behind my eyelids.

His parents' heads turned to follow Lad's gaze, finally acknowledging my presence in the room. They must've known I was there before but hadn't cared to address the fact until now.

I watched in apprehension and fascination as the three of them took turns looking at each other, at me, back at each other. Their expressions went through rapid succession from surprise to anger to puzzlement. At one point, his mother looked emotional and… happy perhaps? But then a harsh look from his father seemed to chasten her, and she looked at the floor.

It was one of the most unnerving experiences of my life. One, because I was clearly the topic of a heated argument. Two, because I couldn't hear a word of it.

Lad's father glared at his son then spun around and charged, fuming, from the room. Lad's mother stayed by his bedside, looking into his eyes and patting his hand. After a few minutes he started to drowse. As his eyes ebbed and closed, his mother's slender hand stroked his forehead and hair the way my mom had done to me when I was little and in bed with a fever.

She loves him. It was obvious, and it reassured me. Whatever happened to me, Lad would be okay.

When his breathing grew slow and steady, his mother rose and walked slowly away from the bed toward the door. Reaching me, she stopped and turned to look right into my eyes. Even if I'd believed she could understand my words, I had no idea what to say to her. She looked at me with a tentative curiosity. After a few moments, she smiled and shook her head slightly.

Then she placed her fingertips lightly on my hands, which were folded tensely in front of me, and she squeezed. A pleasant heat bathed my fingers, and then it was gone. Lad's mother looked back once more at her son, left the room, and left the door open.

I tensed as a guard stepped into the room. This was it—I would be removed now. But he simply stood in the doorway and turned his gaze away, fixing it on the wall. For whatever reason, it seemed I would be allowed to stay.

I went back to Lad's bedside. He still looked sick but so much better than when we'd first arrived at his home. *His home.*

I surveyed my surroundings, finally calm enough to really think about where we were—deep underground, in a cavernous otherworld populated by impossibly beautiful people who didn't speak my language and were very likely somewhere outside this room silently discussing what to do with me.

All I knew was Lad was alive and seemed to be getting better, and for the moment, we were together. Fatigue was starting to hit me. I went to get the chair from the corner and pull it over to the bedside.

First, I picked up the exotic stringed instrument and searched for somewhere else to put it. It was heavy and substantial in my hands, and somehow familiar. I could almost hear a lilting melody in my mind. It must have been the carvings that covered it. They were like the ones on the chest Lad kept in his nest hideaway.

I went back to the bed and held his big hand in mine, wondering how long he'd sleep, whether he felt any pain, and whether he even knew I was still there.

"What a mess, huh?" I said softly. "I'll bet you didn't expect to introduce me to Mom and Dad so soon."

A tiny hint of a smile flitted across Lad's lips. My heart contracted with a sweet pain. I wanted to kiss those lips again, to comfort Lad and make him feel good again. Instead, I brushed my fingers gently through his hair, lightly over his ears and the strong planes of his cheekbones.

He looked amazingly like an angel in his sleep. Not a baby-faced cherub or diaphanous floating vision of an angel, but a powerful, glorious Old-Testament-Gabriel-kind-of-angel, resplendent in masculine beauty and all that poetic stuff.

"I'm sorry," I whispered. "I know your parents blame me for what happened to you, and they're right. It's my fault. I should've come with you when you asked me to hide. I should have listened when you told me we couldn't be together. I'm never going to put you in danger again. Keep fighting, okay? Rest and get better. I'll be right here."

Lad's chest moved in a heavy breath, and his hand went slack in mine.

Chapter Eighteen
Answers at Last

I woke to the pleasurable sensation of strong fingers stroking my scalp. Always a sucker for having my hair played with, I rolled my head dreamily to one side and smiled, still more asleep than awake.

Lad's soft laugh finally opened my eyes. "Good morning, Beautiful," he whispered.

"Is it morning?" I lifted my foggy head to look around.

"It's a whole new day—in more ways than one."

"Oh!" I suddenly regained my senses, the previous day's horrifying events rushing back to me. "Lad—you're awake. Thank God. I was so scared."

He put a gentle finger to my lips to stop my eager babbling. "Let's stay quiet, okay? I want some time alone with you before the others realize we're awake and decide to join us. I sent the guard away earlier, but I'm sure he's not far off."

"Okay." I lowered my voice. "How do you feel?"

"Like I've been shot by a drunk, ignorant hick. And it's a good thing for him he did shoot me because he was about to be a drunk, ignorant, dead hick."

"Oh Lad, don't joke about it. Yesterday was the worst day of my life. I didn't think you were going to make it." I choked a little on the last part.

"I'm not joking at all. I fully intended to kill those men after I realized they wanted to hurt you. If I hadn't been out of my mind with rage, I would have come up with a better plan of attack and avoided all this... nonsense." He gestured at his own wounded body in disgust. "How did you manage to get me here? I can't remember."

I was thankful for that. I fervently hoped he did *not* remember the excruciating pain or my frenzied screaming. I shuddered and tried to push it back out of my own mind.

"I ran and called for help until two of your people found me. They were tall men with wavy hair, dressed like you."

Lad smiled weakly. "Sounds like a description of every male here over the age of thirteen. You must have been convincing to have lured them out into the open. I'm actually shocked anyone responded and went with you."

"Well, I don't think they liked the idea much, but I was waving your necklace and yelling your name over and over."

"You were very brave, Ryann," Lad murmured softly. "I owe you my life."

I shook my head and started to protest. I was the one who was indebted to him for saving me. Lad tried to roll onto his side as he reached toward me but hissed sharply through his teeth and fell back again, clearly in pain. A wave of guilt washed through me.

"Does it hurt a lot?" I touched his chest with my fingertips.

"Not very much," he said, probably lying. "I assume our healer, Wickthorne was here last night?"

"Yes, someone came and removed the bullet and gave you something for the pain. He didn't tell me his name, though. No one here's told me *anything*. Or *asked* me anything. In fact, no one's said a single word... to me or to each other." The frightening fact sank in and reverberated through me.

"Yes... as I told you before, we communicate... differently than you're used to." Lad covered my hand with his much warmer one, pressing my cool fingers harder against his chest. "Poor Ryann, you must be very confused and frightened right now. This is not how I planned to reveal the details of my life to you. In fact, I had no real plans to do that at all. I guess the truth had to come out eventually, though."

"So... what *is* the truth?" Now that he was well enough to speak to me, I was dying to know what was going on.

Lad's brow lowered. "I'm not sure where to begin."

"Well, you can start with the communication thing. Doesn't anyone *ever* talk around here? It's kind of creepy. They come and go in total silence."

"It doesn't sound like silence to us." He chuckled. "We're hearing things all the time. You're familiar with the concept of mental telepathy, aren't you?"

I sat stunned for a second before answering. "You mean, you're all reading each other's minds?"

"No. No, it's not mind-reading. That implies that we know what everyone else is thinking all the time. It's more limited—more…intentional. It's like…" Lad paused, and his eyes brightened as he came up with a good comparison. "…like sending a text. I have to formulate the message in my mind with the purpose of communicating it to the other person, then I hit the mental 'send' button."

"And then everyone hears what you thought?"

"Only the person I send it to. And that person hears only what I want them to hear. They don't know *all* of my thoughts."

I considered it for a minute. It explained a lot. Like the strange, knowing looks Lad's people had been giving each other, and how the two men who rescued Lad had started to leave me then reconsidered and let me follow them here.

"Lad, after you were shot—you told those men to let me come with you?"

His shoulders lifted in a shrug, causing him to wince. "I'm not sure what I told them. Everything is pretty foggy. I kept slipping in and out of consciousness. I only know I was desperate to keep you with me." A small smile bent the corners of his mouth. "I probably shouted it at them. No doubt that made them even angrier with me."

"Angry? How do you know they were angry?"

He looked at me as if the answer would be obvious to the smallest child. "Ryann, everyone's angry with me now. I told you contact with outsiders is forbidden. Now that you've seen this place, you must be starting to understand why."

Actually, I wasn't understanding much at all, but I did get the fact that Lad wasn't quite like the others here.

"*You* talk to me out loud. Are you the only one here who can do it?"

"I'm the only one who wants to. The others could do it, if they chose to. It takes some practice."

"So nobody ever makes a sound? That's so weird."

Lad laughed again. "I can see how you would think so, but for us, it's quite normal, just as speaking out loud is normal for you and everyone you've ever known. It's not completely quiet here, though. We do vocalize. There's singing for instance, and of course, laughing or crying produces sound you or anyone else could hear."

"Do you sing?"

A flush swept across his cheeks. "A little bit. We all do—we're a musical people. But I prefer playing the aelflute." He nodded toward the strange stringed instrument in the corner.

I looked over at it then let my eyes wander around the room. "This is your room?"

"Yes."

"And, the huge rooms they led me through, and the halls with all those doorways? It's all part of your house?"

185

He nodded.

"Wow, you live in sort of a mansion."

"Well, my parents entertain a lot of guests, so the space is useful. And this is a hereditary family estate. This home has been lived in by generations of my family."

"Do you have a big family?"

"No. Most couples here can have only one child, very rarely two. It's me and my mother and father. And well, I have a... um, brother of sorts."

"How do you have a sort-of brother?"

"He's not my biological brother. He's actually my cousin, but we've been raised together since we were boys."

"That's cool. I always wished for a brother or sister."

There was a pause before Lad answered. "Yes. It *can* be. We used to be inseparable, except for the usual he-wants-whatever-I-have rivalry. But lately we've grown apart."

"Oh. What happened?"

"Nothing actually *happened*, until very recently, in fact." Anger flashed through his eyes. Or maybe it was just annoyance. Since I'd never had one, I could only imagine the sort of quarrels that might arise between siblings. "He's always been different, but he can't help it. He's a relative, but their... branch of the family lives by a different set of rules."

I sat forward, enthralled by Lad's revelations. I had longed for even the tiniest trickle of information about his life and family, and now it was pouring forth like a flooding rain. "Like which rules?" I asked.

"The ones pertaining to involvement with your kind, mostly. They're not hesitant to mix with your people, and if it suits them, to take advantage. They use their... special talents to get their way. It was never really an issue with my brother since he was raised with us—but lately he's spent more and more time away from here. He's been gone more and more often this year and barely checked in during the past few months, and he doesn't talk about where he's been or what he's been doing." Lad's eyes narrowed and he scowled. "I think I *may* have a pretty good guess, though."

"What do you mean?"

"Never mind. I... can't really talk about it, and it's going to be resolved very soon. I'll make *sure* of that." His expression told me he was done with the topic. "Speaking of family drama, you met my parents, I guess."

"Yes, last night, if you could consider it meeting them. I watched your father storm in, stare at you, and storm out again. Your mother stayed for a while, though, and she at least looked at me before she left." Remembering the way she'd stopped and stared so purposefully into my eyes the night before, I said, "Oh. I think maybe your mother tried to say something to me. She must have thought I was completely dense."

Lad smiled gently at me. "No, I'm sure she understood you're at a distinct communication disadvantage here."

"She was so upset last night, Lad. I hope she doesn't think I deliberately did something to hurt you."

He reached over and stroked my hand. "Of course not. You may not be able to hear our communication, but you definitely send out messages in your own way. She would have picked up on that."

"Messages?"

"I mean your feelings are pretty loud in there. You must have some latent talent for projection. It makes sense that some of you would. Every now and then I've even been able to pick up a word or two from you." His grin widened.

My face heated as I considered it. "What words?" I shuddered to think which thoughts I'd felt so strongly around Lad they'd been audible to him without my even speaking the words.

He reached out and slid a large hand through my hair, grazing my cheek and neck with his thumb. "Good ones," he said softly. The fire returned to his impossibly beautiful eyes.

My heart started to pound, and I felt a new wash of embarrassment, wondering if I was projecting any revealing words at him that very moment.

"It might be an ability you could develop. It could be useful. I'll help you practice, if you like," Lad offered.

"Okay. We can try, I guess. Send me a message."

Lad smiled then got serious and looked into my eyes intently. I stared back at him and tried to "listen." I didn't know what his mind was saying, but Lad's expression was certainly sending a message—his eyes sparked hot green fireworks. My gaze was torn between them and his lips, which had kissed me so tenderly and passionately before. I was starting to feel *very* warm now and a little weak and shivery.

The memory of those stirring kisses and the desire to touch and kiss him again was almost more than I could resist. Here I was supposed to be focusing on hearing Lad's message, and my own heated thoughts flooded my mind. I fought to rein them in. It took a minute before I was able to discipline myself enough to speak.

"Did you do it?" I asked, a little breathless.

"Yes. Do you know what I said?" He raised an eyebrow and gave me a mischievous grin.

I giggled. "No. What was it?"

"I'm not going to *tell* you. You have to figure it out. We'll have to keep practicing."

At the sound of the door opening behind us, I scooted my chair away from the bed. Lad's father entered the small room, filling it with his imposing presence. He looked between the two of us suspiciously. I concentrated hard on listing state capitols, not wanting any damning "words" to leak out.

He strode to the bedside where he and Lad engaged in what I now understood to be a conversation. I shouldn't have "eavesdropped," but I couldn't stop myself from watching the captivating display on their faces. They were definitely not discussing the weather. Whatever was being said, it was pretty heated.

All traces of the previous night's worry and concern were gone from Lad's father's face. Now he only looked incensed. Lad seemed angry as well, but there was also a subtle sense of respect in his expression as he regarded his father. I noticed a few quick glances in my direction and was momentarily *thankful* I couldn't hear the conversation.

After a few minutes, Lad's father turned on his heel and left the room, bumping shoulders with Wickthorne, the healer, on his way out. Lad let out an exasperated groan, rolling his eyes toward the ceiling. He gave me a quick wink before glancing up and smiling widely at Wickthorne.

The healer looked at Lad with a half-smile, like a tolerant uncle regarding a naughty young boy. He set to work examining Lad, efficiently checking the wound, looking at his eyes, listening to his heart and breathing. When he seemed satisfied with his findings, he gave Lad another dose from his flask.

I expected the healer to ignore me as before, but he startled me by coming directly to my chair and kneeling in front of me. I froze in place as he reached into his satchel and withdrew a soft cloth. He doused it with liquid from the metal flask, and then applied it to the multitude of scrapes and scratches on my legs one by one.

I tried to protest, embarrassed that my insignificant flesh wounds would receive any of his attention when Lad's injuries were so much more severe. But the man simply continued, finishing with my legs and moving to the injuries on my arms and hands.

After a few minutes, I was glad he had disregarded my attempts to stop him. I felt an unprecedented sense of well-being. My skin was warm and tingling in the places where the wet cloth had touched me. Perhaps I imagined it, but the cuts and scratches already looked better.

When the healer finished his quiet ministrations, he nodded to Lad then left the room.

"Well?" I looked at Lad and raised my eyebrows.

"What?"

I stood and went back to his bedside. "What did he say?"

"The healer or my father?"

"Both of them!"

Lad grinned widely. He was purposely tormenting me. He reached out and took one of my hands, playing with my fingers. "Wickthorne says I'm healing well. The bullet did very little damage, other than causing blood loss. My father on the other hand, is considering causing *further* blood loss."

"That bad, huh?" I felt rotten. I was the sole reason for Lad's injuries and family turmoil.

"Well, he let me know I've been foolish and reckless, could have gotten myself killed, and that he's extremely disappointed in me." He gave me a smirk. "The usual."

"It's all my fault. I really should leave."

He enclosed my whole hand in his and squeezed tightly. "No, I want you to stay. Now that I can actually be truthful with you, I don't want it to stop. And don't worry—I've been disappointing my father since long before you came back into my life."

His grin was carefree, but I saw past it. His father's disapproval bothered him.

"Why do you say that?"

"As I told you, he has certain expectations of me. As his son, I have responsibilities, and my father wants me to spend every moment at his heel, learning to perform my *duties*."

"And you don't want to take over the family business? What does your dad do, anyway?"

He laughed and reached up to run a finger softly down my cheek. "You're adorable. The family business—yes, that's one way of putting it. His job is… hard to explain to an outsider. It's not that I don't want to do my part. I just don't want it to be my whole life. I want a certain measure of freedom that's not exactly congruous with the job. And now that I've been out in the world among your people, he and I have some different ideas about how things should be done. My father does not take kindly to 'different.'"

I had a feeling he wasn't just referring to his rebellious ideas. "He hates me, doesn't he?"

Lad rolled his lips in then out, stalling before he answered. "He's afraid of you."

"Afraid of me? Why on earth would he be afraid of *me*?" I pictured the intimidating man who made the atmosphere in a room quiver with the sheer force of his personality.

"You're an outsider, so in his eyes, you're dangerous. You represent discovery and doom as far as he's concerned, and..." He stopped there and looked uncertain.

"And?"

"And he's wondering if he made the wrong decision about you ten years ago."

"Decision about me? What does that mean?"

"I keep waiting for you to remember, but I guess you're not going to." He shook his head, his eyes glinting with disbelief. "You've been here before, Ryann."

"When? The night I was lost? You brought me here?"

"Yes. I was only seven myself. You needed more help than I could give you. I didn't know what else to do. It turned out to be a mistake, though. My father has never let me forget my disobedience almost led to... your death."

I drew back, blinking in shock. "No. You *saved* my life. I was freezing. I would have died."

"The searchers probably would have found you shortly if I hadn't brought you home. And when I brought you here, it caused an uproar. The High Council met for hours discussing what to do with you. Some wanted to put you back outside and make sure you *did* freeze to death. Others voted to kill you outright. A couple of the pacifists thought we should *keep* you here so you couldn't go back and tell anyone."

"What happened? How come they let me go?"

"That was my father's call. He's… pretty influential around here, and he decided on mercy. He said they'd make sure you didn't remember much—even if you did recall something, whatever you said wouldn't be believed because of your age. Come closer. Sit with me."

Lad pulled at my fingers until I sat on the edge of his bed. I was careful not to jostle him, afraid of aggravating his wound.

"I don't want to hurt you."

"You won't," he assured with a sweet smile.

Stroking his arm lightly, I thought about the random images that still sometimes came to me in dreams about that night. I glanced over at the aelflute in the corner. "I was in this room before. And you played that for me."

Lad's face flushed. He nodded. "And I was terrible. But it seemed to make you happy."

"Yes. I definitely remember being happy, which never made any sense to my parents. They couldn't seem to handle the fact that I always had such positive feelings about that night, when it was so painful for them to remember. I think they were worried the whole experience had left me kind of unhinged."

Lad smiled and pushed a strand of hair behind my ear.

I reflected on what he'd said. "You know, I understand your people wanting their privacy and everything—but to actually consider killing a child over it? It's so extreme. I don't get what would be so bad about others knowing your people are here. It's not like you're hurting anyone…

you have amazing talents. People would be excited to know about you."

Lad sat up a little in the bed, his face going severe. "No, Ryann. They wouldn't. It's not about privacy—it's about survival. Your people wouldn't be able to deal with the knowledge. It would alter their understanding of reality, and when that happens, humans don't react well. I've read countless history books that prove it. In 1576 Scotland, a midwife named Bessie Dunlop was accused of sorcery and witchcraft after displaying unusual knowledge and healing talents. She defended herself, claiming to have learned these things from a woman known as the Queen of Elphame—one of us. Bessie was burned at the stake in Dalry. In 1588, Allison Peirson was burned as a witch in Fife, Scotland after prescribing potions and treatments she claimed to have gotten from the same mythical Queen. And, of course, you've heard of the Salem witch hunts, haven't you?"

"Of course." I tried to process what he was telling me. I looked down at the bedcovering then back at his face. "You mean you're... witches?"

"No!" He laughed. "I'm making the point that people are often afraid of what they don't understand, and sometimes when they're afraid, they react violently. We haven't always been so unfriendly and secretive. We *have* reached out to your kind in the past. It usually ends badly for everyone involved, for the people like Bessie and Allison. And... there are far more of you than there are of us. Your kind are much more successful at reproducing.

It's very possible there would be a repeat of some of the lower points in human history if your people ever confirm we exist and discover who we really are."

Cold dread prevented me from breaking the silence for a few moments. I studied the wall, mapping its bumps and crevices, trying to master the unsettled feeling in my stomach. It was finally hitting me that I was dealing with something so far beyond the ordinary, I might not even *want* to know the answer.

But I had to. My throat was dry, and a whisper was all I could manage to produce. "So, you're not human then."

Lad's eyes locked onto mine in a wordless plea, begging me not to make him answer. But I wasn't going to let him off the hook. I couldn't. Even if I never saw him again and had to spend the rest of my life questioning my own sanity, I had to at least know this much about him—who he was. *What* he was.

Meeting his stare, I waited, wondering if he had enough faith in me to confess the truth. Lad's gaze dropped to our clasped hands. He moved his strong fingers over mine in a slow, gentle massage as conflicting emotions warred across his face. Finally, he looked at the ceiling and let out a tortured sigh. His eyes met mine again, and I saw his decision had been made.

He spoke softly, his tone serious. "We were here for at least eight thousand years before your people ever ventured to this continent. My kind live in the desert, in the mountains, in the forests, anywhere there's unpopulated, undisturbed land. A few of us still live near the oceans, though most have been driven out of those habitats because of extensive human development. Wherever we live, we exist in harmony with the land, and in hiding."

My brain was buzzing like I'd chugged a dozen Cokes. I wasn't sure what Lad was leading to, but I knew it would be shocking, maybe even frightening.

"Long ago in this place, we did have close contact with the other indigenous people," he continued. "We shared the land, helped each other. The children played together. We even taught them how to obtain a version of saol water for their own use. But when your people came here, things changed for all of us. The Native Americans were bolder, more welcoming of your kind. We remained concealed and observed the interaction. We saw how their generosity and friendliness earned only persecution for them. Now, they're gone from here, either killed or rounded up and herded onto small pieces of land. Meanwhile, our secrecy and separateness have served us well. Our lifestyle continues as it has for thousands of years."

Thousands of years. It was mind-boggling. People like Lad had lived among humans for thousands of years, and we'd had no idea. It didn't seem possible.

"We've been largely successful at preserving our secret, though rumors and legends about us have persisted—the result of someone among us not being careful enough and being accidentally exposed. But so far, we've been able to happily remain a myth to you all."

I sat silently for a long while, thinking over what he'd said, trying to match what little I'd learned about his people with the legends and myths in books I'd read. A name popped into my head, but I couldn't make myself say it. Better to make him say it than be embarrassingly wrong again.

"What myth?" I barely breathed the question.

Lad gathered my fingers in his warm hand and gently squeezed. His expression said he was finally ready to tell me the whole truth.

CHAPTER NINETEEN
WHO THEY ARE

"Your people call us... Elves."

An explosion rocked my mind. It was impossible. It was crazy. And I knew it was true. "But... you're not tiny."

Lad gave me a gleaming smile. "That's a very convenient misunderstanding... for us. We can thank the Elven playwright William Shakespeare for that. It's why he masqueraded as a human in the first place. Before he wrote A Midsummer Night's Dream, most depictions of us were of human-sized beings, which of course, is dangerously accurate. Then Mr. Tolkein came along and got it almost right again. The myths are helpful though—it's a lot better for us if people are looking for small cookie-making creatures and Snap, Crackle, and Pop."

"There are a lot of you then—all over the world?"

"Our people live on most every continent, or at least they used to. Human cultures around the world have legends of encounters with our kind. Even the ancient Greeks and Romans told stories of Elves. In Iceland, they call us *Huldufólk*. In Germany they call us *Alb* or *Álfar*.

They referred to us as *ælfe* in Old English. The Scots call us *Ghillie Dhu*. The Maylay people of Borneo, southern Thailand, and Sumatra refer to us as *Orang Bunian*. Their legends are so close to the truth it's scary. Some Elves there must have been careless." Lad chuckled.

"Roman mythology called us *Iele*. The ancient Greeks described us as *Nymphs* and *Dryads* and *Naiads*, depending on where they spotted us. The Japanese know us as *Erufu*. In Poland, we've been called *Psotnik*. The Irish call us *Aes Sídhe*. Finnish people know us as *Haltija*, the Danish word is *Elver*, it's *Alv* in Swedish. Many in Europe refer to us as Fae Folk. The names they gave us go on and on."

Lad stopped and studied my face, waiting.

My skin was covered entirely in goose bumps. I suddenly understood how people must have felt when they thought they'd seen a ghost—the disconnect between what you believed was possible and what you saw before your eyes was soul-jarring.

"When you lay it all out, it's obvious people have been running into Elves for centuries all over the world. Now that I think of it, it's a little hard to understand how people could *not* know you exist."

"Some well-placed glamour here and there has helped hide our existence."

My head snapped back from shock. "Glamour? That's real?"

"Absolutely—it's one of our natural defenses. Usually, it's not necessary, though. Most humans need proof of something to believe it." Lad grew increasingly animated as he went on. "It's good that people in modern times *are* so skeptical. Throughout history when we were accidentally revealed to people, their mass communication was limited to quills and parchment and word-of-mouth. Even so, the stories got around, becoming legends, without the aid of twenty-four hour news channels, smart phone cameras, and the Internet."

"Wow. I can imagine what would happen if you were to be discovered in this day and age. The news would be all over the world in seconds."

"That's why my father's so adamant about not interacting with humans. And why he's so furious with me now. Our run-in with the rifle-toting booze brothers unfortunately confirms what he already believed about humans and the perils of the big bad world out there." His tone was sarcastic.

"Well, he was right about those guys—they *were* bad news. And as far as I can tell, a parent's main job is worrying, or it's an engrossing hobby at the very least. My mom would be even worse." Then the terrible realization hit me. "Oh no—my mom!"

I pulled my phone from my pocket and stared at it as if any signal in the world could reach this far underground. Naturally, the screen was dark and lifeless.

"Lad, I have to get to the surface. I have to call my mother. She must've been trying to call me all night. She's probably burning the road up from Atlanta right now because she hasn't been able to reach me. What time is it?"

Without my phone, digital clocks, or even a helpful window, I'd lost all concept of the hour. I was pacing the room.

"It's still early. She might still be sleeping."

"She's going to kill me. One of her conditions for leaving me here was that I stay in constant contact with her—oh no—I probably can't even get a signal above ground way out here."

"It's okay." Lad tried to calm me. "Someone will come any moment, I'm sure. They've undoubtedly heard your voice and will want to make sure the dangerous human isn't doing me harm." He held his hands up defensively, grinning and cringing in mock-helplessness as I glared at him. He laughed and motioned for me to come closer. "I'll ask someone to take you up so you can call her. It will be all right—you'll get a signal. I wish I could escort you myself, but…" He gestured to indicate his bed-ridden state.

In spite of his size, he looked like a little boy, rumpled and warm and sleepy. I was suddenly afraid to leave him. I went back to his bedside and placed the lightest of butterfly kisses on his lips.

"Can I come right back?" I whispered.

With a tender smile, Lad slid a large hand around to cradle my head and pulled my face back to his until our foreheads touched and our breath mingled. "You'd better."

Two men entered the room. They were the same tall, warrior-types who'd come to Lad's rescue in the woods.

"Ryann, I'd like to introduce you to Voldur and Langnon. You'll recognize them, though you have not officially met. I'll ask Langnon to escort you to the surface and then bring you right back to me."

Shifting from foot to foot, I eyed the two mute men. "Yes, thank you. That would be great."

Lad spent a few moments silently giving them instructions. They turned toward me and nodded politely.

"It's... uh... nice to meet you, too," I stuttered, feeling supremely silly.

Lad squeezed my hand tighter. "Langnon will take you now, Ryann. You have nothing to fear from him. He'll help you in whatever you need. Before you go..." He pulled me back down to him, slowly and deliberately kissed me, then glanced back at the guards as if he wanted to make sure they were watching. "Come back quickly," he whispered.

I moved away from the bed, looking back until the last possible moment before following Langnon from the room. My stomach was a bowl of raw nerves as we walked through the labyrinth of hallways in Lad's home.

Langnon's long strides forced me to speed walk along behind him as we passed through the great hall. I surveyed the room from a new perspective, one of informed awe rather than bewildered ignorance. It was large and elegant. The stucco-style mudded walls were hung liberally with beautiful tapestry weavings of fancy parties and hunt scenes and images of tall graceful women with cascading curls.

Mosaics made of the otherworldly glowing stones decorated the walls, floors, and even the ceiling where a huge elaborate central design illuminated the room below in colored light. Men and women moved busily about the room, carrying linens and platters, and vases that emitted a subtle glow. I assumed they were also filled with the phosphorescent mineral rocks.

Then we were back in the relative darkness, moving through yet another hallway, which I now knew would lead us to the cavernous open area in the center of this secret subterranean world.

When we emerged into the public area, I was once again the subject of intense study by everyone we passed. There was no apparent shock this time. Word of the alien visitor must have spread, and my appearance was now a remarkable curiosity instead of a surprise. I returned their gazes, offering a smile. No one smiled back. Lad had smiled at me many times, but I couldn't recall having seen any of the others here smile. Perhaps somber expressions were their way, or maybe there hadn't been much cause for joy since my arrival.

Just before we entered the tunnel to the surface, squealing and laughter grabbed my attention. I turned to see a group of small children looking and pointing in our direction. That answered my question—plenty of happy faces there. The sound of childish laughter was always pleasant, but these voices were something more. They reminded me of my childhood encounter with Lad. I couldn't stop myself from giggling along with the delicious music of it.

The sweet young voices faded as we climbed the dim incline, spiraling toward the surface. I smelled the fresh air even before the sunlight began to filter into the tunnel from above. Outside, the green brightness of the morning nearly blinded me, and I'd never truly appreciated how spectacular the woods smelled before.

As marvelous as the sights and scents above ground were, I was anxious to complete my call and return to Lad. Fishing in my pocket for my phone, I looked back over my shoulder to make sure Langnon was still there. He nodded tersely at me. Poor guy. Stuck with human-sitting duty.

Checking for a signal, my heart fell again. I was right. I had one bar, and it was wavering. Holding the phone up, I turned to one side then the other. No good.

And then Langnon lifted one of my arms and slung it over his shoulder, wrapping one of his hands around my waist.

"Wha—" For the second time in my life, I was on a quick, involuntary ride up a tree. Instantly nauseated, I closed my eyes and gritted my teeth, waiting for it to be over. So, this was what Lad had meant when he'd assured me I'd be able to get a signal. From the top of the enormous magnolia, I'd have a straight shot at a cell tower for sure.

When Langnon stopped moving, I opened my eyes. *Don't look down.* This time I took my own advice and kept my eyes up, taking in the thick trunk and the branches around me. My footing was solid enough, but Langnon kept one hand wrapped around my arm, and I didn't complain. I was, however, motivated to keep the conversation short and sweet.

When I looked at my phone again, there were three bars—good enough. I hesitated a second before dialing. What was I going to tell Mom? Usually, I could talk to her about anything. This was not one of those things. I wasn't in the habit of lying to her, but I had no choice. I'd have to make an exception here, for her sake and for Lad's.

Before the first ring even finished, my mother picked up and launched into a worried rant. She sounded like a woman at the end of her rope—a fusion of bad temper and extreme relief.

"My God, Ryann—where have you been? I was about to get in the car and come home. And I was exactly five minutes from calling the sheriff's office. Why haven't you answered my calls or texts?"

I kept my voice even and light, though my belly clenched at the dishonesty of what I was about to say. "I'm sorry you were worried. My phone must have died last night, and I slept in today. I didn't even realize you'd called and texted until I got it charged this morning."

"Well, you about gave me a heart attack. This makes me wonder if you really are responsible enough to be there alone. I should've insisted on you coming with us."

"No, I'm fine here. I'm sorry. I won't let it happen again, Mom, I promise. How's your visit with Shelly going?" I tried changing the subject, but she wasn't ready to let it go.

"Fine," she replied tersely. Suspicion now colored her voice. "What've you been doing?"

"Oh, you know, hanging out, spending some time outdoors."

"Are you being careful? Are you having fun with your friends?"

"I really am."

"What are your plans today?" Her tone was brightening, the crisis over. This one, anyway.

"Oh, just getting together with some people." *Or some Elves, no big deal.*

"Well, make sure you keep your phone charged from now on. No more giving your mother nightmares, okay?"

"Okay, Mom. I'm sorry again."

"Okay, babe. I miss you. Shelly says, 'Hi.' We're going to the World of Coke and the Georgia Aquarium today. It's the biggest in the world. I wish you were here to see it."

"I'll see it next time. Have fun. Take some pictures for me."

"I will. Love you."

"Love you, too." I didn't know how much longer I'd be staying with Lad, but if it turned out to be more than a day, I'd have to make regular trips to the surface for phone calls. My mother's trust in me wouldn't withstand another long period of time incommunicado.

Next I called Emmy to make an excuse for my absence, but it went straight to voicemail, which was a relief. I left a message saying I was fine, staying with a friend, and promising to explain all later. Hopefully it would satisfy her.

"Okay, I'm done." I turned back to Langnon, knowing he didn't understand my words, but he seemed to get the idea.

I clung to him as he carried me back down the tree, and slipping back into the hole, I followed him down the sloping entryway. My surroundings were losing their frightening strangeness, and I was starting to appreciate how beautiful Lad's home was. Nothing was gilded or delicate, but there was artistry and a sense of history in the décor and the furnishings.

As I once had noticed about Lad himself, there was similarly nothing artificial in this place. All the colors and materials were appealingly natural. The people here had probably never ingested a chemical, worn a man-made fiber or even touched something made of plastic. Their healer Wickthorne must have had a very light work schedule.

Langnon led me to Lad's door then turned and stopped with his back to the wall of the hallway, like a guard at his post, which I supposed was exactly the case. When I touched him lightly on the arm, he looked down at me.

"Thank you," I said.

Of course he didn't answer, but the corners of his mouth edged upward almost imperceptibly.

Lad was sitting up when I entered the room. The bed coverings were folded down around his waist—the smooth exposed skin of his chest and arms looked warm and tan and touchable. Only the cloth bandage on his side betrayed his injured state. He looked better recovering from a gunshot wound than most guys did on the best day of their lives. Inwardly, I chastised myself for lusting after an injured man.

The look on his face when he glanced up at me sent warm tingles down my spine. "You came back."

"Well, I couldn't leave you down here at the mercy of all these mythical creatures." I went to Lad and wrapped my arms around his neck in a cautious hug. He surprised me by gripping my hips with his hands and pulling me onto the bed with him.

"Oh—be careful—your side. You'll hurt yourself."

"I'm feeling much better." Lad grinned wickedly.

"Yes, I can see you are." I giggled and pulled back to look at him. "How is that possible by the way? You were shot yesterday."

Lad raised his hands in a *What can I say?* gesture. "Elf," he offered as a one word explanation.

"So you're telepathic and have accelerated healing powers, too? Not fair."

"Yep. Stinks to be a mere human, doesn't it?"

"Yeah, it kind of does, especially when suffering from a human weakness like hunger." I rubbed my empty stomach. "Don't tell me Elves don't need food either."

"On the contrary, I'm starving." Lad smiled at me and clapped loudly, and the door opened. Langnon poked his head into the room, watched Lad for a few seconds and ducked out again.

"Let me guess, you placed your breakfast order? I've *got* to learn to do that!"

"*Our* breakfast order. And I think you *will* learn to do it. All you really have to do is concentrate on the meaning of what you want to convey to the other person. Try it."

I was doubtful but made an attempt to please him. After a moment he stroked his chin in an exaggerated gesture of contemplation.

"Hmmm. You said... you find me unbearably attractive and have sworn off all other guys forever." He laughed.

Pretty darn close. "Actually, I was wondering what you eat for breakfast around here. No Froot Loops, I guess."

"No Froot Loops, whatever that is, but we'll see if we can tempt you with some of our foods." He grinned widely.

I was amazed to see him acting playful and energetic after all that had happened. Amazed and grateful.

A girl came in carrying two trays laden with more food than two people could possibly eat. Or so I'd thought. Apparently recovering from a near death experience creates a monster appetite because Lad ate quickly and enthusiastically, only pausing between bites to educate me about what was on my plate.

"That's called *koek*." He gestured toward a pancake-like food. "It's made from acorn flour, and of course, you recognize the eggs."

There were wild blueberries and an unfamiliar hot cereal that reminded me of oatmeal. I took a few tentative bites then my stomach unleashed a full force protest against its emptiness. I couldn't get the food into my mouth fast enough. Lad and I looked like we were in a competitive eating contest. We glanced over at each other and burst out laughing.

"You're adorable," Lad informed me, his green eyes brimming with warmth.

"Oh, yes—nothing more appealing than a girl stuffing her face like a hamster."

"Like a yellow-pine chipmunk actually. But they're quite cute." He shook his head, grinning. "I've never in all my life seen a girl eat like you do."

"I suppose Elven girls have impeccable table manners, too."

Seeing my obvious embarrassment, Lad laughed and reassured me. "No, I *like* it. The girls here are all so sedate and reserved. You make me laugh. I have fun with you."

How different and bizarre I must have seemed to everyone there—everyone from *his* world. "Lad?"

"Hmmm?"

"Exactly how much trouble are you in?"

"You mean, about you being here, or about mixing with humans in general, or about getting myself shot?"

"All of the above."

He handed me the platters to put on the bedside table. Giving the mattress a pat, he invited me to sit beside him. "I'm not the most popular person around here at the moment, but that's not your concern. You've done nothing wrong. I need you here. And they all might as well get used to the idea."

"Really?" I was amazed by Lad's willingness to buck his family's opinion and risk his society's disapproval for my sake. And that he believed he'd be able to get away with it. And that he *needed* me.

"Absolutely. In a couple days, I should be ready to move about again, and I'll show you more of my home. "

Privately, I doubted that would ever happen. I felt like I was here on a minute-by-minute pass. His father would probably eject me from the premises as soon as he was sure Lad's health was out of danger. I'd be banished back to the real world, and Lad might be forbidden from ever venturing to the surface again.

Lad seemed oblivious to the future and overjoyed that I was with him in his sickroom confinement. I snooped around his room, and he agreed to play his aelflute for me, though he refused to let me hear him sing.

"Why not? Do you suck that much?" I teased him.

"No." He laughed. "I don't want to unfairly influence you."

"Afraid I'll fall madly in love with you and stalk you forever?"

He laughed. "You're joking, but if you've ever read any lore about Elves and Fae, you've probably seen it mentioned that our singing *can* have a strange effect on humans. Sometimes simply talking to them will do it. Or even a look. That's what glamour really is—it's similar to the way we communicate without speaking aloud—but with a little added persuasion."

"Well, I've read about it in books, but I had no idea there really was such a thing."

His chin dipped and he looked at me from under his brows, clearing his throat before speaking. "I tried to use it on you the day I surprised you at the pool in the woods when you were so afraid of me," he confessed. "I'm sorry. I was desperate."

"Oh—the 'pushy' look."

"Yes, you remember. I won't try it again—I promise. It's better to know how you really feel about me than to trick you into some false emotion."

"Good. I don't think it worked on me anyway—did it? Maybe I'm immune."

"Maybe. I've wondered about that. Influence isn't really my specialty, though."

"Influence? What do you mean?"

"Well, all Elves have a certain degree of influence—we call it Sway—but different family lines have different strengths when it comes to glamour. For some it's a more powerful ability to influence human minds. For others it's emotional connection, musical ability, physical prowess, even…" He blushed. "…even sexual appeal."

"Is that your specialty?" I asked, completely serious.

Lad laughed. "Thank you for the compliment, but no. My father's is leadership and inspiring trust. He says mine is the same. But I'm not very practiced at using my glamour. As a rule, none of us here like to use it. It's one of the main things separating us from the Dark Elves—we make a point of not using our gifts to take advantage of humans—they think it's foolish not to. A Dark Elf would probably be able to glamour you. Some of them are quite strong—they can even glamour other Elves in addition to humans."

"So then, some Elves *do* associate with humans?"

"Oh yes. Extensively."

"And if they're the Dark Elves, what does that make you—Light Elves?" He nodded, and I continued. "So… what? They look different?"

"It's not about appearance. We all have varied skin tones and hair and eye colors. It's more about a difference in world views."

"Oh, like Democrats and Republicans."

He laughed. "Yes, but our politics are the oldest on the planet, and even more contentious. The rift goes back all the way to the First Ones. Naturally, they don't call themselves Dark Elves—that's our name for them. They call themselves "The Beings" and believe they're as right as we believe *we* are. We seem to keep moving farther apart in our approaches to the human race. We *all* protect the secret. But the Light Elves do it by keeping ourselves as separate from the human world as possible, and the Dark Elves do the exact opposite, flirting with disaster by seeking the spotlight and relying on glamour for cover."

"What do you mean the spotlight? I've never seen any."

"You have. They masquerade as humans, but you've been watching them on television and in movies, listening to them on the radio your whole life."

"You're kidding."

"No. As I said, Dark Elves enjoy manipulating humans and crave human admiration. So they're very attracted to the entertainment field, and sports, and politics. They long for the Old Days, when being worshipped and served by humans was the normal order of business. In the beginning, none of us were in hiding. We were the gods of this world, if you will."

"You're telling me there are celebrities and politicians and famous athletes in this country who are actually Elves? How can you tell them apart from the famous humans?"

"Well, naturally *I* know which are Elves and which are not. But you could probably tell if you really tried. The ones who seem almost too good to be true—too perfectly formed, too strong, too talented—that's how you know. Dark Elves have always been the most popular and highly acclaimed celebrities, and it's on the rise, thanks to the fan pod system they've come up with."

"Oh my God—fan pods? Vallon Foster and Serena Simmons. They're Dark Elves?" A cold sensation crept through my stomach. *Emmy.* "What are the fan pods for? What do the Dark Elves want with them?"

"Well, to expand their following among humans, obviously, but we're not sure exactly why. Or why they seem to be increasing their efforts lately. The Light Elves usually stay completely out of it, but my father and the rest of the High Council feel it's getting out of hand now. It will be one of the main topics of discussion at the next Assemblage."

"What's that?"

"The Assemblage is a great gathering of Elves that's been going on for thousands of years, a way of staying in contact with the other "tribes" so to speak. The Light and Dark High Councils and their entourages from all the different regions of this continent will come together to discuss policy. The next Assemblage will take place here. Everyone looks forward to it—there's a lot of trading and mediation of disagreements between the groups, but it's also a time of celebration."

"So it's like a big annual Elf Convention?"

Lad laughed. "Something like that, but the Assemblage happens only once every ten years. It's not easy for such a large number of us to travel undetected on a more regular basis. Envoys from the different tribes visit each other more often, carrying reports and messages between them."

Lad insisted he needed me with him to recover, so I stayed, and over the next few days we talked endlessly. I told him about school, my parents, Grandma, and my friends.

He explained day-to-day life in his underground world. He described growing up there and sneaking away as a child to try to find me again. I smiled, thinking of the mischievous, laughing boy he'd been, the curious, kind boy who'd saved me that night in the woods long ago.

Now he was so much more to me. I watched his animated face as he told a story.

I know him.

A kind of warmth grew in my chest. For the first time, I felt like there was someone who really knew *me*. Lad knew and understood even the part of me I'd been forbidden to discuss with anyone else—and he *believed* me because he was part of it, too.

The dark warm room was our cocoon, where we could transform and grow strong together before we had to emerge and face the harsh realities of the world outside.

Of course, there wasn't *just* conversation. We spent a ridiculous amount of time kissing. It never went further than that—there was still the unspoken danger of the coupled-for-life-thing. And how far could it really go anyway with what amounted to a babysitter posted right outside the door and the possibility of his parents barging in at any time?

I spent overnights in a room next door to Lad's. It was dark and cozy like his. My first night there, either the bed had been extraordinarily comfortable or I'd been more exhausted than I realized, because I'd slept as if under a spell.

When I woke, I discovered several dresses draped over the bed, all made of the exquisite delicate fabric I'd seen the girls here wearing. I chose one and slipped it on, the soft wheat-colored material floating over my skin, light as breath. Though the garment was warm, I had to touch it over and over to be sure it was really there because it felt no more substantial than a spider web on my skin.

The only truly uncomfortable moments came when Lad's parents, who I'd learned were called Ivar and Mya, paid their daily visits. I didn't need the ability to hear thoughts to understand how his father felt about me. It was painfully obvious. Lad's mother might have thought differently, but I couldn't be sure. Mya seemed reluctant to even glance in my direction with Ivar's hostility always dominating the atmosphere.

"Wow, he totally hates me," I said after their third visit. I felt judged and a little angry, but I also understood Ivar's position. If I were him, I would probably have hated me too.

"No. I told you, it's not you, it's—"

"It *is* me. It's not just that he's questioning his decision to let me go ten years ago, or the threat I pose because I'm a human where I don't belong. It's *me*. There's something about me in particular that completely unhinges him. I can see it in his eyes when he looks at me."

Lad tried to protest. "I'm sure you're wrong. What could he possibly hold against you personally?" But I saw I'd made him wonder.

Each day, I made an excursion to the surface to call Mom and return texts. Lad always asked what she'd said, curious about my family.

"I can tell she's a little jealous of her friend Shelly's happy marriage—Mom misses being married."

"How long were your parents together?"

"Sixteen years. They got married because Mom was pregnant with me, but they always seemed happy. Well, until recently, of course. In spite of all the things she says about men, I think she'll end up marrying again eventually," I told him. "That is, if she meets the right person."

"And that's really how it works? You meet someone, and you simply choose each other based on your feelings?"

I wasn't sure where he was going with this. It seemed pretty straightforward to me. "Yeah... why do you have that look on your face?"

"Well, it's just so different. Here, couplings are arranged by families on the basis of strengths and weaknesses and... alliances." He looked down and drew on the bedspread with one finger as he finished.

"What about love? Passion? Doesn't anybody feel that stuff?" I was strangely distressed by the idea of marriage without love, though that was no guarantee—my parents had supposedly started off in love, and look how it had turned out.

"As I told you before, it's a permanent decision for us. It can't be based on something changeable like feelings or passion. My people don't make decisions rashly—probably why we've been around so long."

"What about you? You seem… passionate." My cheeks heated at his slow answering smile.

Lad leaned toward me, his voice gaining a teasing note. "Well now, I'm a rule-breaker, aren't I? Reading about human romance… getting crazy ideas, letting myself be corrupted by a beautiful human girl…" His voice was a seductive caress, low and drawn out. "Of course, if more of us discovered kissing, there might be a great deal *less* practical decision making going on around here." He moved in and took my mouth in a sweet, warm kiss that gave me some crazy ideas of my own.

When he eventually pulled away, I studied his face. "So it's really true then? You'd honestly never even kissed anyone before me?"

"I told you, Ryann. You'll eventually learn I never lie. What about you? Are you the marrying kind? Like your mother?"

"You know what's funny? She's the reason I'm *not* the marrying kind. Or maybe my father is the reason. Anyway, I'm not. I don't know if I'll ever get married. You will, I guess—since that's the only way you can ever have…" My words drifted away in my embarrassment.

Lad nodded. "I *have* to. I have no choice. In fact…" He paused, shifting and looking away. "In fact, I don't have much time."

"What do you mean? Time for what?"

"Soon I'll be eighteen—the age of coupling for the Elven people. When I told you before it was getting harder and harder for me to resist—that's what I meant. As we approach our eighteenth birthdays, the drive to find a mate becomes stronger and stronger. I guess it's Nature's way of ensuring the continuation of our race."

I blinked a few times and sat silently, trying to make sense of his words. "But eighteen is so young. And if you have a… wife…"

It was too obvious to even warrant saying out loud. No matter *how* I felt about Lad, or how he might feel about me, this relationship was going to be short term. Very short. In a few months I'd start my senior year, and Lad would become someone else's *husband*.

I sensed myself heating up from the inside, a state somewhere between fury and despair taking over. My ears burned. I looked away from Lad toward the wall, trying to control my emotions.

His voice behind me was grim. "I'm sorry—I've been trying to tell you. I wish things were different… but I can't help who I am."

"I know." My voice sounded ragged. "I don't wish you were anyone other than who you are."

Lad's response was a whisper. "I do."

He got up and crossed the room to retrieve his aelflute. Returning to the bed, he sat next to me and strummed it. The tune was nothing I'd heard before, but I recognized its sadness.

I should have been sorry for him in that moment, I guess. It would've been the generous emotion—if I never wanted to marry, that was my choice. It was also possible I'd change my mind someday. Again, my choice. For Lad, participating in an arranged marriage was required.

But I couldn't feel anything besides anger at myself and maybe a little embarrassment, too. I mean, really—how many times did reality have to slap me in the face? How had I let myself get in this deep? I knew better. I had to let go of the dream of being with him.

I stood and turned toward Lad, looking down into his mournful face. "I'm tired. I'm going to my room now."

He reached out for my hand. "No. Stay. Stay for a little while longer? It's your last night here."

"I know. I think I should get an early start home tomorrow… in case my mom comes back early."

Lad must have heard the determination in my voice because he didn't argue further. Rising from the bed, he put his hands on my shoulders and bent to kiss me. I dropped my chin, hiding my face.

After a moment's hesitation, he kissed my forehead as if that had been his intention all along.

Chapter Twenty
One Revelation Too Many

I wasn't as morose the next morning. Things were what they were, and I was beginning to accept them. I was going home today—I might never see him again.

But... I was with him *now*, and that was a gift. He wasn't eighteen yet. We had a little time left. And seeing him healthy and moving easily around his room made me happy. I'd accomplished that much. Lad had saved me. I'd saved him back. We were even. I'd think about the rest of it later.

The speed of Lad's recovery was astounding. Any human would've been hospitalized for weeks, if not dead, after enduring what he'd gone through. It had been a few days, and his gunshot wound was almost healed.

"Is it because you're, you know, an Elf?" I asked as we shared breakfast.

"Partly. As you've noticed, our hearts beat faster than yours. Our body temperatures are higher, and our metabolisms seem to be faster. I've never spent this much time close to a human, so I haven't had the chance to make side-by-side comparisons before. But it does appear we heal faster as well."

I considered it. "You said 'partly.' There's more, isn't there? I mean, my legs and arms were so torn up I looked like I'd wandered into a pit bull fight. Now, my skin is as clear as a baby's. Is it the stuff Wickthorne rubbed on me?"

"Yes. The healing solution he used on both of us is derived from the same source as saol water. I don't know how much of the physical difference between our races is due to that and how much we're born with."

It made me wonder. Since taking up temporary residence in Lad's underground world, I'd been living like an Elf, eating their food, drinking saol water daily—still the best thing I'd ever tasted. Each time I had it, its glowing effect flowed through me. I felt better now than I ever had in my life. Maybe it was due to the saol water. Maybe it was being with Lad.

"Feel me," I ordered him.

Lad gave me a funny look. "What?"

"I'm not trying to seduce you, silly. Feel my forehead—you know—to see if I'm warmer."

Lad obligingly placed a palm across the top of my face. "I don't know. You still feel like a cool little river pebble to me."

I rolled my eyes. "Oh, never mind. Anyone would feel cool next to you. What about my pulse?"

Slowly he lifted his hand and brought it to my neck, his long fingers reaching almost all the way around it as he searched for the rhythm beating there. I realized this wouldn't be a very scientific experiment as my pulse skyrocketed in response to his touch. No matter that it was foolish and impractical to be so drawn to him—I was only human, after all.

"It is a bit faster," Lad whispered, his green eyes glowing with enticing playfulness. "Not an Elf *quite* yet, though."

I sighed in disappointment. It was true. I *wasn't* one of his kind. I couldn't help wondering who this Elven child-bride of his would be, what she'd look like. Was she one of the beautiful girls I'd already seen here?

No—stop.

I couldn't go there yet. I'd have plenty of time to torture myself with those thoughts later in the privacy of my own room where I could mope as much as I wanted to.

Reluctantly, I pulled away from him and stood. "My mom said they'd be home this afternoon. I should go home and clean up. I have to be at the house when she gets there."

"I know. I'm well enough now to take you, but would you do me a favor? Let's put it off a little while longer. I want to show you some things first. I'll get you back in time."

I changed into my own clothes and met Lad in the hallway. I'd been hurriedly escorted through the public areas here many times now but never with any real opportunity to interact with its residents. Now I'd be by his side, clearly his guest, and I had no idea what to expect. Would the Elves fear me? Attack me for being different? Would their reactions change the way Lad saw me?

I followed him through the dimly lit hallways of his home, and he pointed out rooms, explaining their purposes. Lad said the great hall was frequently used for large formal gatherings.

"Like a ballroom?"

"Something like that."

Whenever we talked about his family, I got the impression Lad was trying to *underwhelm* me. Judging from their huge and opulent home, they were people of considerable importance here, but he seemed reluctant to say much about them.

We emerged from the tunnel into the enormous common area, and Lad became much more talkative. He almost ran as he pulled me by the hand, pointing out things along the way. The ground floor of the cavern seemed to comprise a village. At the base of the cavern wall, people entered and exited warmly lit cave-like openings. It reminded me of the huge, bustling shopping mall we sometimes visited in Memphis, the nearest large city.

Punctuating the open area were small huts—walking paths weaved between them. The structures looked too small to be dwellings. I peeked in the open doorway of the closest one as we passed.

A startling thrill of alarm shot through me when I spotted the white crown of a spiral-curled head bent over a large loom. For one eerie moment, I thought I was looking at my grandma, that somehow she'd found out what I'd been up to and had come to find me down here. But the woman looked up from her work, and of course she was a stranger. I raised my fingers in a sheepish wave, and she stared after me in curiosity until we left her sight.

Lad dragged me past one noisy hut where hissing steam and glowing light filled the air. "This is a metal shop where our tools and dishware are made."

"Where does the metal come from?"

"From the earth." He looked at me as if I must have been slacking in geology. "We harvest large lumps of native copper and iron ore from the ground, and our metal workers fashion it into whatever is needed. Many of the vessels we use we make from clay, but other things are better made from the copper and iron."

We walked in the direction of the underground river. The path was a busy thoroughfare, with people coming and going. I noticed a peculiar reaction from those we encountered, not just to me, but to Lad. Everyone—men, women, and children included—made a deferential nod to him when we crossed their paths. Some even stopped and looked down until Lad and I passed by. He didn't seem to notice.

"Here we are," he said with satisfaction as we arrived at the riverbank. "The source of our greatest treasure."

I looked across the wide crystalline river toward the dark opening in the wall from where it flowed. "What treasure?"

"The water. It feeds us, heals us, gives us strength, energy, and health." He kneeled and scooped some from the river's edge, cupping it in his hands for me to taste. I obliged him, taking a sip as he tipped some into my mouth. It tasted cool and pure, but not like the sweet, simmering otherworldly drink I'd come to know as saol water.

"It tastes different."

"I said this is the *source*, but it's only the beginning of the process. Follow me." Lad got to his feet again and offered his hand. We walked along the river, enduring some amazed stares and the respectful nods and bows of everyone we met on the way. The path under our feet was earth and stone, worn smooth by centuries of Elven foot traffic.

We neared the base of one of the long-reaching root columns. Its size was simply astonishing. From a distance, I'd imagined them as sinewy, twisted vines hanging from the soaring ceiling down to the earthen floor of the cavern. Now I realized they were colossal supports, as vast in size and strength as any column in a magnificent Greek ruin.

These huge columns, spread throughout the grand space, and the complex web of intersecting roots answered my question about how the tremendous ceiling was supported.

Bustling activity surrounded the pillar. Young Elven men carried large containers back and forth to the root column. Elven women worked at its base, attending what looked like taps driven into the gnarled skin of the roots at various intervals. Clear liquid dripped from the taps into the large empty vessels placed below them.

Lad stopped a few yards away and pulled me close to his side, whispering a narration of their activities. "Do you know what they're doing?"

"They're taking something from the roots. Is this where the saol water actually comes from?"

"It's almost saol water at this point. The roots draw water from the subterranean river and pull it upward. It will eventually reach the trunks of the trees above ground, and be drawn all the way to the ends of their smallest branches. The natural sugars produced inside the roots mix with the pure water from this underground source to provide nourishment for the trees. We tap it here at the lowest levels where the sugar is the least diluted."

"Does it hurt the trees? Aren't they… you know, hungry?"

Lad laughed and wrapped an arm around my back, settling one large hand at my waist. "No, there's plenty to go around. They hardly notice the trifling amount of sap we take. There's one more step in the process. Come and see."

He steered me away from the river toward one of the wide caves in the foot of the cavern wall. Roaring fires glowed in each corner of the rectangular room, the smoke being drawn up into dark, sooty holes in its ceiling.

The delicious scent would have told me we were in the saol water processing room, even if I hadn't seen the tall, muscle bound Elves laboring over steaming bowls of liquid. I counted twelve of the huge concave discs made of hammered copper. They contained glowing stones of various hues and different levels of clear liquid and were attended by large Elven males, each one as fit and perfectly formed as the next.

The men were all shirtless and barefoot, dressed only in short breeches. They looked like a Chippendales fantasy version of factory line workers, armed with heavy tongs, lifting and carrying blistering hot mineral rocks between the corner fire pits and their gleaming vaporous bowls. I wondered if their lack of clothing wasn't dangerous, considering the obvious high temperatures of the substance they worked with.

There was something else unusual about their appearance as I observed them in the steamy, sweet heat of the room. Their skin and hair seemed to glisten and even sparkle in the light as they moved. *Some other subspecies of Elf, maybe?*

Then it occurred to me—they were covered in sugar. In the process of distilling the root sap down to saol water, the workers placed heated mineral rocks into the bowls. The hot rocks caused steam to rise from the naturally sugared water, coating the men with a sheer mist of sugar crystals. I imagined after a full day of this work, they were quite sticky.

I was thinking about this, wondering about the practicalities of underground showers—I'd found a hot bath waiting for me in my room each night, and they obviously had created some sort of drainage system beneath the floors for bathrooms—but I hadn't seen any showers here. I realized Lad was staring at me.

"Are you all right? You seem... thrown off by the workers. Do you find them attractive?"

"No... I mean... yes, of course. But not like *that*." Lad broke into an amused grin as I continued fumbling through my explanation, my blush deepening. "It's just *everyone* here is so attractive. It's not normal."

Lad's smile as he looked down at me was meltingly warm and as sweet as the air we'd left behind in the sugar room. He placed a kiss on my forehead, making me feel like a treasured little girl.

"Mmmm, now *you* taste sweet." He laughed, tugging at my hand, urging me to walk with him. "Well now, *I* think humans are rather attractive, actually, because their appearances are so varied, so interesting. You must have noticed we all look quite similar. Some would say when everyone is beautiful... no one is beautiful. Now you see what I meant when I told you I'm nothing special."

I didn't see that at all. Even among all the unnaturally perfect men of his own world, Lad stood out.

"You *are* special," I said as I turned something over in my mind. "Speaking of 'special'… do you even notice how everybody acts when you're around? They're almost—what's the word—reverent, I guess. I mean… it's strange… like you're Prince William or something."

Lad winced before straightening out his expression.

A sharp shock went through me, my mind scrambling, putting together the things I'd witnessed the past few days here in his mysterious home. I stopped walking.

"You are… aren't you?"

He just looked at me, his lips forming a tight, grim line.

"Oh my God. I'm such an idiot. The nodding and bowing, the guards, the enormous house and servants—they *are* servants, aren't they? Oh, man, you have servants!" I had to stop and breathe a minute. I was headed toward hyperventilation.

"You're part of some kind of… royal family. And your father, with all of his *Lord of the Manor* attitude and his insistence that you do your duty and learn at his knee… that's why, isn't it? Is he a king? Yeah? And you're… are you a… *prince?*"

Lad's expression was miserable. I hoped he was. How could he keep such a secret from me?

"*That's* why your men broke the rules and responded to me when I ran through the woods with your necklace, screaming your name. They weren't going to take any chances with the life of the prince, were they? That's why I was allowed to come with you. And stay. Why I'm allowed to be walking around here now with you. No one else would get away with blatantly breaking the rules, would they? But they can't stop you—because… you're their ruler."

Why was this so shocking after the discovery that I had fallen for an Elf? I wasn't sure—but the knowledge that he was, in fact, an Elven *prince* was just about to send me over the edge.

"No," came his quiet reply.

"No, you're not a prince? I thought you never lied." My tone was surly.

"I'm not their ruler. Not yet. My father is the ruler of the Light Elves. I am his heir." Lad didn't seem proud of the fact. His voice was quiet and solemn. When I didn't reply, he looked over at me, his brow furrowed. "Are you okay?"

"No!" Several heads turned in the direction of my raised voice. "No," I began again more quietly. "I am definitely not okay. I never even believed in Santa Claus for God's sake—not the Easter Bunny or the Tooth Fairy or… or… Cinderella and Prince Charming."

Lad's forehead furrowed. "Don't most children in this country believe in those legends?"

"Yes," I hissed in irritation. "But not me. Oh no—my parents didn't want to fill *my* head with make-believe— that would have created confusion between what's real and what's fantasy. Ha! And now, here I am—me—talking to the Prince of Elves in his magical underground kingdom."

My sarcastic sing-song tone made Lad's eyes turn sorrowful. But I was finally, *finally* beginning to get it through my head. Sure, I felt closer to Lad than I'd ever felt to anyone other than my parents and grandma. Lad understood me. He cared for me—I knew it. But This. Was. Impossible.

I looked at my hands and realized they were shaking. Tears were sure to be next—the pressure was already building behind my eyes.

Lad pulled at my hand, and I stiffened my legs like a mule refusing to be moved. Then he placed one arm around my back and gently guided me along the path as it sloped upward into the dark river cavern.

His voice was soothing, low, and quiet. "It's all right. Everything's fine. Come on, Ryann. We'll sit and talk."

I shuffled along beside him in silence. After walking a ways in relative darkness, we came to another open space, lit by a crevice in the rock overhead. In the center was a basin of crystal clear water, fed by a waterfall. From the surface above, it must have looked like a rocky hillside. Underneath, from our vantage point, the crack served as a perfect skylight to illuminate the beautiful underground pool.

Lad sat on a rock at the water's edge and gathered me into his lap, cradling me in his arms. The gurgling sound of the flume spilling into the pool began the work of soothing my sprung nerves. He rocked me gently, allowing me no wiggle room as he crushed me against his chest.

I started sweating from the heat of his body, and still, I didn't move, just sat passively on his lap with the side of my face pressed against his sauna-like warmth. That felt real, if nothing else in the world did at the moment.

"This is why I didn't tell you," he softly crooned to me. "It's too much. You're okay, my sweet girl." He continued the gentle rocking motion, petting my hair, trying to give me comfort.

Finally I lifted my head and looked at his face. Lad smiled at me. Then he laughed softly at my expression, a light coming into his eyes. "Oh no, don't tell me... you're going to ask me if I'm real again, aren't you?"

"Yes. Yes, I am. Tell me I'm not crazy, Lad, please."

"Of course I'm real, love. I'm still just me. And you are perfectly sane—unfortunate, but sane. It's my fault—you've simply become involved in something you were never supposed to know about. As I said, it's too much for humans to handle. It makes you question reality. Do you see what I mean now? Imagine if others found out about us, too. If Elves are real then what else is possible? Ghosts? Aliens? It's too frightening for humans to believe." He pressed his nose and lips softly against my cheek. "Are you still mad at me?"

"No." I realized it was true as I said it. I wasn't mad anymore. I understood why he didn't tell me, and I was starting to accept what it meant for us. I sat safely wrapped in his arms for a long time. My breathing calmed, and my mind gradually cleared.

I became aware of splashing noises coming from the pool and lifted my head to look. A group of children, probably two or three years old, were swimming and playing, their perfect tiny naked bodies the closest thing I'd seen to chubbiness since arriving in this unreal place. Shrieks of delight and peals of musical laughter filled the air and echoed off the cavern walls and low ceiling.

Several young women sat at the edge of the water supervising the toddlers, silent except for the occasional responsive laugh. They looked slightly older than me and possessed the physical markers I'd come to learn were common to all Elven females—long, curling hair, luminous skin, slender, muscular bodies. Put simply, they were flawless. The whole scene had the atmosphere of a classical oil painting depicting bathing nymphs.

"They're so gorgeous," I whispered, watching the lithesome babysitters adorning the shoreline. In the presence of these perfected beings, I felt like a dumpy extra on a film set. "They must look at me and wonder why you would bother with a human at all."

"Ryann." Lad sighed, shifting me to the side so he could stand and stretch. "What will it take to make you believe me? You are the prettiest girl I've ever seen— probably the prettiest girl in the world."

"You must not have seen much of the world," I muttered, but I couldn't help feeling a little pleased. "Or maybe *you're* the one who's crazy."

He walked over to the tiny beach, glancing back at me and looking one hundred percent adorable. I had to grin at him. His answering smile almost hurt my heart, but I wouldn't let it. Not now. These were probably my last few moments with Lad. *I should enjoy them.*

Lad abruptly stooped and swept his hand through the water, purposely splashing me and laughing.

"Oh... you've done it now. Prepare to get soaked, Your Majesty." I leapt from my perch on the rock to the shoreline.

Lad let out a laughing yelp as he contorted and swerved to miss the payback splash. The lovely caretakers silently gathered up the children and left the pool area, sneaking glances at us as they passed by. From the kids, I got some funny faces and even friendly grins.

When Lad and I were alone again, he stretched his hands out to me, inviting me to come to him. I walked slowly to face him and placed my hands in his palms.

"There's one more thing I want to show you before we go." A sly smile crept across his face.

"What?" I was suspicious, but not suspicious enough.

"This!" With a loud whoop, he grabbed me and jumped into the water, pulling me under with him. We both came up laughing and dripping.

"Well," I huffed with feigned indignation, wiping water out of my eyes. "That is not exactly regal behavior fit for a prince."

He swam backward a few strokes. "I'm not a very regal prince. As I've told you, I'm an utter disappointment."

"Maybe..." I swam after him, enjoying myself. "...you're sowing your royal oats before settling down with a nice Elven girl and getting to the business of running the kingdom, like a good little monarch."

"Hmmph," Lad growled then disappeared under the surface.

Warm fingers closed around my ankle and jerked me under the water. In a flash, Lad's arms were around me. He brought me back up with him, my body pressed against his chest in a tight embrace. He shifted one arm, sweeping my legs out from under me, to cradle me against him in the water. Our faces were level now, giving me a breathtaking view of his green eyes, which looked almost turquoise reflecting the pool.

I shivered once in spite of the comfortable water temperature. "Hey, why am I not freezing right now?"

"It could be thanks to your own personal water heater." He dipped his chin in a gallant gesture. "Or it might be because there's a hot spring emptying into this pool."

Lad walked in slow circles, carrying me like a baby while I enjoyed the pleasant warmth of the water swirling around us. My gaze wandered over the sides and ceiling of our rocky enclosure. They were encrusted with sparkling clear crystals and dotted with the now-familiar multi-colored luminescent stones.

"It's magical here," I whispered. I needed to remember every detail of this place. And of him. I looked back at Lad and drank in the sight of his wet face, beads of water dripping from his dark golden hair and glistening on his face. Leaning in, I playfully licked one from his top lip.

The sharp intake of his breath echoed in the quiet stillness of the pool cavern. He went perfectly still for a moment, though I detected a rush of heated thoughts charging behind his eyes. Then he released his pent-up breath.

"I have to take you home," he hissed, tension evident in his voice. "If we start what I'd like to start right now, I may never let you go back."

CHAPTER TWENTY-ONE
SWEET GIFT

The woods seemed overly bright compared to where I'd spent the last few days. On the walk home, Lad moved as gracefully as he had before his injury.

"How do you feel?"

"Good as new." He squeezed my hand.

"I'm surprised your father let you leave with me—I'm surprised he let *me* leave at all."

"Well, truthfully, there was some disagreement on the issue. I assured him it would be fine with me if you stayed indefinitely. That, of course, convinced him you should leave as soon as possible." A small bitter laugh left his lips. He looked sideways at me, checking my reaction.

"I'm sure. And he's not worried I'll tell someone about y'all?"

"Well." He twisted his mouth then let it widen into a grin. "I *sort of* promised to glamour you until you couldn't remember your own birthday."

"Are you going to?" I teased him, sticking my chest out, daring him to try.

"No. Of course not—even if I *could*. I trust you. Anyway, I'm recovered, you're on your way home, and as far as my parents are concerned, life can go back to normal now."

"Yes, I bet there'll be a big party in Elf Land tonight—Ding Dong the human is gone."

"*I* will certainly not be in a celebratory mood. And please... don't call it Elf Land. That sounds absurd."

"You're right. Elves on the TV and radio, an entire secret kingdom right under our feet—perfectly reasonable. Calling it Elf Land—absurd."

"Really. We *do* have a name for our home that doesn't make it sound like an amusement park. Altum. Translated into your language, it means roughly, 'deep water.' It's named for our subterranean river."

"That *is* a little better than Elf Land," I conceded.

As we neared my house, I was surprised to see a man turning away from the front door and descending the steps. Stopping in the yard, Lad stood tensely beside me but made no attempt to hide. Apparently he wasn't willing to leave me alone in the presence of a stranger again.

The guy was clean cut and wearing a suit—not exactly dangerous looking—but then Grandma's house was rather off the beaten path for a traveling salesman, and with my mom out of town, I didn't like his timing. He looked up, spotting Lad and me, then changed direction and started toward us, a huge smile plastered across his face.

"You must be Ryann!" he bellowed.

"Um, yes, and you are?"

"Tom Barr." He stuck out his hand, looking at Lad and back to me. "You kids been swimming?"

"Yes." I watched the man survey the property in search of a swimming pool and reached out to shake his offered hand.

"I came by to see if I could catch your mother but didn't get an answer at the door."

I was confused. She hadn't told me she was seeing anyone new. "She's… out right now. Are y'all… dating?"

"Oh, no," he chortled.

My relief was instantaneous, but I still didn't know who this guy was and what he wanted with my mother. He obviously read my expression.

"You may be asking yourself, 'Who is Tom Barr?' I work for Meyer Industries." He widened his oily smile. "We're a paper products manufacturer in Yalobusha County, and we offer local timber growers fair prices for their crops. I've been talking to your mother about a super business deal."

"But we're not timber growers."

Barr stretched his arms out and twisted side to side, resembling a ringmaster under the big top. "Looks to me like you've been growing some fine timber right here for quite a while."

He still wore a slick smile and looked as if he might wink at any second. All he had to do was call me "little missy" and the smarmy picture would be complete.

My mind raced, trying to comprehend the meaning of his words. Was *this* my mother's last resort plan to come up with the money for the IRS? The one she wouldn't tell me about until it became necessary? *No wonder.* How could she even think of chopping down and selling all the trees? Especially to this guy.

"Well, there is no fair price for the trees on this land. They're not for sale."

"I'm afraid your mother disagrees. I'll go now and let you discuss this with her when she gets home. You two kids be good."

And there was the wink. My skin crawled. Tom Barr walked to his shiny car in his shiny shoes, got in and drove away. I looked over at Lad, feeling on the verge of tears.

"I can't believe my mom's considering this. Grandma will be devastated. What are we going to do?"

He came to me instantly and folded me against his warm chest. "We have to do something—that's for sure. If he succeeds in buying the timber here, and clear cuts this land, my people will be forced to leave."

"But... you live underground."

"Yes, but our whole existence here depends upon the trees. Our home is supported by the living system of roots around it, and our main form of sustenance comes from those trees. We can't survive without them. When the trees are gone, the wildlife living among them will also be gone. Our shelter, food, and mode of transportation will all be gone. We must stop the sale."

"You don't happen to have a big pot of gold somewhere do you?"

"No." He laughed in a sad-sounding way. He stroked my hair while pressing my face closer to his chest. "We're not leprechauns. And we've never had need of human treasure before, though now I do wish I had enough to save your home… and ours."

"Are you going to tell your father?" I pulled back and looked up at Lad's face.

His arrested expression told me he hadn't considered that yet. "I'll have to. We must prepare in case the worst does occur." His eyes widened and then closed. He breathed out loudly. "I just realized… my father will be convinced it's your doing. He'll never believe it happened coincidentally right after you found out about us. He's so determined to keep us all separate from human life, he doesn't know about things like overdue taxes and greedy corporations. I assured him you wouldn't talk, but he'll believe you revealed our secret and the land is being destroyed in an attempt to exterminate us. It will reinforce every negative thing he already believes about humans."

"And about me. Lad…" I could hardly find my voice. "We won't just be separated. We'll be enemies." Hot tears leaked furiously from the corners of my eyes.

"That will never happen. No, no, Ryann… shhh… please don't." Lad wiped my tears with a fingertip then hugged me close to his body. "We'll think of something.

Come here." He sat on the back porch step and pulled me onto his lap. "I could never be your enemy. All I want is to be with you. Sometimes it feels like nothing else matters."

I nodded, wiping my wet face on my sleeve. "I feel the same way. But other things do matter. We have to be realistic."

He shook his head in denial. "We'll be together again soon, I promise."

My heart wanted to believe it, but my head knew a relationship with him was impossible. *Say it. Say it, chicken.*

I couldn't. Instead, I said, "You should probably go. Mom and Grandma will be back soon, and you don't want to meet up with them."

"I do want to meet them. You met my family."

"Yes, and that went *so* well, didn't it? What's the point?"

His expression was wounded. "The point is—I'd like to meet these women I've heard so much about."

Dang it. Looking at his sweet face and obviously hurt feelings it was nearly impossible to say no. It didn't make any sense to keep doing this—we were only postponing the inevitable—but I found myself agreeing.

"All right, but you're going to need a wardrobe adjustment, unless you care to explain your traditional Elven garb to them."

"No, that won't help anything. I'll wear my library clothes when I meet them."

"Library clothes? You mean the ones you were wearing the day I met you at the pool?" I wrinkled my nose, smiling. "*Where* did you get those?"

Lad's face reddened. "I took them off a scarecrow in a field over in the next county. I've always been worried that one day some farmer will spot me in them and say, 'There's the one who stripped my scarecrow. Get him!'"

We both dissolved into a fit of giggles. "No offense, but I don't think those clothes will work if you're actually going to meet my family. Dressing like scarecrow beefcake won't accurately represent the kind of person you are."

"I thought the idea was to *camouflage* the kind of person I am. What's wrong? Ashamed of me?" he teased. "Don't worry. I'll find something better to wear."

"No, I'll handle it. It's easier for me to go shopping than it is for you. I'll pick up something for you."

Before he left, Lad suggested we try once more to communicate in the Elven fashion. I was sure it was hopeless but agreed to make him happy.

"Focus on me, Ryann. I know you can do this." Lad held my shoulders in the warm grip of his strong hands and placed me directly in front of him. He bent his head so our faces were close. *Dang.* I was losing focus already, before we'd even begun.

"All right," I said shakily, "Go."

I stared into his melting green eyes, but as before, my thoughts drifted to the times Lad had kissed me. The feel of his lips on mine, the way his breath had come in rough winded gasps when he held me close. I couldn't stop the pull of my eyes down to his lips.

I forced myself to look back up at his eyes, but it seemed they were much closer. He was moving in toward me—no, it was me. I was inching my face closer to his, without seeming to have any control over it. Finally, I pressed upward, bringing our lips together.

Lad responded immediately and enthusiastically, a low hungry noise humming in his throat. He wrapped his fingers around the back of my head, kissing me with a fierce passion he'd never shown before. It was shocking. And exciting. We swayed together as we stood at the back door of my grandmother's log house. I would have been content to stay right there, doing this all day, but after a few minutes, Lad pulled back and looked at me. I'd completely failed again. Why was he so convinced I could learn to communicate the way his people did?

"I'm sorry. I… I couldn't concentrate with you so close to me. I—"

"Ryann, you did it. You *heard* me," Lad interrupted, looking as thrilled as I'd ever seen him.

"I did?"

"Yes, I was telling you to kiss me—like I did when we tried this before. You heard the message this time, didn't you?"

He seemed so pleased, I hated to deny it. And maybe he was right. All I could think of the first time was kissing him, too. Of course, that was what I wanted to do whenever I was close to him anyway, so it probably wasn't a very good test. And it certainly wasn't helping me to control my feelings for him. Or say what I really *should* say. *Chicken.*

"I don't know. You probably should've picked a topic that doesn't come as easily to me, like hockey stats or the rules of Call of Duty."

"What's that?" Lad asked.

Yep. Dream guy.

"Oh, I almost forgot. I have a gift for you." Lad pulled a beautiful tooled metal flask from a leather pouch at his side and placed it in my open hand. It was lightweight and cool and covered in intricate Elven designs.

"It's pretty."

He chuckled. "The gift is what's *inside*. Saol water. I was thinking you could try it in your tea recipe—a fusion of your traditional drink and mine. And the sweetness of saol water is so concentrated, the tiniest amount would equal a great quantity of sugar. Besides that, saol water has health benefits sugar can't provide. It's rich in minerals and vitamins, even protein. Worth a try, isn't it?"

Actually, the anticipation of experimenting with it was the only thing making me feel marginally better about the coming separation from Lad.

He didn't seem worried at all. "I'll let the situation cool down and give my father a few days to come to terms with our relationship then I'll meet you at the pool in the woods at the end of the week—Friday afternoon," he said.

Say it, Ryann. It took great effort but I pushed the words out. "Maybe we shouldn't."

"Shouldn't what?"

"Maybe we shouldn't... see each other Friday. Maybe we should just, you know, let... go."

Lad gripped my arm and looked down at me with a stern expression—not something I was used to from him. "No, Ryann. I *will* see you again. I'll work it out."

I opened my mouth to argue, but he jumped off the porch and ran to the edge of the woods. He turned around again and yelled back to me. "Friday."

I nodded and watched his muscled back and tousled golden hair disappear into the trees. While I went inside to await the return of my mom and Grandma Neena, Lad was going home to face the consequences of "consorting with a human," or whatever they would call his terrible offense.

No matter what he'd said, I had to prepare myself that he might not be coming back. Not Friday.

Not ever.

Chapter Twenty-Two
Secret Ingredient

"Mom, a guy came by today. He said he was from Meyer Industries."

She paused then continued unpacking her suitcase while I sat cross-legged on her bed watching. She was obviously trying to act casual.

"Oh, did he leave a business card?"

"He told me what's going on, Mom. You can't sell our trees. What did Grandma say?"

She pushed the suitcase aside and crawled up onto the comforter beside me. "Ryann, honey, I'm sorry. I don't want to—Grandma doesn't want to either—but I don't think we have a choice. The innocent spouse plea failed, and Lee says I'm out of options. Would you rather see a few trees go, or have us lose everything, including the house?"

"Of course not, but it's not a few trees. Mom—they're going to clear cut the land. They're going to take *all* the trees. Do you have any idea how bad that is?"

What I really wanted to say was that she had no idea how many *lives* would be affected by this, but I couldn't. She could never know about Lad's people. I had to somehow prevent this catastrophe while preserving their secret.

She pursed her lips and drew her eyebrows together, tilting her head to one side. "Calm down Ryann, you're getting hysterical. I can't think of any other way to come up with so much money, can you?"

"How much is it, Mom? Tell me."

"Almost two hundred fifty thousand dollars."

"Oh my God."

"I know." She looked a little nauseated.

"So how much would Meyer Industries give you for the timber?"

"About two hundred thousand. I'd have to come up with the rest of it somehow. Maybe I can get a loan at the bank. Maybe I'll talk to your father and see if he might possibly consider thinking of someone other than himself for a change."

"How much time do we have to pay? I could talk to Daddy next weekend when he's here to visit. Maybe he'll be ashamed enough to do something about it if he knows that I know."

My mom laughed bitterly. "I doubt he's in the mood to do me any favors. And as far as I know, he doesn't have any way to get that kind of money, but it's worth a try. The payment deadline is four months away. We have to try anything we can at this point."

"Please don't sign anything with that Meyer slime ball yet, okay? I know something's going to work out. We have to save the trees."

"My daughter… the tree-hugger." Mom planted a kiss on my forehead. "Okay now scoot. I need to get some sleep before work tomorrow. I'm exhausted."

It looked like a pretty happy exhaustion to me. "You had a good time, huh?"

"Actually, I did."

Her mischievous smile piqued my curiosity. "Hey, what's going on? Did something happen in Atlanta this week?"

She actually giggled before answering. "I can't believe I'm saying this. I met someone—a friend of Shelly's husband. Well, actually, I met him a long time ago, but we ran into him at a restaurant in Atlanta, and he remembered me."

"What? Who is he? What's his name?"

"Davis. He's single, employed, nice hair, incredibly charming." She laughed, looked down at the bedspread almost bashfully and back up at me again. "He's a senator."

"A senator? You mean Davis *Hart*, the senator from Georgia?" I'd seen him many times on CNN student news when they played it in our classrooms. He was in charge of some powerful committee or something.

"Yes. Isn't that strange? I worked on his campaign back in college when I was at Georgia Tech. He and Shelly's husband Rob have been friends for years. We started talking at the restaurant, and it was like not a day had passed."

"Wow." I didn't know how to react. It *was* strange. First of all, Mom had never told me she'd worked on a senator's campaign—she wasn't the least bit political now—she never even watched the news. But the strangest thing was her obvious enthusiasm for this guy. Her eyes sparkled in a way I'd never seen, and I'd never known her to act like this—she was like one of my friends gushing over a guy. "Well... you seem to like him," I said.

"I do. I... haven't felt like this in a long time. I thought maybe I never would. But he's like no one else I've ever met. I think you'll like him. He's planning to visit in a couple weeks."

"That's good. I'm glad. You deserve to be happy."

"I am happy." She yawned widely, her eyelids droopy, though she still wore a sappy smile.

"Okay, I'll let you get to bed. See you in the morning." I closed her door and went to the kitchen, still shaking my head over the change in her.

Reaching into my pocket, I pulled out the vial of saol water, the parting gift from my own amazing guy. Just holding it made me feel close to him while making me lonely for him at the same time. I was eager to find out how using the saol water in my sweet tea recipe would work.

I stayed up way too late, experimenting. Naturally, I sampled it as I went, and I had to admit, it tasted pretty unbelievable. Since the only thing that had changed was the substitution of saol water for sugar, I had to give the Elven sugar-making hotties their due.

For a while now, I'd been toying with the idea of taking a sample over to the manager at the Food Star grocery. Maybe now was the right time. With some luck and my new secret ingredient, I might be able to sell my tea there and help us inch out of the financial abyss.

Tuesday morning, I got up and dressed early. I planned to take a few gallon jugs of tea to the store before Grandma needed her car for the day. On the way I'd drop one off at The Skillet for Dory. She didn't have me on the schedule until tomorrow, but she was always eager for a sweet tea delivery.

When I walked into the kitchen, Mom and Grandma were already at the table, having breakfast and sampling the tea I'd left out for them.

"Ryann, this last batch is the best yet," Mom effused. "I've always said your tea was something special, but this... don't you think so, Momma?"

She looked over at Grandma Neena, who didn't answer. Grandma had closed her eyes after taking a sip, held it in her mouth, and finally swallowed. Then she opened her eyes and stared at me with such intensity I started feeling uncomfortable.

"Are you okay, Grandma? Does it taste all right?"

She waited another long moment then seemed to snap out of it. "Oh yes, honey. It's wonderful," she replied, once again the same twinkly warm Grandma I knew.

But when I sneaked a glance back at her while heading out the door, Grandma was staring after me, and the probing look was back in her eyes.

At The Skillet I gave Dory the tea and chatted with Emmy, whose breakfast shift was a little slow this morning.

She dragged me over to an empty corner, whispering, "So, *what* is going on with you? We didn't hear a peep from you out at the lake. And I can't believe you turned down the Atlanta trip. I would die for a little 'city time'— any chance to get out of this po-dunk place. So, let's have it."

"What? There's nothing to tell. I just needed some down time. I was…"

She wasn't buying it. At all. Her hands came to her hips, one eyebrow practically grazing her hairline.

"Okay—I was with someone," I confessed.

"I knew it!" Her squeal nearly took the roof off the diner. She looked around at the gawking patrons and lowered her voice. "Who is it? Do I know him? It's Nox, isn't it? Y'all are like, secret luvahs—I knew it." She giggled and slapped the counter next to her.

"What? No." I shook my head in irritation. "It's somebody else. But... I can't tell you who."

She leaned in eagerly. "Why? Is he like, really old? Is he in *college?*"

I was shocked to find myself wanting to talk about Lad. Emmy and I had had so many conversations enumerating the glorious qualities of Jake McKee, and Lad was the closest thing I'd ever had to a serious boyfriend. Couldn't I tell her just a bit? Change a few details, withhold the critical stuff, gush about his perfection for a minute?

The eager look on Emmy's face made me giggle. I made her promise complete and absolute secrecy before agreeing to say anything.

"He's *not* old. He's perfect. Beyond cute—the best-looking guy I've ever seen. And he's sweet and he reads a lot. Remember the guy I told you about a few weeks ago? The home-schooler?"

More gleeful laughter and squealing from Emmy was accompanied by an ecstatic little tippy-toe dance. I doubted she was ever this excited on Christmas morning. "Oh my God—Hot Geek Alert! You are *so* lucky. I never meet anyone new."

"But listen—I haven't told *anyone* about him. I don't even know if we're... dating or whatever, and my mom will flip if she hears I've been seeing someone she hasn't even met. You have to promise not to say anything. To *anyone.*"

Emmy's face took on all the solemnity of a Chuck E. Cheese birthday party as she attempted to convince me of her trustworthiness. "I won't. I promise." She gave me the zippered lips signal and then a huge grin.

I was really glad I hadn't revealed more.

She gripped my forearm. "Well, now I have some news to tell *you*. Get ready for it... guess who got into Vallon's fan pod?" She let out a scream. "I'm leaving for L.A. July first. One month. Can you believe it? I'm *in*."

Every good feeling left my body in a rush. "Oh no, Emmy. You really shouldn't do that."

Her smile melted into an offended frown. "Hey, not fair. I know you're not into the whole celebrity thing, but don't be a snob."

"It's not that. It's... I don't think you really know what you're getting yourself into."

"Yes I *do*. You said it yourself—nobody knows more about this stuff than I do. This is what I want, Ryann. More than anything I've ever wanted. I was happy for you—why can't you be happy for me?"

I *couldn't* be happy for her, and I couldn't tell her why. I left the restaurant eaten up with worry. Maybe Lad could help me keep Emmy out of that fan pod where she'd be glamoured and used by a Dark Elf. I needed him—right now. How was I supposed to wait until Friday to see him?

What could I say to persuade her? I suddenly wished for a bit of glamour of my own. "It's just... Los Angeles is so far away. And how do you know you'll be happy there?"

She lifted her chin, her eyes hard and defensive. "I *don't* know—I *believe*. It's fine if you want to live a bottled-up life Ryann, but I'm going to go with my gut.

And I'd appreciate it if you'd stop trying to bring me down."

"I'm sorry."

We stared at each other, both troubled.

"Well, I have to go. We'll talk about it more later."

"Let's not," I heard Emmy mutter behind me as I walked to the diner's exit door.

When I reached my car, Nox called out to me from the sidewalk—on his way to The Skillet, no doubt.

"Hey, where you going? Want to have some breakfast?" He smiled at me as if it had been months since we'd seen each other instead of only days.

"No thanks," I said, still a little distracted. "I'm on my way to Food Star."

He joined me beside the car and opened the driver's side door for me. "You need groceries?"

"No. I'm not shopping. I'll be attempting to *dazzle* the manager with my tea-brewing skills."

"Well, that shouldn't be hard. I've tasted it. It's great. But why?"

"We need a serious cash flow increase at my house. Dory's been great, but if I could get more customers, I could help my mom a little more."

I climbed into the car, and Nox shut the door for me. He leaned into the open window. "Let me come with you. I'll go in and testify on your behalf. I can be very persuasive, you know." He grinned wickedly at me.

"Oh, I know," I said dryly. "But that's okay. If I'm going to attempt to be a businesswoman, I guess I should do this all by my big-girl self."

"Well, at least give me a lift over there. I need to do a little shopping, too. And you *owe* me a ride."

"Really? Okay then. Get in."

Nox sat in the passenger seat and moved it all the way back, but his legs still looked cramped. I'd never thought of Grandma's car as small. Nox had a way of dwarfing everything around him.

As we drove across town, he asked, "How was your holiday weekend?"

"Quiet." An understatement, considering I'd spent it in a place where no one spoke out loud. "But it was good. What about yours?"

"Great—but why was yours quiet? You didn't get to do much in Atlanta?"

I glanced over and saw his puzzled half-smile. Training my eyes back on the road, I considered how to answer. "I... didn't go after all. I decided to stay here."

"What? If I'd known you were around, we could have hung out. So what did you do the whole time?"

"Um... spent a lot of time in the woods. I guess I just needed to be alone." *With my beautiful boyfriend, who, as it turns out, is an Elf.*

There wasn't much about the past few days I could share with Nox, or Emmy, or Mom, or any other human being for that matter. Nox's smile had disappeared. I guessed he was hurt I'd chosen to spend the weekend "alone" rather than spend any time with him.

"Okaaay…" He dragged out the word, sounding a little surly. No doubt he believed we still weren't quite as "fine" as I'd said we were. "Will you be continuing your exclusive love affair with nature this week, or do you think you could squeeze me in to your busy botany schedule at some point?"

I pulled the car into a spot in front of Food Star and put it in park, turning to face him in the front seat. "Hey—don't be mad." I tried to appease him. "It's nothing personal. I didn't see any of my other friends, either."

His expression brightened, his usual humor returning. "All right, I'll overlook your cruel standoffishness… as long as you agree to let me whisk you away later today for a play date."

"Sure. Well, we're here. I guess I'd better do this thing." On the short drive to the Food Star my confidence had faded, and now my stomach felt like a Jell-O Wiggler. "That is *if* I can speak without my voice shaking."

Nox started to say something, but my cell phone rang and interrupted him.

"It's Dory," I said, looking at the screen. "I just saw her and dropped off some tea—mind if I answer it?"

"No. Go ahead."

"Hello? Dory?"

I had to pull the phone away from my ear as her excited voice came through a few decibels too loudly.

"Girl... what on God's green Earth did you put in that sweet tea?"

My heart dropped. "Why? What happened? Did somebody get sick?"

Her cackling laughter hurt my eardrum. "Heavens, no. We sold out already. Once the first customer tasted it, my counter was basically mobbed until the jug ran dry. I hope you're ready to get to work tomorrow *and* bring your secret recipe."

"Yes, I am—I will," I told her, feeling dazed, "See you in the morning, Dory."

It hadn't been my imagination or my mother's flattery. The tea really was better. I felt even more hopeful my sales pitch would be successful.

Opening my car door, I looked over at Nox. "Wish me luck."

He opened his own door and got out, grabbing the tea containers from the floorboard. "I'll do you one better— I'll carry the jugs inside for you. Come on."

Inside Food Star the woman at the customer service counter paged the manager for me while I stood shifting my weight from foot to foot, listening to Karen Carpenter explain why rainy days and Mondays always got her down. My mom had always loved that song for some reason.

Instead of going off to do his shopping, Nox insisted on waiting with me. I was about to shoo him away when a thin, buttoned-down guy appeared at the service counter. He was younger than I'd expected. Still managerial, though.

"Hello. I'm Heath Marston. What can I do for you today, Miss…?"

"Carroll. Ryann Carroll." I'd never made any kind of sales presentation before. My palms were wet and my tongue was dry. *What the heck am I doing here?* With a quick, panicked glance in Nox's direction, I opened my mouth and started my speech, trying to make my product sound as appealing as possible. And yes, my voice was shaky.

"I make a specialty sweet tea I've been supplying it to The Skillet for a few weeks now. I'm expanding my business, and I'd like to give you the opportunity to carry my product line in your store."

Mr. Marston's eyebrows shot up, followed by a bemused smile. "Well, Miss Carroll, we already carry several brands of tea."

"Yes, I realize that. But mine is different—secret recipe. You could carry it as a local gourmet brand. Maybe you could try it and see what you think? Please?" No decent Southern gentleman could refuse the double whammy of a potent feminine smile and a "please."

Apparently Heath Marston hadn't brushed up on the unwritten rules of Southern chivalry. "I'm sorry, Miss Carroll, but this is not—"

Nox hefted the jugs to the countertop, plunking them in front of the manager. He stared down at the shorter man, but he was smiling, as usual. "You *really* want to try this stuff, sir. Believe me—you won't regret it."

The manager lifted one of the tea containers and looked back to me. "All right, young lady. I'll give this a taste and get back to you."

It was hard to contain my excitement. Inside I was doing a victory dance, complete with fist-pump. "Thank you sir. My number's taped on the containers. I hope you like it."

As the manager walked away, I turned to Nox, beaming. He held up his open hand for a high five, which I delivered with enthusiasm.

"You did it," he said.

"Well, actually, I think you did it."

"Nah—I just made a suggestion. You were the one who was brave enough to come in here and ask in the first place."

"Well, thanks anyway. It was nice of you."

He swatted the air as if the matter deserved no further consideration. "No problem. Friends don't let friends flame out on their first big business deal, right?"

"Right. I guess. So... you're grocery shopping now?" I asked, having difficulty forming a mental image of Nox Knight pushing a cart through the dairy aisle.

"Yeah—running short on a few things."

"Unfortunately, I can't wait around. I have to get my grandma's car back to her so she can make it to her oil-painting class at the senior center. How will you get home?"

"I'll walk. It's not far from here."

"Okay. Well, I guess I'll see you later then."

"Yep—I'll pick you up in a couple hours."

It wasn't until I was almost home that I remembered why the idea of Nox food shopping had seemed so strange to me—he had told me he ate every meal at The Skillet. *Maybe he's learning to cook for himself?*

Maybe he'd made up an excuse to come along and help me for some reason.

CHAPTER TWENTY-THREE
HISTORY LESSON

Grandma Neena was sitting at the kitchen table when I got home. In front of her on the tabletop lay the distinctively carved copper cylinder Lad had given me. She picked it up and rolled it between her hands, looking at me, but not saying a word. I glanced around the kitchen at all the wide-open cabinet doors and drawers, their contents spread across the countertops. Grandma had been busy.

She'd apparently discovered the bottle in its hiding place on the highest shelf behind the canned vegetables none of us really liked. Beets. Brussels Sprouts. Wax Beans. Was it possible she'd been specifically looking for it?

"Hi," I said cautiously. "What've you been doing?"

"I think the question, Ryann, is what have *you* been doing?"

My heart went into overdrive. I didn't know what was going on, but the question unnerved me. I tried to interpret her knowing expression, to gauge how much information she already had. No point getting myself into more trouble than necessary.

Maybe for some bizarre reason she thought I'd shoplifted the flask. Maybe she thought it contained alcohol. But that wouldn't explain why she'd dismantled the kitchen looking for it in the first place.

"What do you mean?" I bluffed.

"Ryann… I know what this is. Now I want to know where you got it."

Impossible. Yet the look on her face assured me Grandma Neena really did know. *But how?* My shocked response came out in a strangled whisper.

"A boy gave it to me… as a present."

"A boy? Where? When did you meet him? While we were gone?"

"Don't tell Mom."

"I won't make any such promise, although I certainly won't be telling your momma *all* the details, and I think you know why." She looked at me pointedly, her tone deadly serious.

My head was swimming. *What* was going on? Grandma waited, staring at me with the sharp blue gaze I'd known all my life—there would be no b-s-ing her.

I swallowed hard. "I met him in the woods shortly after we moved in with you. A few days later I was out walking and came upon a dead doe. I was almost attacked by a pair of coyotes, and…" I stopped.

"Go on." She never let the expression on her face change.

"…and Lad saved me. I saw him again after that. And again. I stayed here over the weekend to spend time with him."

"And you were with him the whole time we were gone?" Her expression was still neutral, but I expected a severe blessing-out any minute now.

"It wasn't anything bad. I swear nothing happened. Well, a lot of stuff happened, but not the kind of stuff you're thinking."

"I believe you, Ryann because I know the kind of person you are. And… I'm pretty certain I know the kind of person *he* is." She raised her eyebrow meaningfully.

It was obvious she knew more than I would've ever dreamed, and the whole truth would be coming out right here at the kitchen table.

"I tasted it." Grandma ran her fingers lightly over the carvings on the surface of the tube. "Quite nostalgic."

My heart pounded. I could hardly breathe as I waited for her to continue.

"I noticed the flavor as soon as I tried your tea this morning. I didn't know how, but I had no doubt you'd put saol water in it."

I was stunned. "How… how do you know about saol water?" My mind cast about for possible explanations. "Have you met… you know… one of them?"

"One of whom, Ryann?" Grandma Neena's eyes sparked with a challenge and a gleam I'd never seen in them before.

Random images and bits of conversations flashed through my mind—Grandma's wild ringlets, the loom worker in Altum, the old men reminiscing at The Skillet, the fact that she never talked about her childhood or where she was from, the fact she'd never remarried in spite of being widowed and uncommonly beautiful at age twenty-two, her reluctance to leave this much-too-large house in the middle of the woods. Her woods. Her home. The home of... her people.

I momentarily forgot how to inhale and exhale. "You *are* one of them—aren't you?"

"We need to talk, sweetheart."

I wasn't the only one in the family capable of a mighty understatement. My heartbeat had climbed up into my throat, and I made my way to a kitchen chair before my shaking legs could give way.

"How? How is this possible? How did this happen?"

Grandma Neena set the copper container aside and reached across the table to pull my hand inside of her soft, unwrinkled ones.

"There's no need to be afraid or upset, Ryann. I'm not sure how much you've seen or heard, but obviously this boy you met has told you something about us. You two must be close for him to have given you this saol water. Frankly, that concerns me. But before I ask you to tell me any more about him, I'll explain some things about myself to you."

I nodded mutely.

"You're right. I am..." she paused a long time before continuing. "I am one of the people of the trees, of Altum, of the Elves." Grandma Neena exhaled with a tense laugh and wiped the underside of her chin with the back of one hand. "Ahh, mercy. It feels strange to say. I haven't talked of such things for so long now, it doesn't even seem real to me anymore. But, it's the truth of my past. You understand why I couldn't give you a real answer when you asked me about my childhood home the other day."

"But why aren't you with them?" Then the thought occurred to me that maybe in a way she still was. "Wait— do you go back to Altum sometimes?"

Grandma Neena's eyes became moist, and her hand patted mine. "No, honey, I'm not welcome there anymore. I would dearly love to see my old home again, but... I made my choice long, long ago. You see, when I was a girl, a year or two older than you in fact, I did something quite unforgivable among my people. I fell in love with the wrong person. I had a bit of the wanderlust, and I used to love to explore and venture as close to the human settlements as I could without being caught. One day I got careless, and I did get caught, by a young man who was out hunting in these woods. He spotted me and called out to me. Instead of escaping as quickly as possible, like I should have, I went to him. He was exotic, and so handsome. It was curiosity, I guess... fascination."

"My grandfather."

"Yes. Benjamin was as taken with me as I was with him. He tried to talk to me, and of course I couldn't understand him, but he kept coming back to that spot day after day. I did, too. I couldn't help myself. Eventually we learned to communicate with each other. Our desire to know each other kept growing. Finally, when I turned eighteen, I had to make a decision. I was promised to be married to a young man of my own kind. He was a fine person—quite a catch really—and I did care for him. But it wasn't the same as how I felt for Ben. I'm ashamed to say I took the cowardly way out. Instead of telling that young man face-to-face of my choice, I ran away and married your grandfather."

"Did your fiancé ever find out what happened to you?"

"Oh yes. He came looking for me. When he found me here, he was crushed. And so angry. I'm afraid I broke his heart." She looked as if she was living that anguished moment all over again.

"So then you pretended to be a human? You chose an average human life over life in Altum?"

"There hasn't been anything average about it. I've had an incredible life. Not too many people can say they've lived in two entirely different worlds."

"But you lost your husband so soon—after all you gave up for him. Didn't you ever wonder if you made the wrong choice?"

"Benjamin and I didn't get to have a long life together as we planned. But I did have true love in my lifetime.

And I had your mother, so a part of Ben is with me always. And I have you." She smiled and squeezed my hands.

"What about your other family? Your Elven one?"

Grandma Neena's face looked more troubled than I'd ever seen her as she mentally went back in time. "Yes… that was hard. I know I hurt them, and I shamed them. They were of some social standing there, you see. I never had the chance to apologize to them. I did try to go back once to explain, but…"

She paused for such a long time I thought she'd finished. I began to ask another question, but she picked up her story again softly. "Hopefully they were able to go on with their lives in spite of the scandalous thing I did and didn't suffer too much in the eyes of society there. I don't know—young love is a powerful force. I was mostly feeling at the time, not thinking about all of the things that would come after."

There was something I could definitely relate to. Sometimes common sense just wasn't happening. It occurred to me that maybe I wasn't the first one to share Grandma's secret.

"Does Mom know?"

"Lord no. And don't you think about going and telling her, missy. I promised myself the consequences of my choice would be entirely on my shoulders. I may have broken my engagement, but I would never betray my people. I've never told a single soul. Even Ben never knew. He accepted I had a past I could never speak of, and he loved me in spite of it, bless his heart. Now, speaking of secrets, you have some explaining to do yourself."

In spite of my tremendous shock over Grandma Neena's revelation, I was starting to feel light... happy. Maybe it was the relief of finally being able to unburden myself and discuss the amazing things that had been happening in my life. It all seemed somewhat less crazy now.

"I've been there," I whispered, though no one was around to hear.

"You have? To Altum? Oh my goodness. So *that's* what you were doing while we were gone."

I told Grandma it had been Lad I'd met in the woods as a child.

"I always suspected it was one of us." She nodded and gestured for me to continue.

I explained how Lad had saved me twice—once from coyotes and then from the drunken hunters—and how that had led to his being shot and to my unplanned visit to his underground home.

"Mercy me, right now I miss my home more than I have in decades. I wish I could see it just once more."

"Well, you never know... it could happen."

"No, what's done is done," Grandma said with a faraway look in her eyes. "So, tell me about this Lad."

I couldn't suppress my smile. The chance to talk about him was such a relief. "He's incredible. Amazing."

"Oh dear..."

"What?"

"Well, I may have fallen in love with a human, but that doesn't mean you need to go falling in love with an Elven boy."

"Who said anything about love?"

"Ryann…" She shook her head at me, a lifetime of wisdom behind the gesture. "Honey, I know you don't want to hear this, but you really need to stay away from Lad and let things run their natural course."

I couldn't believe my ears. As much as I loved my grandma, she was being astoundingly hypocritical. "Why? You didn't."

"And that's exactly how I know what I'm talking about."

"But I thought you had no regrets!"

"No, I said I've had a good life. But it's a tough row to hoe, Ryann. You have no idea what you could be letting yourself in for. Ben and I loved each other, but it wasn't easy. Combining two separate lives into one is hard enough. It can be even tougher when people come from different ethnic backgrounds and cultures, or two different religions. But you and Lad come from two different worlds. Benjamin's early death was devastating, but it also prevented our having to deal with a lot of the repercussions. If he had lived, all the secrets and background issues might have eventually torn us apart."

Of course I was aware of the potential problems. It was all I'd been able to think about since coming home from Altum. But I wanted it to be *my* decision.

"You said it was all worth it."

"For me. And maybe it's worth it for *you*, honey. You're young, and if you try it and things don't work out, you can move on with your life and be fine. But what about Lad? Did he tell you how it is for our people? Have you considered all he would have to give up if you two continue on this path?"

I felt a twinge of conviction. "Well, he told me it's a permanent choice, and if he makes a mistake he can't take it back. He told me there's a severe grieving process if a bonded couple is forced to part, and a lifelong mark, but…" My words dropped off into nothingness as it hit me. "That's what happened to your hair, isn't it? That's the mark?"

Grandma Neena nodded and placed her hand firmly on my forearm. "Will you think about what I said about Lad? About what's best for him?"

"Sure. Yeah, I will—" My text tone interrupted our conversation. I looked down and saw Nox's name on the screen. I'd completely forgotten he was coming.

-I'm here.

"Shoot—Nox is waiting for me out in the car. I'm sorry, I've got to go." I couldn't bail on him—not after what he'd done for me at the store today. I got up and started for the door then turned back. "Oh. Grandma, can you still communicate like they do?"

"Honey, I sure don't know about *that*. It's been ages since I even tried."

"Maybe we could try it together sometime. Lad seems to think *I* could do it if I practiced, but I don't know. I mean, I'm not—" My mouth dropped open as it hit me like a thunderbolt. I was mostly human, of course, but if my grandmother was Elven… then *I* was—

"I guess I haven't lost it completely, Ryann because I can tell exactly what you're thinking right now. And yes, honey… you are."

CHAPTER TWENTY-FOUR
MEET THE FAMILY

It was official—this was the longest week of my life. I thought about Lad, tried not to think of him, and thought about him some more. I couldn't stop wondering if he'd be there on Friday afternoon, and whether I should show up or just let it end.

Right—like I wasn't going to show up.

Emmy and I seemed to be okay. We'd called a truce—we wouldn't discuss the fan pod situation, which meant I just worried silently. On Wednesday night, she threw one of her famous girls-only "Fat Pants" parties, where all the guests wore their most forgiving sweatpants and pigged out on chips and chocolate, cookies, and high octane soda, no diet drinks allowed.

It helped get my mind off things. By the end of the night I could hardly move but was deliriously happy and ready to resume eating sensibly for a couple of months until the next Fat Pants party. Of course, I went bearing all the sweet tea my girlfriends could drink. Everything was polished off without a hint of apology. There's no such thing as a polite portion at a Fat Pants party.

I went for a run the next afternoon in a remorse-fueled effort to make up for some of the excess. Normally I hated running. Okay, I always hated running. It hurt. As a general rule, I avoided things that hurt. By the time I was red-faced and wheezing my way back down the driveway toward the house, I'd sworn off Fat Pants and anything else that might lead to masochistic exercise in the future.

There was a Harley parked near the front steps. I walked inside, and my father jumped up from the couch.

"Ryann Rabbit!" He came to me in long strides, sweeping me up in a hug. He'd grown a beard. It felt strange against my face. I hadn't seen him since he'd hit the road six months ago to "discover himself" and write a book.

"Daddy—I thought you weren't getting here until Saturday. Hey Grandma."

She nodded to me as she entered the room from the kitchen and joined us.

"The weather was good, the ride was smooth, and I kept on driving through the night. I couldn't wait to see my girl. Besides, I saved money by not getting a hotel room." Super. *Now* he was fiscally prudent.

"Well, okay. Um, did you want to go somewhere?" It was weird to feel so awkward around my own father. But with all that had happened I felt almost like I didn't know him anymore.

"I thought we'd go to Taylor Grocery for an early supper."

"Oh. Well, let me grab a quick shower first."

Grandma looked like she hoped I'd medal in Olympic speed-showering. I guessed she and Dad weren't having a happy reunion.

"I think I'll take a walk outside while I'm waiting." Dad was already headed for the door as he said it. He must've picked up on Grandma Neena's vibe and wasn't anxious to spend any more quality time with his soon-to-be-former mother-in-law.

I met him twenty-five minutes later in the driveway and checked out the big black and silver Hog. "So you're a biker dude now?"

"A little early birthday present to myself. Actually, with the cost of gas, I thought it would be more economical to drive than the car. I sold the Lexus and got this baby. I had a motorcycle when I was younger. I kind of always wanted another one." Of course. A relic of lost youth recaptured. Check another one off the midlife crisis shopping list.

"Should be *fun* this winter. So, should we take Grandma's car to Taylor? Mom's still at work in hers."

"No, let's take this. You'll love it." He handed me his helmet to put on and straddled the huge bike. Oh well. He'd made it all the way from Miami on the thing alive.

Taylor was only a fifteen minute ride away. How bad could it be?

Fifteen minutes later I had my answer. There was no future for me as a Harley Girl. Each minute had felt like an hour on the curvy country back roads. I'd clung to my father's jacket and sent up a silent prayer each time we leaned into a turn. Dad, however, couldn't have looked happier. He wore a huge grin as he climbed off the bike.

"Some ride, huh?"

"Yeah, some ride." I could've kissed the red dirt under my feet.

Taylor, Mississippi made Deep River look like Metropolis. It was situated halfway between Deep River and Oxford. There were cotton fields, houses, more fields, and a tiny curve in the main road cradling a post office and Taylor Grocery, which contrary to its name, did not sell groceries.

At one time, of course, it had. It was built in 1889 as a dry goods store, and the condition of the exterior suggested that was about the last year any sort of building update had been done. A couple had bought it in the 1970's and turned it into a catfish joint, and it had remained one ever since. In spite of, or maybe due to its unpolished appearance, Taylor Grocery was quite the happening spot, especially for the college crowd from nearby Ole Miss, aka the University of Mississippi in Oxford.

I tried to fluff my helmet hair as Dad and I walked toward the faded brick building where a rusted tin Coca

Cola sign proclaimed, *Eat or We Both Starve*. I only trusted the sagging wooden porch to support us because it was already holding groups of decked-out college kids sitting on benches, laughing and smoking and drinking out of bottles wrapped in brown paper sacks. Taylor Grocery was BYOB, as long as you carried concealed.

As we approached, a guy wearing a striped tie and buck oxfords gave me a grin and a wink from under the disheveled hair falling over his forehead. Only an Ole Miss frat boy could manage to look that hedonistic in a sport coat and khakis. I stared at my feet and hurried up the steps.

Dad opened the squeaking screen door for me. We walked in to the tempting smells of spicy shrimp gumbo, hushpuppies, and frying catfish. In other parts of the country, catfish has kind of a dirty reputation. But Mississippians know the catfish you get in restaurants here have spent their entire lives in meticulously maintained pools on catfish farms, eating nothing but soybeans, corn, and wheat. Not a bad life when you think about it. Taylor Grocery served it blackened, grilled, or fried.

Dad and I ordered the breaded filets then sat and listened to two guys, who were both named Jeff, playing music in the corner while we waited. I watched one of the Jeff's hands as he strummed his guitar, and my mind drifted to Lad then drifted further to the night at the club when I'd watched Nox play. Dad interrupted my reverie, leaning over the table and speaking louder than usual, thanks to an amp system too large for the small room.

"I said," he repeated himself for me, "It's good to be back home again."

"Oh. Yeah, it's been awhile since you've been here. Do you really still think of it as home?"

"That's one of the things I wanted to talk to you about tonight, Ryann." *Oh no.*

"They held my position at Ole Miss—I'm considering coming back."

"Daddy, you're not planning to move back here to stalk Mom are you?"

"No. It's mostly to see you. And you can't stalk your own wife."

"Yes, you definitely can. I saw it on Lifetime. Fair warning—it won't do any good. She. Is. Done." Mom had been doing so much better lately. I really didn't want my father to come here and get her all messed up again.

He raised his eyebrows at me. "Well, I'll keep your opinion in mind. But I have a meeting at the university tomorrow. And we'll see about your mother. There are a lot of things you don't know about our problems—and you shouldn't. They're for *us* to work out."

"You *really* think that's going to happen?" My tone expressed my extreme doubt.

He held my gaze for a minute then dropped his to the basket of bread that had just been delivered to our table. "I don't know, Ryann. I hope so. There's no one like her in the world. We've both made mistakes, but I still love her."

Okay. So there was the possibility of a lot more Dad-time in my life soon. I wasn't sure what to think of that.

My mother would be less than thrilled. Whatever her *mistakes* were, they couldn't have been equal to his affair. She definitely didn't want anything to do with him, and she'd be pleased if I felt the same. It was hard for her to fathom why I'd want a relationship with him at all anymore.

But I *had* been feeling the need lately for *some* sort of relationship with my dad—maybe it was disloyal—I didn't know. The thing was, I was only going to get one father in this life. Maybe an imperfect, somewhat disappointing one was better than no father at all.

Besides, being angry at him all the time only made me feel worse. I wasn't interested in his side of the story yet—the wounds were still too raw to accept any kind of excuses, but I could probably handle a little more time with him here and there.

Our fish platters arrived, steaming and fragrant, and we gave them our full attention, punctuated by only the most casual conversation for the rest of the evening. It was a start.

We reached the log house after dark. Mom's car was in the driveway, and seeing the shape of her head silhouetted in the kitchen window made me nervous, like I was cheating on her or something. She was going to flip about the motorcycle thing, too.

"So where are you staying tonight?" I asked.

"I got a room in Oxford for a few days. I have my meeting on campus in the morning, but I'd like to see you again tomorrow afternoon."

After almost a week of forced deprivation, I was supposed to finally see Lad the next day after work. I didn't think I could wait a minute longer.

"Sorry, but I have some plans I can't cancel. How about breakfast Saturday?"

"Okay then. See you Saturday. Sleep tight. Don't let the Heffalumps bite." Our inside joke from my early childhood days. He chuckled and leaned over to kiss my cheek. Scratchy. I just couldn't get used to the beard.

"Night, Dad."

His bike roared up the drive and out of sight. My father. On a Harley. Okey Dokey. Mom and Grandma Neena looked at me expectantly when I walked into the kitchen.

"How's your father?" Mom made an admirable attempt at keeping her face pleasant.

"He's good." My voice up-ticked on the last syllable, sounding weird. "He seems fine. He has a meeting at Ole Miss tomorrow about his old job."

Bye-bye, pleasant face. "Wonderful. That's all I need—just when I'm starting to find a little bit of peace for myself."

"He said he wasn't going to bother you. He wants to move back here so he can see me more," I explained. For the life of me, it sounded like I was trying to defend him. Which I wasn't. I figured I'd better throw in a disparaging remark for balance. "But you know *him*. Who knows what he's up to."

It seemed to placate her. Now that she sensed *I* was bothered, Mom was all about comforting *me*. "Well, Ryann, I wouldn't worry about it. He probably won't even follow through on it. It's probably another whim he's tossing around. Next thing you know, he'll be calling from California."

The following day moved torturously slow, thanks to the anticipation of seeing Lad and my nervousness about introducing him to Mom and Grandma Neena. I was still hoping to persuade him against it, but if he insisted on meeting them, he'd need something to wear. Of course, I didn't know Lad's sizes.

He was almost as big as Nox, so I finally used that number he'd given me and texted him.

-Hi. What size do you wear?

-Large shirt. Size 34 jeans, extra-long. Pretty much Large everything. Why?

Poor guy. He probably thought I was planning to get us matching outfits now that we were all buddy-buddy again.

-Just curious. What about shoes?

-Thirteen—you know what they say about guys with big feet.

-Yep. Big feet, big EGO.

-Like I said—Large everything.

I drove Grandma's car to the Hook 'N' Bullet, right off the Route Seven bypass. In addition to hunting and fishing gear, the store carried a small selection of practical work clothes. Feeling conspicuous browsing the men's

Wranglers and shirts, I finally settled on a John Deere t-shirt and a dark blue pair of jeans. Hardly fashion-forward, but not outside the norm for guys in this area. I skipped getting shoes because I still wasn't sure about Lad's size and I couldn't imagine how to tell him I'd estimated based on the size of some other guy's feet. I hoped he'd think to bring some.

At home I freshened up, changed into some walking shoes and headed out, noting with rising hope that Grandma was still out for the afternoon. Maybe she and Mom wouldn't make it home in time to meet Lad today after all.

He was already waiting when I reached the pool, somehow looking better than ever. I was excited, nervous, and... relieved. Part of me had believed until that moment I'd never actually see him again. No longer bothering with holding back, I ran to Lad and jumped into his arms.

"Hi," I said with a breathless laugh.

"Hi." He beamed back, squeezing me tightly against him and peppering my face and neck with kisses. "You look beautiful. I missed you. Tell me all about your week."

"It was fine. Long. Boring. Tell me what happened with *you*. That's the important news. What about your father? I can't believe he let you out into the light of day again."

"He would rather not have. In fact, he literally had me locked away in my room for most of the week."

"Oh no. How did you get out?"

"No elaborate escape or anything. I asked to speak with him. He probably expected me to apologize and abide by his will, but actually, I told him about the threat to our woods and to Altum."

"Oooh." I winced. "What did he say?"

"He immediately started planning the exodus of our entire population. The worst possible timing, since the Assemblage is a few weeks away. I assured him that would not be necessary as long as he let me leave Altum to see you. I told him we're working together on a plan to save our home."

"Good thinking. So, what's the plan?"

His cheerful expression wilted. "I was hoping you had come up with one."

"Oh. I've been trying and trying to think of something, but it's such a huge amount of money. I'm going to see my father again tomorrow—he's in town, by the way. Anyway, when I see him I'll talk to him and find out if there's any possibility he can help stop this."

"Yes, perhaps. Well, it *will* work out somehow because it has to." Admirable faith, baseless as it was. Lad gestured to the bag I carried. "What's that?"

"These…" I said pulling them out like a shopping channel host on TV, "are your snazzy new human-clothes. You know, for meeting my family, that is, if you still want to. If you've changed your mind, it's totally okay."

"No. I have not changed my mind. That's the first thing I wanted to do today, well, the second thing." Lad bent down and kissed me. "All right, *now* to meeting your family."

"Try them on then, I guess."

I turned my back to give him privacy—kind of pointless considering he was usually barely clothed anyway. I heard rustling and zipping and snapping, and then he touched my arm. I turned around and did a double take.

"Wow. You look... normal... kind of. Well, better than normal. You look nice. Very presentable and... human." Truthfully, he looked much, much better than the average human, even in his farm boy outfit. At least dressed like that, he didn't look quite as much like the fairy tale character he was. "You definitely don't look like an Elven prince in those."

"Excellent." He smiled, breathtaking as always. "I brought my shoes." He reached down beside a large rock to retrieve some beautiful handmade-looking leather sandals and put them on. "I keep these in my treehouse for visits to the library."

"Good call. I didn't know what we were going to do about that. It's no shirt, no shoes, no dating in my mom's book."

Lad looked at me quizzically. In spite of all his reading, there were some phrases he'd apparently never encountered.

"Never mind, it's not important. Ready to go?"

We set off for the house, talking about the various activities that had filled my week. He was very interested in my reunion with my father, but as we neared the house, I cautioned him to drop the topic.

"Better not mention Dad in front of my mom and grandma, okay? Touchy subject. And—oh my gosh—before you meet my grandma, there's something I really should tell you."

Lad put his finger gently to my lips to stop me. "You know what? I'd prefer to just meet them both and form my own impressions, okay?"

"No, I really think you—"

"Trust me, Ryann. I can handle it."

I went along with it, but when he found out what I'd wanted to tell him, he might regret not letting me forewarn him. All of my cowardly hope of avoiding the meeting faded when I spotted my mom's car in the drive. Grandma's car was home now as well.

"Okay, they're here. Sure you want to do this? Last chance to chicken out…"

"Yes, I'm sure." Lad smiled and gripped my hand securely inside his, and we walked up the steps to face my family. Inside, he looked around with an expression of wonder. It was funny to see him so agog over the interior of a very average home. But then, I'd probably looked the same way when seeing his home.

"I've never been inside a human house before," he leaned down and whispered excitedly into my ear.

"Okay," I shushed. "No more of that. My mother will be shocked enough when I tell her I actually have a boyfriend. If she finds out you're also an Elf, we'll have to resuscitate her. And stop looking so amazed. Pretend this is what you're used to."

"I'll try." He smiled a little too big.

My mom walked into the living room from her bedroom where she'd changed out of her work clothes into some jeans and a t-shirt. She stopped.

"Oh, Ryann honey, you startled me." She looked curiously at Lad, and then down at our clasped hands. Her eyes widened. "And I see you've brought home some company..."

I dropped Lad's hand and went to stand beside her. "Yes. Mom, I want you to meet someone. This is Lad. He's a close friend of mine. Actually, we've been... seeing each other."

My mother's head whipped around as she looked from Lad back to my face again. She couldn't even begin to hide her astonishment. After a moment, though, she regained her composure and stepped forward with her hand extended.

"Lad, it's so nice to meet you."

I prayed Lad would figure out what to do with her hand. I'd never told him about the custom of shaking hands in greeting. I hoped he'd read about it.

He handled it beautifully, reaching out and taking her hand in a firm, but not tight, grip and then letting it go. "It's a pleasure to meet you as well, Mrs. Carroll." Lad smiled.

I noticed my mom's face soften in approval. She was a sucker for good manners and good teeth.

"Well, I have to admit, this is a surprise. Ryann didn't mention she's been dating someone. Do I know your family, Lad? What's your last name?"

Yikes. I wasn't prepared for that one. I blurted out the first thing that came to mind. "Prince. Lad Prince. I don't think you'd have met his family, Mom. They don't really spend a lot of time in town, and Lad is home schooled." *So far so good.* I could tell my mom was about to burst with curiosity, but she managed to resist firing a barrage of questions at Lad.

We'd just taken our seats in the den when Grandma Neena came down the hall. She started talking before seeing we had a visitor.

"Oh my. I tell you, I was so tired. I had to lie down for a little—" The sentence died on her lips as she spotted Lad.

He stood up respectfully, and all the color left Grandma's face. I really hadn't expected her to be so surprised. Unlike my poor mother, she'd at least had a clue about what was going on. I stood and joined them.

"Grandma, this is Lad. He wanted to meet you and Mom, so I brought him by today…" I studied Grandma with concern as she walked slowly toward Lad, her fingertips lightly holding her own face as if she wasn't quite sure it was still there. Mom gave her a puzzled look as well.

"Lad," I said, sounding strangled, "this is my grandmother, Neena Spears."

He reached out to her and said gently, "Mrs. Spears... so very nice to meet you." After taking her hand, he darted a quick glance at me and raised an eyebrow. He knew.

"Lad..." Grandma whispered. She looked at him as if she'd never seen a boy before. It must've been the shock of seeing one of her own kind after so long.

"Well..." Mom laughed uncomfortably. "Why don't we all go into the kitchen for some iced tea?"

Sitting around the table with my mother, my grandmother, and Lad was an almost out-of-body experience. Grandma recovered her composure somewhat, and Lad did an admirable job of pretending to be ordinary, but there were some strained moments when he was forced to be evasive about his background.

My mother's eyes narrowed slightly at those points. She would no doubt attempt a thorough vetting of his family history tomorrow in town. *Good luck with that.* After an excruciating half hour, I was more than ready for some relief and some alone time with Lad. I pushed away from the table.

"Well, we have plans, so I guess we'd better get going," I announced. "Lad?"

He walked to the door with me, exchanging pleasantries with Mom and Grandma. Before we could step outside though, my mom stopped us with a hand placed lightly on my arm and an apologetic smile.

"You know what? I've remembered there's something I need Ryann's help with this evening. Lad, I'm sorry to

AMY PATRICK

interrupt your plans. I hope you don't mind if I steal my daughter tonight."

"Mom!" I started to protest, but Lad smiled and assured her it was no problem at all, much to my annoyance.

She turned back to me. "Honey, why don't you walk Lad out, and I'll see you in a minute, okay?"

I grumbled inwardly, already knowing what she wanted to see me about. I walked outside with Lad to say a begrudging farewell. "I'm so sorry. She's just doing the mandatory mom freak-out thing. Can I see you tomorrow after I go out to breakfast with my dad?"

"Of course." Lad took me in his arms for a gentle hug. "She loves her little girl, and I can't blame her. So... I see what you wanted to tell me—your grandmother is one of us."

"What do you think?"

"I think it's great." He laughed. "And it explains a lot. Now I know why I can hear your thoughts sometimes." I saw another realization hit him. "And why my glamour doesn't really work on you."

"Well, I'm only a little bit. I don't think I got too much out of the Elven gene pool."

"You—got all the best parts," he said and tickled my ribcage, making me giggle and squirm away from him. He took my hand and pulled me back. "I'll see you around midday tomorrow. I've got something important to tell you."

"Oh? Tell me now."

"It can wait until tomorrow. Goodnight, Sweet Ryann," he said, placing a chaste kiss on my forehead, well aware that my mother was watching from the window.

Back inside, I shut the door and gave her an exasperated expression. "Well? What is it you so suddenly need my help with?"

"Understanding what on Earth is going on, that's what. Where did all this come from Ryann? And if you've known this boy for weeks, why am I just now hearing about him for the first time? This is not like you. You're usually so open with me."

"I didn't tell you before because there wasn't really anything to tell. I met him and I liked him, but it didn't become serious until recently." *Oops.*

My mother seized on my unfortunate word choice, her tone rising. "Oh, so now it's *serious*? I don't know, Ryann. I'm not sure about this guy. How old is he? He seems nice, but there's something… off about him. I mean, how much do you really know about him?"

"Enough," I insisted. "He is kind of different, but please don't judge him. You don't understand. I really like him. I've never felt this way about anyone."

"Oh, I understand better than you think. I just want you to be careful. Your father was the good-looking, mysterious type. I know how irresistible that can be to a young girl. Please think about what you've seen me go through. I don't want that for you. *You* don't want that, believe me."

"Mom," I bellowed. "He is *nothing* like Dad." She was being impossible. My dad wasn't a toad or anything, but objectively, he wasn't all that good-looking. And he hadn't been mysterious a day in his life. Besides, this conversation was about *my* life, not about hers. "This is totally different."

"What about Nox?"

"What about him?"

"I like Nox." Mom had met him *once*. Like all other women in his sphere, she'd been immediately overwhelmed by Nox's apparently limitless charm. She'd mentioned him over and over again since then.

"Why don't *you* date him then? He's got a lot of women your age throwing themselves at him, actually."

"Ryann, watch your mouth and stop being ridiculous. Why *don't* you date Nox? He has excellent manners. I can tell he really likes you, and he's handsome, and charming, and talented…"

"Because I don't love him."

She looked like I'd poked her with something sharp. "And you love Lad?" she asked in her ultra-calm, dealing-with-an-emergency voice.

"I didn't say that."

"Listen, honey, you know I'm only concerned about what's best for you. I'm worried. I can't put my finger on it, but there's something funny going on with that boy. I know he looks like an angel, but I feel like he might be… I don't know. I wish you would date someone a little more…" She seemed to be searching for the magic word that would persuade me without sending me the other direction and prompting me to elope with Lad.

"More like Nox?" I finished her sentence for her, "Like Jake McKee?" She looked at me silently, clearly preferring both examples to the guy she'd just met. Lad didn't like to use his glamour, but I wished he'd thrown a sprinkle or two her way.

"What do you think Momma?" She turned to Grandma Neena, who'd been sitting quietly, listening to the whole exchange.

"I think I'd like to chat with Ryann privately."

My mother's brow instantly lifted, and she breathed out a sigh of relief. She believed she had an ally and was clearly counting on Grandma Neena to get through to me where she'd failed.

"Well, I'll leave you two to talk then. I think I'll go to my room and call Davis—find out how his day was." She was so obvious, rushing out of the kitchen to give us privacy for a little heart-to-heart.

When Mom was out of earshot, I sat down at the table across from Grandma, eager to hear her impressions. But instead of offering any, she had a question for me.

"Ryann… you never told me about Lad's family. Who are they?"

The heart-pounding feeling was back. "Why?"

"Because… Lad looks exactly like my old fiancé."

CHAPTER TWENTY-FIVE
FACING REALITY

"*That's* who you were supposed to marry—Ivar, Lad's father?" I gasped.

"Now you can understand why breaking my engagement was such a scandal."

It took me a few minutes to find the instruction manual for my tongue. "So that means... you would've been Queen of Altum. Wow. You really did do a big no-no. No wonder why he hates humans so much... one of them stole his bride." It would also explain Ivar's extreme personal prejudice against me. "Grandma, people always say I look like you did when you were younger. I think Lad's father must have recognized who I am. The way he looked at me—no wonder you could never go back."

She surveyed my face, nodding. "Well, you do look enough like me. And I swear, Lad looks so much like his father, when I saw him standing in my living room tonight, I thought I was looking at Ivar. Lad is the spitting image of his father the last time I saw him."

"That was, how long ago—forty-something years? And Ivar is your age? I don't get it. He doesn't look..." My voice faded away in bewilderment.

"Ryann, I thought you said Lad told you about the Elves."

"He did tell me... a lot. What do you mean?"

"Sweetheart, think about when you were in Altum. How many Elves did you see who looked like me? Who looked old?"

"Only one. Everyone else was..." My hand flew up to cover my mouth. "Oh my God."

"So Lad didn't tell you everything then. He didn't tell you... Elves are immortal."

"No," I whispered, stunned. "So, then... you are? Immortal? How does that work? How were you planning to explain that to everyone when you're still around and still strong and healthy, like, when I have grandchildren?"

"Well, of course I've had to start thinking about that lately since I'm getting up there in human years. I guess I'll do what the Dark Elves who become famous do— disappear from the public eye when the cover story is no longer believable. They can claim Botox or plastic surgery or airbrushing for a while, but eventually they have to pretend to develop a social phobia, or overdose on drugs, or die in a car crash. I'll pretend to die of old age."

I blinked rapidly, hardly able to believe my ears. "But... you *won't* be dead. If you can't go back to Altum, what will you do? Hide in the house?"

She leaned further over the table, reaching to cover my hand with hers, as if to lend me the strength to handle what I was about to hear. "I'll have to go somewhere where no one knows me. This is the consequence of the decision I made, Ryann. That's what I'm talking about when I ask you to think of Lad. And now that I know the whole truth of his identity, I'm even more certain you two have to end this thing."

My fingers clenched into a tense fist under hers, but she didn't withdraw her hand. Instead she rubbed it over mine in a soothing motion that matched her consoling tone. "Lad will be king someday when his father steps down. He has to marry, honey, and the time is near for him. I know it won't be easy to give him up. It's going to hurt like all get-out, but it will be so much worse if you wait."

Now I yanked my hand away. "But you said to *trust* in love—that it could be good."

"I know honey." Her eyes were wet. "I'm sorry. Sometimes loving someone means letting them go. Every day you're with Lad makes it more dangerous for *him*. If he does fall in love with you and the two of you decide to bond—which is going to get harder and harder to resist—he won't ever be able to take an Elven bride and carry out his duties as the leader of his people. The royal lineage will stop with him. And someday he'll lose you. You're only partially Elven—there's no guarantee you'll have an extended life span. You don't want him to end up alone like me, do you? You have to find a way to let him go now, Ryann, for *his* sake."

"No. I can't lose him. And I can't lose you! There has to be a way."

I ran outside, slamming the screen door, and collapsed into the cushions of the bench swing. I shouldn't have yelled at Grandma. But I couldn't help it—it was all so hopeless, and that made me furious.

For a long time I rocked and squinted up at the sky through tears, thinking about what I'd ultimately have to do and wondering how much time I had left with Lad until I had to do it.

I drove to The Skillet the next morning, still in a deep funk, hoping my puffy eyes didn't attract too much attention from the late breakfast crowd. There was only so much concealer could do.

Dad was there already—his Harley was parked in a spot outside the front window where he could keep an eye on it. He'd been living in the city too long. He was more likely to run into Lady GaGa on the sidewalk here than to have his motorcycle stolen.

"Hey." I slid into the booth opposite him. "Still drinking your coffee black, I see."

"Yep. Only now I don't drink it after noon, or it keeps me up all night."

"Or maybe it's the guilt," I suggested sourly under my breath, then louder, "You should try the sausage biscuit sliders here. They're awesome."

My father glanced up from the menu to give me a hard look from under his brows. I could tell he was trying to decide whether to scold me for my rude remark, which he'd clearly heard. I halfway hoped he would.

We'd been seated in Emmy's section, and she came to our table, pad in hand. "Hi Ryann. Morning, Mr. Carroll. It's been a long time. You back in town now?" Her tone was cautious, but she offered my dad a polite smile.

"Looks like it," Dad said. "I have to say—it's good to be back."

She laughed. "Well, I'm glad for *you* then, but I can't wait to get out of here."

"Oh—you planning a summer getaway?"

"Maybe even longer. I'm heading out to Los Angeles in a few weeks. I might stay."

"Well, I couldn't blame you. I've been there, and it is quite a place. I wish I'd travelled and followed my dreams when I was *your* age—I'd probably have figured out a few things sooner—or at least gotten it out of my system."

They shared a grin of agreement as I silently seethed. Emmy took our breakfast orders and winked at me in a *See, I'm right* expression before hurrying off to turn them in.

When she was out of earshot, I muttered, "Since when are you and Emmy B-F-F's?"

My father's lips compressed into a thin line. "Something bothering you this morning, Ryann?" His tone dripped sarcasm.

"You could say that."

I'd just spent one of the worst nights of my life, he was encouraging my best friend to make the worst *mistake* of her life, and I was annoyed that he was planning to invade the contented little world my mother had constructed for herself here. I was also sick to death of the whole financial mess we were in because of him. Add it all up, and I was ready to unload.

"You have *no* idea what bad advice you gave Emmy. And Mom is about to lose her family's land, thanks to your funny business with the IRS. Not that it affects *you*."

He nodded, his expression contrite. "I'm sorry about that. It's no excuse, but I did spend all the money on your mother and you. I always felt... how can I explain it? I always felt so lucky to have your mom—like she was this amazing gift I didn't deserve and might lose at any moment. I wanted to give her everything, and I made some stupid financial mistakes trying to provide a lifestyle beyond my means."

"If you were so smitten with her... why did you cheat?" There it was—the question that had been eating at me. I could hardly believe I'd asked it. My heart pounded as I waited for his response.

Dad stared at me with sad eyes. It was obvious he wanted to give me some sort of answer but wasn't quite sure what to say. "I was… hurt. And I made a terrible, immature decision. It was only the one time, and I regretted it immediately." Taking in my incredulous expression, he sighed deeply, defeated. "And I *don't* have the money for the IRS right now. I'm sorry. We may just have to let a few trees go."

I huffed a humorless laugh. "We? They're not *your* trees."

"Would you rather see me go to jail, Ryann?"

"Don't ask," I snarled.

At his wounded grimace, I back-tracked a bit. "No, of course not. It's just not fair that Mom has to face the music while you cruise around playing Easy Rider. And where have you been for the last six months? Why show up now after not bothering with one visit and hardly a phone call?" If my parents had a horrible fight, if they'd both been at fault, well okay. But he hadn't just left *her*, he'd left me, too. "I mean, if it's freedom you want, go for it. Grow a beard down to your knees, join Hell's Angels and ride off into the sunset. You have my blessing."

My father's face was deep red by the time I finished my tirade, though he kept his voice calm and low when he replied. "Ryann." He paused and breathed deeply, "I've admitted I made some mistakes."

"Hmmph." I folded my arms across my chest. Understatements ran rampant throughout the entire family, it seemed.

"I know I messed up—especially with you. That's why I want to move back here and try to fix things. My meeting at Ole Miss went well yesterday. I looked at some apartments in Oxford. And for the record—I have called—you don't answer the dadgum phone. I shouldn't have stayed away so long, but I needed some distance. I needed to think. The feelings between your mom and me were pretty raw, and I couldn't handle being around her. But I'm much better now. I've missed you more than I can explain. And If I come back to my job at the university, I can collect a paycheck again, help y'all financially, and be close to you... and to Maria."

I shot him a warning look, and he responded by holding his hands in front of him in a defensive posture.

"I know. I know what you said, but sooner or later your mom and I have to find some closure between us. And yes—I'd love to earn her forgiveness and maybe even her love again someday. I know I don't deserve another chance, but I can't just let go without trying. There's no getting over her. She's special, kiddo." He gave me a weak smile that pleaded for understanding.

Yeah, right. "Good luck with that." My tone contradicted my words.

"Well, thank you very much for that sincere wish. And... my luck *is* pretty good so far. I talked to her last night as a matter of fact."

My chin lifted, my eyes narrowing. "About what?"

"About you, mostly. She's concerned about the boy you brought home, and I have to say, I agree with her."

Great. The first thing my parents had agreed on in the past year, and it was the death of my love life. It was too much. I jumped up from the table and threw my napkin back into the booth.

"*You...* are the last person who should be handing out relationship advice. Pardon me if I've lost my appetite for cheese grits."

I rushed for the door, catching Emmy's sympathetic look on the way out. Struggling to hold in tears, I backed the car onto Main Street, spun the wheel and aimed for home. What the hell was going on? I'd just about come to terms with the fact that everlasting love was a load of you-know-what, and now my dad was back, all sorry and sappy and love-sick.

And there was more than a slight possibility that if he showed true remorse and repentance, my mother would give him another chance. *And* it infuriated me that everyone had something to say about Lad. Mom. Dad. Grandma. And that they were all right.

They were right if you looked at the situation from a logical point of view—our relationship couldn't work—it should never have happened. But I wasn't feeling very logical at that particular moment. I was feeling angry, fiercely defensive of Lad, and... in love. *Oh God, no.* I didn't love Lad, did I?

I did. *Dang it.* Not now. It was my worst nightmare and sweetest dream all mixed up into one tasty bite. So much for "icing on the cake." I'd let Lad become the whole dadgum dessert menu.

I would see him in a few minutes. I should probably have at least grabbed a biscuit at The Skillet before stomping out the door because my stomach felt all squishy. Would he be able to tell? Maybe he *already* knew. But what did love even matter when his life was governed by duty and Elven law? The whole thing was hopeless. I had to let him go. *But not today.*

Part of me wanted to get it over with. The other part wanted to stretch out our time together until there was no other choice. *Not today.* Not right now. He might not have been human, but he was the one person I felt I could trust completely.

I breathed unsteadily as I walked toward the pool in the woods. As soon as Lad came into focus, his buoyant mood was obvious. There was a new lightness to his face. The green of his eyes seemed brighter, if that was even possible, and his smile was wide.

I couldn't manage one myself. I approached him slowly, cautiously. He didn't seem to notice any change in me. He greeted me by grabbing me and administering a mind-erasing kiss. When I didn't respond with the usual enthusiasm, he loosened his hold on me and searched my face.

"What's the matter, Ryann?"

"Rough morning."

"Your father?"

"Among other things."

"Well, I have some news that will cheer you. Here, sit with me."

We sat in the ferns at the edge of the pool. I trailed my fingers across the surface of the cool water, waiting for the big announcement. Lad said nothing. I looked up at him. *Why is he stalling?* He seemed nervous.

"Well?"

He took a deep breath before speaking. "Remember I told you about the upcoming Assemblage?" I nodded, and he continued. "The date is set—it will take place in two weeks."

I wasn't sure what it had to do with me. "That's good."

"And remember how I told you I must marry at age eighteen?"

I nodded slowly.

"My birthday is a week away. My father has planned a grand wedding ceremony during the Assemblage." He paused. "My parents have selected a bride for me—well actually, we've been betrothed for some time, since we were twelve years old."

Ooof. That one hit me like a body blow. He was *engaged*. Had *been* engaged. For years.

"This is the news that's supposed to cheer me up? What do you want me to say—congratulations?" I jumped to my feet. "*That* would have been nice to know a little earlier. You lied to me."

"I didn't lie." Lad reached out and caught my hand, pulling me back to sit on the ground with him.

I sat but tried to tug my fingers away. "Not telling me something so important is the same thing."

He gripped my hand tighter, giving me a reassuring smile. "Ryann, wait. Let me finish. What I wanted to tell you today is that I've made a decision. Having this deadline before me has caused me to think about what I really want for my life. It's helped me to weigh my family obligations and duty to my people against the feelings I have for you. It's forced me to consider the incompatibility of being with you and living in Altum, and so, I had to choose."

"Yeah, I get it. You have a duty, blah blah blah." I jerked my hand from his grasp and wrapped my arms around my knees.

What an idiot I am. I'd known this day was coming. I'd been crazy to even keep seeing him this long. *It's okay. This is good. It's for the best.* He was saving me from having to do it.

"I choose you," he said. His smile was stunning.

My response was a gasp. "What?" It was a good thing I was already sitting because I would have fallen over.

"Yes." Lad nearly shimmered with joyful energy, laughing. He couldn't stay still. "I guess I'll have to get used to those strange human houses and those horrible clothes because I've made my decision. I don't even care what's right or wrong anymore. I couldn't do it—give you up in order to fulfill some ancient, outdated tradition and take a bride I care nothing for, living out the rest of my life in resentful obedience. Not when I feel this much lo—"

"No!" I interrupted him in a panic—clapping my hand over his mouth. I was out of time. All hope of putting it off was gone. I'd been given no chance to strategize, to prepare a speech that would end things neatly between us and make Lad see it was for the best. And I did have to end it. For his sake and for mine.

"No, Lad. I don't want that." I scrambled up and stalked away from him, twisting back in time to see his expression turn from joy to confusion.

"I don't understand." The usual deep melodic quality of his voice had been replaced by a hollow whisper.

My gut churned at the look on his face, so I glanced away, at the ground, at the trees, anywhere but his troubled eyes. "I know you don't understand, and I'm sorry. I... haven't been honest with you. I've led you on, and now it's gone too far. We... we can't see each other anymore."

He bolted to his feet and started toward me. "What are you saying? No... no! What's happened, Ryann? How can you say that, after what I've just told you... knowing how I feel about you? I know you feel the same."

I swallowed a painful lump in my throat and forced myself to say words I despised. "I'm sorry, but you're wrong. With your lack of experience around humans, maybe you're not very good at reading our true feelings. I feel bad for taking advantage of that. It wasn't fair."

I was thankful I hadn't eaten breakfast after all because every organ inside my body was revolting against the words coming out of my mouth. I had to turn away and clench my stomach muscles, pressing my fingers hard into them to keep from retching.

"It's not true..." he whispered.

When I looked back, Lad's eyes showed me that my razor sharp lies were hitting their mark, slashing him, wounding him.

He shook his head side-to-side, his voice thick with bleeding emotion. "Ryann, I love you. I thought you loved me, too. I was ready to leave everything behind... live as a human for you. I want to. I want *you*." He took a step toward me then another, raising his palms toward me. "Come here. Let me just touch you... please."

"No—I don't want... don't..." I stepped back to preserve the crucial distance between us. If he reached me and pulled me into his arms, it was all over. I'd grab him and never let go again.

The pressure built behind my eyes, Judas tears threatening to reveal my true feelings. I had to end it fast and get out of there, making sure he'd never try to see me or speak to me again. It was his only chance to have a happy life. The life he was born for.

"When you told me about the Assemblage, how you'd be expected to take a bride at eighteen, I felt..." *devastated* "... happy. Relieved, actually. I was already trying to figure out how to tell you my interest in you has faded. This is perfect timing, really. You should go back to your family, to your home. Go back and be with someone of your own kind."

"You are my kind, Ryann."

My heart ripped further. I was starting to crumble. I reached for the final dagger that would release the last of the lifeblood from Lad's feelings for me—something that would convince him, before his entire life was ruined, along with the lives of all his people. And before I found myself committed to the most dangerous kind of relationship, one where I was deeply in love. I steeled myself and made my voice as hard as possible.

"That's... unfortunate because I don't want you. I've found someone else. You may remember him—Nox—the one you saw me with in my yard? At the time I wasn't sure which one of you I wanted, so I lied. But now I realize *he's* the one. You see, the truth is... I love him."

I would remember the look on Lad's face for the rest of my life. And for the first time, I realized the word "heartache" was based on a real biological phenomenon. A physical pain gripped my heart, squeezing until I thought I might pass out from the sensation.

I wanted to sink down, melt into the ground like rain. The simple act of standing while forcing myself to continue to wound him was too much. I wasn't sure I could keep it up. I locked my knees and willed myself to remain upright. Lad backed away from me slowly, his voice sounding choked.

"No, no, no," he repeated as if in a trance. "It's not true. I know what I saw in your eyes. I know what I heard from your mind."

"You're wrong, Lad. I don't have that ability. It was your imagination. You heard what you wanted to hear. If you don't believe me, watch. Nox is coming to take me out tonight. You'll see."

I'd somehow have to put off falling apart a while longer, long enough to call Nox and beg or coerce him into picking me up and making it look like we had a date.

"Believe it Lad. Go home and get on with your life." Turning, I stumbled away from him without looking back.

I forced myself to walk in case he was watching, though I wanted to run. Run away from the horrible lies I'd told, from the devastation I'd seen on his face. I prayed he would run in the opposite direction, toward the life he was always meant to have. Toward home and family. Toward eventual peace and happiness... and lasting love with a girl of his own kind. It was the best thing for both of us.

Once I was out of his sight, the tears came, finally overpowering all ability I had to control them, flowing freely as I let myself break into a run at last.

CHAPTER TWENTY-SIX
DATE WITH DISASTER

At home, I rushed past Grandma to the safety of the shower where I could camouflage my tears, and if possible, drown. When the hot water ran out, I emerged, cold, wet, and unfortunately still alive and reminded myself the job wasn't finished.

I had to call Nox and arrange to put on a show in case there was any piece of Lad's heart still left unbroken. Nox agreed all too eagerly and promised to pick me up at six.

Pulling on my sleep mask and putting in my ear plugs, I crawled under my covers, seeking an escape from all thought and feeling for a few hours. My dreams weren't much more pleasant than reality, but at least the pain in them was somewhat dulled.

When I woke, there was barely enough time to dress and put on some makeup before Nox came. I wandered to the kitchen where Mom and Grandma were preparing a meal for Davis, who was scheduled to arrive from Atlanta at any time.

"Oh, hi Sweetie. Are you not feeling well? Grandma told me you came in and took a shower and went right to bed. I looked in on you a couple times, but you were really knocked out. Everything ok?" Mom walked over and held her palm against my forehead as she did any time I felt less than perfect. Even if it was a splinter, a fever check was in order as far as my mom was concerned.

"Yeah, I'm fine," I said dully. "My breakfast with Dad didn't go so great. We kind of had a fight."

"Oh..." She nodded in understanding, assuming my funk was all due to my father. That was easy for her to believe, and for now, I'd let her. I was far from ready to discuss my breakup with Lad. Grandma Neena looked at me with sympathy. I directed my attention to her and willed her not to say anything. She seemed to get the message and stayed silent.

"I have a date with Nox tonight. He'll be here in a few minutes."

"Oh, that's *good*," Mom said a little too brightly. "But you're going to miss meeting Davis. He's really interested in getting to know you, Ryann."

"I know. Sorry. Next time, okay?"

The doorbell ended the conversation and compelled me to dig into my reserve tank for a smile and some forced enthusiasm. Not that I didn't want to see Nox—I didn't feel like seeing *anyone*.

In fact, I didn't feel much of anything at all. It must have been the numbness some people describe when recounting a trauma they've lived through, a temporary lack of feeling that enables people to do what has to be done until the crisis is over.

With that going for me, I opened the door, determined to continue playing the role I had to play for Lad's sake a few hours longer. Mom joined me at the door. Her giddiness annoyed me.

"Nox, it's so good to see you. I read about your record deal. How's everything going?" she gushed.

"Great, Mrs. Carroll. Thanks. Our new agent is working on booking a tour for us after we finish in the studio. We'll probably hit the road this fall."

"How wonderful. So exciting. So, where are y'all headed tonight?"

Instead of answering out loud, Nox leaned over and whispered something into my mother's ear. She broke into a delighted grin and her eyes widened. Then, her brows pulled together slightly as she continued to listen and momentarily considered something.

"No, I'm afraid not. I don't think that would be best. The rest of it sounds fun, though. Back by curfew, right?"

"Right," Nox said, smirking.

As we walked away from the house together, a flash of movement drew my eye to the periphery of the woods. It might have been a deer, but it probably wasn't. Well, good. He'd seen us together. It was done then.

Instead of walking to his car, Nox turned and grabbed my hand, leading me directly toward the woods.

"What are you doing? Aren't we going out?"

"We are out." He raised his hands to the sides and flashed me that mischievous grin of his. "You'll never guess what I have planned. Don't even try. And don't argue—I put a lot of work into this today."

This wasn't happening at all as I'd intended. I'd wanted Lad to see me *leaving* with Nox as I'd told him I would. Then he would let me go and return to his own life with his own people. Now it seemed Nox intended for us to spend the evening on Lad's turf and probably right under Lad's watchful eyes.

I couldn't object, though, after what Nox had just said, so I went along with him into the dark woods. His flashlight clicked on, illuminating a narrow footpath and not much else.

"How do you know where you're going?" I asked.

"Oh, I'm full of hidden talents. Relax. I'm not going to lead you astray."

The trail ended at a wide gully. During a rainy stretch, the gully would've been filled with runoff, running fast and wild and reaching halfway up the banks. But this evening, only a narrow stream flowed through the center of it, leaving a sandy shore on either side of the trickling water. Nox had set up a campsite there—a small nylon tent, a log for sitting, and a barely smoldering fire in a pit lined with river rocks.

"We're camping?"

"Yes, but this is only an *evening* camp for young ladies with eleven o'clock curfews. I asked your mom if she'd consider letting you camp the night out here with me, but as you heard, she shot me down. I guess her trust in me goes only so far. Very wise woman."

He chuckled to himself, refreshing the smoldering campfire with dry wood until it was blazing. Nox reached into the tent and came to sit beside me on the log, holding marshmallows and two long sticks. He put me to work roasting the marshmallows while he threaded hot dogs onto another skewer.

"None for me. Sorry, but hot dogs are gross."

"Oh no," he said, "not these. When cooked over an open fire under a starlit sky, hot dogs rise to the level of epicurean delicacy. Really, they become something altogether different."

I laughed. "Well, that's good news because I *had* thought you wanted me to eat meat slurry, sodium, and fillers on a stick."

Of course, by the time I smelled them cooking and recalled the fact that I'd walked out on breakfast and slept through lunch, I was ready to wolf down my hot dog and fight Nox for his, too. And he was right. They were pretty dang good.

At first, I kept glancing nervously around us at the dark spaces between the trees, expecting at any moment to see accusing green eyes staring at me from the shadows. But after an hour of watching the dancing flames and listening to Nox strumming his acoustic guitar and softly singing, I relaxed.

A heavy sense of well-being washed over me with the music. It was sort of like the night at the club, which should've alarmed me, maybe, but I wasn't feeling very concerned with "should" and "shouldn't." I found myself forgetting for entire minutes at a time about the morning's gut-wrenching exchange with Lad. The relief was heavenly.

"Ever made shadow puppets?" Nox asked, putting down his guitar and nodding toward the shadows we cast on the tent in the firelight.

"I learned some in camp when I was a kid. I'm pretty good, but I'd hate to show you up," I teased.

"Oh, you have no idea who you're talking to. I hereby challenge you to a shadow puppet duel." Nox arranged his hands and executed a flawless butterfly, fluttering across the side of the tent.

"Oh yeah? Think you're something, huh?" I did my dog, my bunny, and an eagle, but Nox completely outdid me each time, somehow forming entire moving scenes with a few turns of his hands and twists of his fingers.

"Okay, I give up. You're too good. And I'm totally out of ideas."

"Come on. One more," he said.

Sighing, I held up my arm, made a simple head with my hand, and undulated my wrist, attempting to pass it off as a snake. The shadow of Nox's arm joined mine on the tent, becoming a snake as well. Somehow, his snake performed maneuvers my pathetic reptile could only have dreamed of. And then, Nox's arm wrapped around mine, and our snakes were intertwined, their fingertip mouths pressed together in a serpentine kiss.

My heart skipped. I turned to look at Nox, nervous about what I would see in his face. His incredible hazel eyes crackled with gold, mirroring the campfire, and I sensed not all the heat in them was coming from the reflection. *Oh God. What do I do here?*

I couldn't seem to do anything, actually, immobilized as I was by those eyes and the intensity of Nox's expression. My pulse raced like a water bug skittering across the surface of a lake, but the rest of me stayed perfectly still. He took the matter out of my hands, using our tangled arms to pull me closer. Lowering his head, he pressed his lips against mine, still humming softly in his throat.

I couldn't think, and I couldn't breathe.

And then he kissed me. This time it was different. Still self-assured, but seductively gentle. It was… very *very* nice if I was being honest. In fact, if I'd never met Lad, I'd probably have been in paradise.

I wouldn't be human if I didn't feel *something*, and for a moment I found myself succumbing to the drugging sensation, returning the kiss and allowing Nox to deepen it.

I was nowhere near ready to move on—I still could barely admit to myself that I'd lost Lad for good. But I could lose *myself* in this—use Nox like an anesthetic to avoid the pain that was inevitably coming when I did face the terrible truth.

No.

I couldn't do that to Nox. He didn't deserve that from me. As good as it felt, these weren't the lips I dreamed of, the impossible sweetness I'd come to crave. I pulled away slowly. His eyes were filled with satisfaction and a new fragility.

There was a loud rustling in a nearby tree. I jumped, and Nox wrapped his arms around me protectively. "It's just a squirrel... or some other little pest. It's gone." His voice softened, "Hey, I hope that was okay. I didn't plan to kiss you tonight."

"Why did you?" I whispered.

"You," he said with a seductive dip in his voice, "are too tempting. I can't be this close to you without wanting to kiss you."

I didn't answer. I didn't know what to say. On one hand, this was good. If Lad was out there somewhere watching, this unexpected turn of events completely supported the fabricated story I'd given him. My heart lurched painfully at the thought.

But what about after tonight? What about Nox? He'd expect more than I could give him, more than I might ever be able to give. I was trying to think of how to explain it to him, but he spoke again.

"I've been thinking, Ryann... about the tour. What would you say about my staying here and going to Ole

Miss in the fall instead? I could still play the area bars, frat parties, play up in Memphis now and then."

I drew back and looked at his face. "What? Why would you do that? You have a record deal. You have to go on tour. It's your dream. You would be insane to pass it up."

"*I* think I would be insane to pass up another opportunity that's only available right *here*." He reached up and stroked his fingers softly under my chin, lifting it up toward his mouth.

"No!" I yelped.

Nox pulled back, looking stung. I'd probably startled him, but he needed a shock—he wasn't thinking clearly. If he turned down this chance he'd regret it for the rest of his life.

"Why not, Ryann? I'd still be doing my music, but I'd be closer to you…"

"Nox—what is the matter with you? Why are you talking like this? We can still be friends if you go on tour. We have phones. You'll come home on breaks and we can hang out then."

"I don't think the occasional phone call and 'hang out' is going to be enough for me. I need to see you more often, like every day, for instance," he said, laying it on the line and shocking the daylights out of me.

No. No no no. I couldn't take two excruciating emotional scenes in one day. Why was I suddenly having to convince every guy I knew not to throw away his future?

"I don't think that's… necessary," I said.

Nox's expression changed, gathering clouds and growing darker. "Necessary. *Necessary?* No, I guess *you* wouldn't think so. I can't believe how stupid I am," he growled. He poked the fire hard with the end of his skewer, sending sparks skittering up into the dark sky.

Wow. I'd disappointed him, maybe hurt his feelings a little, but I couldn't imagine why he was getting this emotional. He was a player, a bad-boy Rock God.

"Why do you sound so mad?" I asked in a small voice.

"Come *on,* Ryann." His voice had turned savage. "What is so hard to understand? How could you *not know* how I feel about you? I mean, it's obvious. It should have been obvious to you for weeks now. If the fact that I try to spend every free minute with you didn't clue you in, maybe you should've figured it out when I lost total control and basically threw myself on you the other day."

My mouth opened, but no word or sound emerged.

Nox made a visible effort to calm himself, holding his hands in front of his body and pushing down, as if quieting some invisible symphony orchestra. He gentled his voice. "Ryann... you don't have to be afraid. I understand you're not very experienced. I realize this... stuff with your parents has you skittish on the whole relationship thing. But I can be patient. God—I've *been* patient, haven't I? We'll take things as slowly as you want."

"That's not it, Nox. I just don't—"

His hands gripped my shoulders. "No. Stop right there. You can't tell me you don't feel something for me. I may have been blinded by hope, but I don't think I could have been *that* wrong. We have a great time together, we're obviously attracted to each other. You *responded* to me when I kissed you. And what about that day on the swing in your yard? And then you called, wanting to see me tonight? Come on. Help me out here. Did I imagine all that?"

Oh Dang. This is awful. "You're right. But, it's... I can't give you what you're looking for. I'm not the one you want."

His voice descended into an angry growl. "*Don't* tell me what I want and what I'm looking for. If there's anything I *am* sure of here, it's what *I* want." Nox looked at the ground, drawing unsteady breaths. "Ryann... please. Isn't there *something* about me, anything you could want?"

"Of course. Everyone wants you."

"Everyone but *you*. Is that it?"

The hazel eyes were swimming with hurt now. It was killing me. "Nox... I do love being with you. I love your sense of humor and your voice and your ridiculously big brain. I love the way you look. It's just—"

"I'm hearing the 'L' word being tossed around quite a bit here," he interrupted.

I shook my head. "But not like that, Nox. It's—"

"No. It *is* like that, Ryann. I know it is... I can *feel* it. You feel it too."

He dragged me back to him again, pressing his lips hard against my mouth, crushing me against his body.

Working my hands in between us, I pushed against his chest forcefully and turned my head away from him.

"Nox—stop it. *Now* you're scaring me."

He stood abruptly, and backed away, his hands shaking. "You know what kills me? You don't even want to try. I mean it's not like there's someone else. *Right?* Well, you know what? I'm not going to try anymore either. I'm done. You want to be alone? No problem. You're going to end up alone. Enjoy." He threw the poker, and it vanished into the leafy darkness outside the campfire's ring of light.

He walked away from the campsite in long fast strides, leaving me staring into the dark woods where he'd disappeared. I sat back down and watched the fire, thinking of what I could say to him when he calmed down and returned, to fix things, to make it all better, to let us somehow stay friends.

When I finally accepted he wasn't coming back, I put out the fire. All the while, I worried about whether he'd made it safely back to his car in the dark. He didn't know the woods like Lad did, like I did. And as I trudged home with the flashlight I agonized—had I done the wrong thing?

He was right. There was no one else. Maybe I should have encouraged him, told him what he wanted to hear, let him hold me and kiss me the way he wanted to.

I kept coming back to this—I couldn't justify hanging on to Nox when my love had already been given away to Lad. It wasn't fair to him, and it was too late for me. My heart had already made its choice. I'd met my soul mate in these woods ten years ago. I'd experienced love. I couldn't keep it, but I couldn't live with anything less either.

Maybe I had more Elven blood in me than I realized. I wondered briefly... when I got home and looked in the mirror, what color my hair would be.

Chapter Twenty-Seven
Bad News and Good News

Sorry I left you out in the woods. Not cool. P.S. Don't worry about me. I'm fine. Totally over it.

Nox's text was the only glimmer of light in an otherwise miserable Monday. I'd spent the past two nights grieving over Lad and fretting over Nox. Today, I'd been barely functioning, forcing my soulless body to go through the motions at work, forcing myself to smile at the lunch customers, trying not to think of the hideous way I'd rejected Lad and annihilated my friendship with Nox.

Trying not to focus on the fact that I would live the rest of my life without love.

I read the words of his life-giving message over and over. At least Nox didn't seem furious at me. The thought of it lifted my spirits, giving me hope. I would find him at the ballpark tonight and apologize, ask if we could start over and be friends again.

The bell jangled as The Skillet's door opened. I looked up from wiping a table to see Nox stroll in. Dropping my towel on the tabletop, I hurried over to him, mentally rehearsing my speech.

"Hi. Listen, can I—" The words died on my lips as Savannah Ford, as in cheerleader-Homecoming court-class-beauty-Savannah Ford, followed Nox into the diner. My gaze lowered to their joined hands. I'd never had a problem with Savannah, but she was never one of my close friends either. Apparently she was one of his now.

Stopping right inside the doorway, he pulled her close and gave her a kiss that could've fried all the eggs in The Skillet's breakfast orders. Then he moved an apathetic gaze over me and raised one eyebrow.

"Yeah, Rye?"

Savannah suddenly noticed my existence and smiled like we were best friends—I guess when you're walking around in a cloud of pheromones, everyone's your buddy. "Hi Ryann!"

"Hi," I answered through a throat dry as unbuttered toast.

Nox kept his eyes trained on me, daring me to object or react in any way. Stammering and blushing ferociously seemed to be the best I could do.

"Uh… table for two?"

"Yes. We'll take this one." Savannah flounced past me heading for a round two-top near the front window and pulling Nox behind her. "Come on, sweetie."

"Okay fine," I mumbled to no one in particular. I walked over to the counter where Dory was working and asked to go on break. Before going to hide in the employee break room, I peeked back over my shoulder at Nox and Savannah. She was studying a menu, chattering happily.

He was looking straight at me.

And so began two weeks of unadulterated hell. I reminded myself forty times a day that I'd done the right thing. In both situations. I believed it was true, but the fact that both Nox and Lad were better off without me was beyond depressing. Lad was gone. Nox didn't want to be friends—he wanted to punish me—and I probably deserved it.

Emmy was moving forward with her plans to go to Los Angeles, and she'd forbidden me to say a word against it. And the clock continued to tick toward the day the IRS would take Grandma's home—our home—and land away. There seemed to be no solutions for any of it.

Just as I had after my parents' separation, I kept on keeping on. I went to work, I saw my friends. I didn't even try to date, though. It was way too sad.

Grandma Neena was the only person I could talk to honestly. We were running errands before heading home to share an exciting Friday night of microwave popcorn and *Friends*. I wasn't up to going out tonight.

"Is it ever going to stop hurting?"

"I can't say it ever goes away entirely." She reached over and patted my back gently. "But it does get easier to live with. I think when you truly love someone, a piece of you stays with them forever. But you're very young, and there's a lot of life and love left for you. Someday you'll meet someone else who's special to you. When you do, you'll be able to share the piece of your heart that doesn't belong to Lad."

I appreciated what she was trying to do, but I suspected the part left over might be too infinitesimal for anyone else to bother with. My cell rang. I looked down to check the screen—Mom—no doubt calling to say good-bye. She was heading to Atlanta for the weekend. At first, she'd been happy I'd broken up with Lad, but I knew she was getting more and more alarmed at my mood.

"Are you going to be okay? Want me to call Davis and tell him I can't make it this weekend? I wouldn't mind. Really. I'd rather stay here with you, if you need me."

"No, Mom. Don't worry. I'm fine. Grandma's here, and you and Davis need to go ahead and get everything worked out." I put on the happiest voice I could manage.

She and Davis would be having "the discussion" this weekend. My father had accepted the job at Ole Miss and was living in an apartment in Oxford, making it easy for him to drop in on us frequently. Anytime Mom happened to be around, he made it obvious he'd jump at a second chance with her.

It had her constantly shifting between states of annoyance and nostalgic longing. She was clearly still attached to my dad, but then she'd talk to Davis and be all swoony over him. I didn't know what to think. She'd promised to consider it seriously and not leave them hanging on indefinitely. I expected her to come home from Atlanta Sunday night with either an engagement ring or an announcement that she was taking my dad back, and I had no clue which one it would be.

"Well, I'm only a phone call away," she said. "You call me if you need anything. I'll turn around and come right back."

"Okay. Have fun and be safe."

"Oh, wait—Ryann—could you and Grandma do me a favor? I forgot to do it before leaving town. Go by Rooney's and pick up some flowers for the Douglas family's visitation tonight. Their daughter Allison died out in Los Angeles. They just got her back here today. Such a shame, a beautiful young girl. I don't think you met her—she was a good bit older. I feel bad about not being there tonight, but... Ryann? Can you hear me?"

"Uh, yeah. Okay, I'll do it. Bye Mom." My chest couldn't have felt worse if the airbag had deployed and hit me full force. Allison Douglas—the girl from Deep River who'd been *lucky* enough to get into a glamorous fan pod. That was it. I had to stop Emmy from going. She was scheduled to leave for L.A. in a week.

I picked up my phone and dialed her but got her voicemail. Before I could even put the phone back in my purse, it rang again. I expected to see that Emmy was calling me back, but it wasn't her number.

"It's a Deep River number, but I don't recognize it," I told Grandma. "Hello?"

The caller identified himself as Heath Marston, the manager of Food Star, and said he had some news for me. He asked if I was sitting down.

"I hope you are because you might not believe this. I tasted your tea all right, young lady. You weren't kidding. It really is something special. I contacted our corporate office in Memphis the same day about striking a deal with you to market your tea line at our store, and they instructed me to send them what I had on hand that night. Well, I did it. You need to come on by the store to hear the rest. Can you do that?"

My head was spinning. So much was happening so fast. "Yes sir. I'll be there in five minutes."

Luckily nothing was more than five minutes away in the town of Deep River. The way my heart was hammering, I might not have lasted much longer. Grandma drove us to the Food Star and went in with me. Mr. Marston led the way to his office, which was one floor above the store aisles with a large picture window overlooking the meat section. He invited us to sit across from his desk in bright yellow molded plastic chairs with metal legs. He sat back, smiled, and continued delivering the unlikely news.

"Well, like I said, I sent your sample up to corporate. They loved it. They lab-tested it. I don't know how you did it Miss Carroll, but apparently your tea is loaded with calcium, potassium, manganese…" He glanced down at the report on his desk. "… magnesium, phosphorus, iron, vitamins B2, B5, B6, niacin, biotin, protein, folic acid, fifty-four polyphenols, and somehow has an impossibly low calorie-count." He threw his hands up in a happy-baffled gesture. "They're not sure if we should market it as a dieter's dream come true or the ultimate health food product. And here's the best part—are you ready?"

I nodded, already wondering how I'd meet the demands of a grocery store on top of what I made daily for The Skillet.

"They want to stock your tea in *all* their stores. Do you know how big that is, Miss Carroll? That's a hundred and ten stores across the Southeast. And it's just the beginning. If it takes off, they want to develop the brand to market nationwide."

Thank God I was sitting down. "Wow." I had trouble making the word audible. "This is unbelievable. I don't know what to say. Thank you Mr. Marston."

"Thank *you*. The head honchos at Food Star think you have a winning product on your hands, and they don't want you to get away. Of course, I got some pretty good kudos for discovering you." He grinned widely. "Now… you've got some work to do. They want you up and running in four months, working in an approved facility, ready to provide product to all their stores. Can you do that?" He looked at me and then at Grandma, seeking some adult assurance of my competence, I guess. She nodded her head, beaming.

"Yes sir," I said.

I had no idea how I'd manage it, actually. But I knew I *would* do it. I had to. It was our answer. Lad's gift combined with my hard work might be enough to save my family's land and his home as well.

"Well, now here's the contract. There's some mighty big numbers on this little piece of paper. You know any lawyers, Ryann?"

"Yes sir. Lee Porter," I said, naming Mom's divorce attorney.

"Good. You have him take a look at it, make sure you're happy, and then let's do some business together. Sound good?"

"Sure does, Mr. Marston." I stood and shook his hand. Grandma did the same. "Thank you again, sir. You won't be disappointed," I said.

"I know that, Ryann, not if you keep making tea like you do, and it sells like we expect it to. Hey, what are you gonna call your company?"

I didn't even need to think it over. "Magnolia Sugar. Magnolia Sugar Tea Company."

When I climbed into the passenger seat and looked over at Grandma Neena, I felt a genuine smile emerging for the first time in weeks. "Well, we're in business."

We both stared at the contract in my hands. It was enough to get my company started. It was enough to pay off the IRS debt. It was a way for me to take care of myself in the future so I'd never have to depend on anyone else. Grandma drove straight to the lawyer's office, and I left the contract with his secretary. On the way to the flower shop, my mind flew faster than my mouth could follow.

"Okay, I'll need supplies—pots—big ones, mixers, containers, boxes, labels, a delivery truck, workers. It's going to take huge amounts of raw ingredients… oh my goodness, Grandma…" I glanced over and saw the realization hit her as well. "I have to tell Lad. His people have to know there's no need for them to leave their home now. Grandma, do you think you could find Altum again?"

She huffed indignantly, but then she broke into a grin, and her blue eyes sparkled. "I may be out of practice, but I *am* still an Elf."

"He won't exactly be glad to see me again," I said.

"I won't be the most welcome visitor, either."

"Well, we have to tell them—there's no choice—and we can't exactly call them up. For this plan to even work, I'll need a steady supply of saol water to make the tea. The Elves will agree, knowing what's at stake, won't they? I want to tell them right away. Can we go in the morning?"

"There's nothing I'd rather do."

Already, I was filled with anxiety over the prospect of seeing Lad. On one hand, I was shamefully eager just to look at him once more. On the other, I was dreading the way he would undoubtedly look at me. He'd had plenty of time by now to get over the shock of our last conversation and be well on his way to hating me.

It didn't matter. I had to find him and somehow hold myself together long enough to tell him what his people needed to know. Afterward when I was alone, I'd deal with the re-opened wound of being close to him again and walking away. Again.

I called my mom, who was still on the road, to tell her the amazing news. She gave me the screaming, joyful reaction I'd expected. I tried Emmy again. No answer. Then I sat staring out the windshield with the phone in my hand, debating about who else to call. That's when it hit me. I'd gotten exactly what I'd wanted—financial independence. But it felt like a hollow victory.

I could share this information with Lad, for the sake of his people. But I couldn't share the *moment* with him— not the way I wanted to. Together, we had saved both our homes, but *we* weren't together anymore. I was safe now, but essentially alone.

It took a long time to fall asleep. I woke again and again from dreams where Lad looked at me with hard, cold eyes and ordered me out of his home, and from an even more painful one where he told me he loved me and asked me to stay. I wondered if Grandma Neena was having any more luck trying to sleep, knowing she'd be returning to Altum tomorrow for the first time in more than forty years.

CHAPTER TWENTY-EIGHT
BACK TO ALTUM

We set out in late morning. Naturally, Grandma didn't move through the woods the way Lad did, but she was sure-footed and confidently followed an internal compass toward her childhood home. I kept up, trying to plan what I'd say to Lad when I saw him. Every time I thought about it my heart squeezed painfully.

"How are you doing?" I asked Grandma after we'd hiked for a while.

"Oh, I'm fine. A mite nervous I guess."

I might have been imagining it, but she seemed younger and younger the closer we got to Altum. She walked faster, her posture was more erect, her expression more alert and alive than I'd ever seen it before. When we reached our destination, I regarded my grandmother with a new wonder and respect. She'd led us right to the foot of the impossibly huge, ancient magnolia tree without a single step in the wrong direction.

She stopped, clearly intending to go no further. "You know what to do from here, sweetheart."

"Oh, no, you have to come with me. I can't go down there alone, and you want one more look at it, don't you? Isn't that what you said?"

"I don't think I should… but if you really need me…"

"I do." I grabbed her hand, searching for the hidden entrance. We found it and slipped inside. I prepared myself to be rushed and tackled by a couple of giant Elven linebackers, but there was no one in the tunnel entrance. Grandma Neena and I proceeded in silence down the spiraling earthen walkway, holding hands like a couple of kindergarteners.

"What will you do when we get there, Ryann?" she whispered. I looked over and saw her eyes glistening with emotion and glowing eerily in the multi-colored light.

"I have no idea. I'm planning to wing it."

We reached the end of the tunnel and stepped out into the grand common area. It looked so different from a few weeks earlier. Something big was going on. The cavern was crowded with Elves, coming and going in groups and couples.

Some wore the kind of light, naturally colored clothing I'd come to expect from Elves, but others wore completely different attire. A group in long deep blue robes walked together near the river. A family of three wore little more than patches of red fabric, strategically placed for modesty.

A pack of younger guys even had on jeans and t-shirts—Dark Elves, maybe?

There was light and music and elaborate decoration. A multitude of small temporary huts dotted the floor of the place. It was like an exotic carnival. And then it hit me...

"The Assemblage," Grandma Neena said it before I could get the words out. She stood perfectly still and stared at the scene around us.

Suddenly the view was blocked by wide chests, brutally hard midsections, and long arms, tensed with muscle, prepared to draw the knives at their sides. The linebackers had arrived. I looked up into one of the unfriendly, unfamiliar faces.

"Lad? Please?" I squeaked.

We were escorted, or rather, surrounded by guards as we made our way to Lad's family quarters. My stomach rolled in cold waves, my chest was weighted. I was about to see him again.

They took us to the entrance of the grand hall where a guard opened the door and went in. Music and laughter drifted from the room through the open doorway. A glimpse of the interior revealed an elegant celebration.

Beautifully-dressed people danced in the center of the ballroom. Others sat at tables around the periphery of the dance floor. It was a party of some kind. No doubt Lad's parents were entertaining the visiting dignitaries here for the Assemblage. This looked like a particularly formal event.

I glanced over at Grandma Neena's face. She was as nervous as I was.

The door opened wide, and Lad burst out into the hallway, followed immediately by his father. Ivar stopped abruptly, his eyes widening in obvious shock at the sight of my grandmother. As concerned as I wanted to be about her reunion with her former fiancé, I could not pry my attention from Lad. He was glorious. Tears flooded my eyes instantly when he looked at me.

I blinked hard and prayed for strength, battling an irrational hope that he might still want me, that if I asked, he'd offer me a second chance. I'd gladly trade my newfound "success" and security for the opportunity to put my heart at risk for him. None of it was worthwhile without him. I had been so stupid to push him away.

My breath felt like it was trying to get into my lungs through one of those tiny coffee-stirring straws. Lad didn't look like he was doing much better. The muscles in his neck and upper body were visibly tense. His gaze raked over me, and his chest rose and fell in a rapid rhythm, the color in his face unusually high.

His expression was neutral, but there was a spark of wildness in his eyes, something that slipped out from under his fiercely held control for a second before he mastered it. He must have been furious to see me there.

Even then, when he was possessed by hatred for me, I couldn't stop myself from longing for him. He was just as perfect—no—more perfect than before. I'd never seen him in such fine clothing. Light-colored pants of some fine soft fabric extended all the way down to his bare feet. His form-fitting shirt was snowy white with an intricate pattern stitched around the open V neckline.

Clearly, he'd continued his habit of roaming the woods because his skin gleamed a light copper color that only intensified the gold of his hair and the impossible green of his eyes.

It was painful to look at him and know I'd never have him, never be close to him again.

"Ryann..." Lad surprised me by sounding as breathless as I felt. "Are you all right? Are you in trouble?" His posture was restrained, his hands staying clenched at his sides, but there was a surprising note of concern in his voice.

"No... I'm fine. I'm fine," I lied.

"Then why have you come here?" he demanded. Now his voice took on the tone I'd expected, his face carved into the harsh mask from my worst dreams last night.

"I... there's something I need to tell you. I hope I'm not interrupting anything too important."

An ethereal figure drifted out of the doorway to Lad's side. A girl about my age with shining platinum curls placed a hand softly on his shoulder and looked inquiringly up into his face. She was dressed in a flowing white gown. Pale, beautiful, delicate, she reminded me of an exquisite lunar moth.

Raw pain pulsed through my insides as I watched them together. Lad turned his attention to her, no doubt attempting to explain our presence. She smiled her adoration up at him then darted her wide blue eyes in my direction before slipping back inside. Lad looked back at me, expressionless.

"I don't have much time. What do you want, Ryann?"

"I'm sorry. I wouldn't be here if it wasn't important. I have some good news. Your people don't have to leave Altum. I'm going to be getting some money—enough to pay the debt to the IRS. There won't be any need for my mother to sell the timber now, and the woods will be safe."

Lad's tight jaw loosened, his mouth falling open slightly. For a moment he looked a bit dazed. Then he turned and stared into his father's face intently for a few seconds, translating, I assumed. Both of them turned back to me.

Lad was still guarded, aloof, and... regal. Ivar must have been very proud. "That is... excellent news. My father extends his gratitude and congratulations to you and your family."

"Yes, we're very relieved. There's something else, though. To earn the money, I've agreed to produce a whole lot of sweet tea on a daily basis. I can't do it without a regular supply of saol water to sweeten it. It was your idea about using the saol water in my recipe that saved Altum... and my home, too."

He gave me a stiff smile in response. "Well, some good has come of all of this then. Of course we will do our part. We can arrange some method of delivery that will be... comfortable for all of us."

I assumed he was referring to the fact he never wanted to lay eyes on me again and would have to find another delivery boy for the essential special ingredient.

I glanced over at Grandma Neena and Lad's father. They stared at each other without blinking. I'd never seen Ivar's face look anything other than incensed, so it was shocking to see the tender expression he now wore. Their exchange was so intimate, I averted my eyes—realizing I'd intruded on something that was none of my business.

Lad noticed it, too, and did a double take before looking back at me. To fill the awkward silence, I blurted out, "Thank you. I know it's not easy to say 'yes' to anything I have to ask of you."

He stared at me with a look that contained some strong emotion I couldn't identify. When he spoke, his tone was low and intense. "Saying 'yes' to you was always too easy for me. Don't you know... there's nothing I would not have done for you, Ryann?"

How could he say that to me after the things I'd said to him? My mind flooded with images of the two of us together—images I'd worked so hard to repress. Was he showing them to me? Why would he do that if he no longer cared?

My heart squeezed painfully, spurred by a tiny hope. We *had* done something good together that had helped both our families. We'd been happy. Was it possible we could make it work? I was miserable without him—safe, but miserable.

Ivar gripped Lad's upper arm, a signal to return to the ballroom. The sweet, torturous images filling my brain were suddenly gone. Lad looked first at Grandma Neena then at me, giving us a slight bow, his tone crisp and polite. His gaze was cold again.

"I must go. Thank you again for bringing us this welcome news. Now we have one *more* reason to celebrate today." He looked at me with glittering eyes. His hoarse voice was edged in bitterness. "Oh, that's right, you could not have known, of course. It's my wedding day. Wish me well?"

My intake of breath was audible. I should have responded of course, but I couldn't.

"Good bye Ryann." Lad whirled and jerked forcefully out of his father's grasp, disappearing inside the doors.

I don't know how much time passed as I stared at those closed doors. When I'd broken things off with Lad, I had thought I was living my worst nightmare. But this… he was really and truly lost to me forever. I'd allowed myself to love someone, and now he was going to spend his life with some other girl. And it was probably the best thing for him.

Grandma reached over and took my hand, and my tenuous control over my tear ducts started to fail. I would've loved to run for the exit tunnel, but we were still surrounded by the huge guards, and they weren't budging. For some reason, Ivar had stayed. At first I assumed it was to say farewell to Grandma, but he stared right at me.

As I looked back at Lad's father, my mind filled with the things I wished I could tell him. I tried one last time to communicate in the Elven way. I put all my will and my heart into my message to him—that I didn't hate him or even fear him anymore—I didn't care what he thought of me. I'd love his son forever whether he approved or not, whether I ever saw Lad again or not. Even if it always hurt, I couldn't stop loving him, and I was no longer afraid of the pain. Most of all, I told Ivar how much I wished for Lad to be happy, even with some other girl, if that's what was best for him.

I silently willed his father to take good care of Lad and make sure he had the fulfilled, good life he deserved.

There was no reaction from him at all. Ivar turned away and directed another long glance at my grandmother, and then he was gone. The guards still didn't move.

"He wants us to wait," Grandma whispered to me.

"Why?"

"I'm not sure. But what choice do we have? Are you okay, honey?"

"No. Not really. Are you?"

"Yes, actually. I feel better than I have in... oh, decades," she answered with a shaky laugh.

"Did you... talk to him?"

"Yes, I guess I've still got it. It wasn't quite what I imagined, seeing him again."

"What do you mean?"

"Well he was *nicer* than I expected. He's not angry with me anymore. I think that surprised him, too. He loves his family. He's had a good life these past forty-two years." Her eyes were warm as she mentally reviewed the conversation they'd shared. "I'm glad I got to see him. It really helps to know… well, that life went on for him. It will for you, too, Ryann. I promise."

I wanted to agree, to make her feel good, but I couldn't. I'd never get over this. Not in forty-four years or a hundred.

"Do you think Lad will be happy? With the marriage?" I asked weakly.

"I can't say, but his father is convinced this wedding is the best thing for Lad and all his people. The bride is a member of one of our clan's—well, *enemy* clans would be putting it too strongly—but her father is the leader of the tribe we've had the most trouble with over the centuries."

"Dark Elves? I thought they were bad."

"Depends on your perspective. *They* don't think they're bad. They think they're keeping up with the times, and that the Light Elves are slowing down progress. This union will go a long way toward smoothing over our differences of opinion and creating a lasting peace between our peoples."

"Great." I was trying really hard to be on the side of peace and Elven unity but not having much luck.

After a few minutes, a servant appeared at the door and directed his gaze at Grandma Neena. He waited as she explained to me what was happening.

"My family is here. Ivar has decided I may stay and see them and remain for the rest of the Assemblage if I want to. You're also invited to stay, Ryann. He knows now that you mean them no harm. Come with me, meet your family."

She was obviously thrilled at the prospect of seeing her people again. I wanted her to, but there was no way I could stay. Not after what Lad had told me. What, would I try to catch the bouquet?

"Grandma, that's wonderful. You stay. But I'm going, okay? I have to. I couldn't bear to see…" I couldn't finish the sentence. My throat was closing up.

"Oh sweetheart." Grandma Neena hugged me close to her. "I'll go with you. Come on, let's go." She started to pull me away from the doors. I stopped and held her in place.

"No, Grandma, you stay. Please. This is what you've wanted for so long. Your people are in there waiting for you. I know the way home now. I'd really rather be alone anyway."

Grandma promised me she'd be home the next day and followed the servant into the celebration. I went with the guards through Altum, back toward the tunnel to the so-called real world. I didn't even look up at the festivities as I walked, too absorbed in managing the crushing pain that threatened to drop me on the spot.

Staring at my feet, focusing on putting one in front of the other, I nearly ran into a large Elven man coming out of the tunnel. I automatically looked up to apologize.

My words dried up and blew away.

It was Nox.

"Ryann—what are you doing here?" His shock was obvious.

"Shock" didn't begin to describe my condition. I looked at Nox, shirtless except for the leather breeches that all Elven men typically wore. It took me a few moments to find my voice, and when I did, it came out sounding shaky and strange.

"What am I doing here? What am *I* doing here? Oh… I'm a total moron. The black sheep brother. It's you. You… phony. I was *worried* about you!" I shoved at his chest and the guards started toward me, but Nox stopped them with a don't-bother gesture as I continued to rant. "I *sacrificed…* let you go for *your* sake because I thought you deserved better than what I could give you. But it was all a lie—the whole time. You've been lying to me since the day I met you."

He shook his head and reached toward me. "I never lied to you, Ryann."

I took a step back. "You never told me the truth either. I guess I shouldn't be surprised. Lad told me what his 'brother' was like."

"Lad." Nox spit out the name like it was a dirty joke. "Don't waste your love on Lad, Ryann. He doesn't care about you. He's already replaced you. He forgot about you the minute you were out of his sight."

"Shut up. Don't even talk about him. Is that what all this has been about, some kind of twisted sibling rivalry? It was *you* who saw us together that day up in Lad's tree, wasn't it? And then you set out to take me away from him, to take what was his."

A guilty grin. "I'll admit at first I thought it would be fun to—no, don't leave yet." He grabbed my sleeve as I tried to push past him. "Listen, Ryann, at first, you're right, my motives weren't good. But as soon as I got to know you, things changed for me. *You* changed me. What I feel for you is absolutely real."

"What you *feel* for me? You don't care anything about me. And the fact that you instantly hooked up with Savannah proves it."

He laughed. "I was only pretending with that silly girl to make you jealous—to make you see you actually do want me as much as I want you. And see? It worked."

"No. I don't want you. Not at all. I never did."

He huffed another disbelieving laugh. "Now who's a liar? And I don't know how you can say I don't care about you after I got that job for you at The Skillet. And made the store manager at Food Star give your tea a chance."

I staggered backward. "You... glamoured them." My breath was wheezing in and out of my lungs as if I were allergic to the air around me. "You glamoured *me*."

He took a step forward, following my retreat. "No. I didn't. If I had, you'd be with me instead of embarrassing yourself chasing after a guy who *doesn't* want you. I *still* want you, Ryann." He reached out a hand to me.

I stared at it then looked up. His mesmerizing eyes locked onto mine. For a moment I was nearly compelled to put my hand inside his.

"It's not too late for us." His melodic low voice was almost like a song.

I jerked my gaze away. "There *is* no *us*."

I pushed past him and ran for the tunnel. Though I was closely followed by the guards, they really needn't have bothered making sure I was leaving. I had absolutely no interest in ever seeing this place again.

When I surfaced, the bright daylight was a cruel contrast to the way I felt inside. It was the blackest day of my entire life. *Lad's wedding day.* I could hardly bear to think about it, but of course I couldn't stop the images from coming. Was the beautiful girl who'd touched his arm the one? His bride? I wanted to throw up. I wanted to cry.

I walked in the general direction of home, but without even realizing it, I ended up at the foot of Lad's special hideaway tree. The place we'd first met as children. Looking high up into the branches, I spotted the nest he'd made there and started climbing. A fear of heights doesn't hold you back when you're no longer particularly disturbed by the idea of falling to your death.

Reaching the nest, I crawled inside, knowing I had no right to be there. *It's all right*, I told myself. It was my final indulgence. Lad would never even know. I needed a few more minutes of feeling close to him, and then I'd go, somehow manage to keep breathing, get on with my life, and let Lad get on with his.

But, oh, it felt good to be there, in his special place. Crawling over to the carved chest, I opened its lid, gently touching the things he'd collected or made in his childhood. A slingshot, a beautiful feather, a perfect pinecone. And of course my treasured Book of Virtues, which had become the Rosetta Stone for our relationship. I crawled back across the nest, finding a comfortable spot in the soft lining to settle into. The fabric was warm and smelled like Lad. I inhaled deeply and accepted the painful ache that came as the tears leaked from the corners of my eyes.

Opening the worn book, I curled up and read the words I knew by heart, letting the familiar phrases and illustrations soothe me like a lullaby. Eventually I drifted off, cuddling my book like a security blanket as I had when I was a child.

My dreams were much, much better than my reality. In them, Lad loved me and I was free to love him. There was music and dancing. Smiling Elven people surrounded us as I walked down a long, flower-strewn aisle toward Lad.

He waited for me, dressed in the fine clothing I'd seen him wearing today, his golden hair gleaming, his smile blindingly white. His green eyes glistened with moisture as he watched me. Tears of happiness streamed from my own eyes. I wanted to run to him, but I kept my pace slow and even because this was a—wait—the platinum-haired girl was there. She stepped up beside Lad in her flowing white gown, her otherworldly beauty drawing the admiration of every eye in the room.

The tears flowed now because I realized I was seeing the guy I loved marry someone else. "Lad…" I called out to him, but there was no sound. He gazed at the impossibly beautiful girl next to him, unable to see or hear me. Tears kept coming, running in rivers down my face and into my mouth, and they tasted sweet, like saol water. The sweetness washed over me, filling me up.

I opened my eyes. My heart was a vibration inside my chest because my dream had shifted again and seemed wonderfully real. Lad was there with me, kissing me with his delicious sugar-sweet mouth, wrapping his arms around me, holding me against his inhumanly warm strength, his steady, rapid heartbeat.

Sobbing with happiness, I kissed him back feverishly. This was the best dream of my life, and I prayed I'd never wake from it. After this, real life held no more appeal for me. I captured his beautiful face in my hands, ran my fingers through his thick curls and over his hard shoulders and back, kissing him with frantic passion.

He felt so good, so real, and I didn't feel guilty for kissing someone else's husband because this was *my* dream. In my dream he belonged to me, not to her, and I was not about to let him go for any reason.

"Ryann. Ryann—" Dream-Lad said with a smothered breathless laugh as I refused to let him up for air. "Hey, calm down. I'm glad to see you, too. But let's talk for a minute."

He gripped my arms lightly, enforcing a slight distance between us. I looked at him and began to cry all over again because the melting heat was back in his eyes the way it used to be, and it was there for me, no one else.

"No, no, sweet baby, don't do that," Lad whispered, kissing the tears before they made it halfway down my cheeks, "There's no need to cry."

His warm whisper drifted across my wet cheeks. The sensation was so physical, distinct, undeniable. I put my fingertips lightly on his lips and felt his moist breath. I had to ask. "You're... real?" My voice sounded ragged from a mixture of anguish and passion. Lad's answering smile spread slowly across his face.

"Are you going to say that to me every time I see you?" he teased softly, seductive warmth oozing from every word.

"Are there going to be... other times?" I was still afraid to trust my senses.

His smile was like heated honey. "There will be lots and lots of time for us. If that's what you want."

"But how... why are you here? You're getting married today... and I thought..." I was hopelessly confused. If I wasn't dreaming, what was happening?

"My father changed his mind. After he saw you and your grandmother today, he asked to speak with me. He told me I'm free to make my own decision about when and *whom* to marry. He called off the wedding. I left immediately to find you."

"But what about the girl? Your fiancée?"

"Vancia. Someone will talk to her. I don't even know her really."

"Won't her family be mad?"

"Probably. But her father's never happy anyway. Now he has something new to be grouchy about."

"Oh." I tried to take it all in. The sudden turnabout had me feeling like I'd just ridden the teacups at Disneyland. "How did you know where to find me?"

"Nox told me, actually. He followed you when you left." Lad paused and his brows lowered. "We need to talk about all of *that* by the way. Apparently when he saw where you went, he turned back around and came home. I ran into him outside of Altum. Luckily I didn't knock him out before he could tell me where you'd gone." Lad's eyes softened again, glowing with their own verdure illumination as he wiped a tear from my face. "I found you weeping and calling my name in your sleep."

"I was dreaming. You were getting married... to someone else."

"No." Lad shook his head and wrapped me tightly in his arms again.

"But why would your father change his mind? He was getting what he wanted. He hates me."

"No he doesn't. In fact, he *told* me to come find you."

"I can't believe it. What in the world did Grandma *say* to him?"

"It wasn't what *she* said, Ryann. It was what you said to him."

"What I said?"

"Yes. He *heard* you. How you care for me. How you were willing to give me up if it was best for me. And when you asked him to watch out for me and make sure I had a happy life, that's exactly what he decided to do. It turns out he was reminded today about young love. I guess it's not something only humans indulge in, after all."

"It's too wonderful. I'm afraid to believe it."

"Believe it, Ryann. I *am* real… and I'm in love with you. Now… tell *me*. Tell me what *you're* feeling, and don't speak aloud." He looked at me, expectation glowing on his face.

I wrapped my arms around his neck, looked deep into his eyes, focused my mind, and told Lad I loved him, without saying a word. After that, there was no need for words. Our mouths were kind of busy anyway.

❧

So now I have my icing… and my cake, too. And I plan to enjoy every morsel. We don't have all the answers. A few months ago, that would have driven me crazy. Now I know sometimes you have to just take life for what it is instead of worrying about what might happen.

Lad's still an Elf, an Elven prince, to be exact, with all the responsibilities that entails. And I'm still human. Well, mostly human. I'm still not sure how much the Elven part of me will manifest itself now that I'm aware of it. I hope it'll make me at least a little more acceptable to his people. I also hope it means my ability to communicate with him in the nonverbal Elven way will continue to develop. And who knows what else I might be able to do?

Lad and I are still tied to our two separate worlds. He has a kingdom to run... someday. In the meantime he has a lot to learn. And there are some pretty hacked-off Dark Elves to contend with now as a result of the broken marriage contract.

As for me... I guess I won't be able to avoid Nox forever. He's part of Lad's world, which means he's part of mine, whether I like it or not. I also have to stop my best friend from running off and unknowingly enslaving herself to a Dark Elf in his fan pod. And there's the small matter of trying to maintain passing grades in high school while running a beverage manufacturing company.

But I know whatever is coming, Lad and I will face it together. How do I know? I heard it straight from his heart.

EPILOGUE

The nest rocked. Both of us sat up straight, the tender moment displaced by alarm. Lad jumped to his feet as two large hands came over the edge, gripping and pulling, and then Nox's head appeared. Lad's body tensed, his hands curling and clenching.

"You are *the last* person I want to see right now. What do you want?" he demanded. Our happy reunion had lasted all of thirty minutes before this unwelcome interruption.

Nox hesitated. I'd never seen his face look so serious, so completely free of any attempt to charm. When he spoke, his voice was grave.

"Lad, you have to go back to Altum. Now."

"Nice try, but you had your shot. We were kind of in the middle of—"

"It's your father." An excruciating pause. "He's dead. Lad—you're king now."

I was still sitting in the nest's floor. Beside me, Lad's legs swayed. I reached out and placed my hand on his calf, trying to impart some small amount of strength to him, to comfort him somehow. He looked down in my direction but not exactly at me. I'd seen the same expression on my mom's face the night my dad told her he had been with another woman. Nothing else looks like that particular combination of shock and blinding pain.

Without a word, Lad moved toward the edge of the nest. He was going home. I scrambled to follow him, still on my knees.

"I'll come with you."

He whirled to face me and barked out a harsh "No!"

Stunned by the ferocity of it, I sat back down and looked at him.

"I... I'm sorry, Ryann. I think you'd better not." He looked like he might say more to me, but he didn't. He raised his hands to his temples and grabbed a fistful of hair in each one. The veins in his forearms stood out clearly.

He squeezed his eyes shut, and when he opened them again he turned to Nox, who had stayed in place, half-in, half-out of the nest.

"Take her."

And then Lad was gone, over the edge of the nest. Within seconds, I heard the scuffle of his feet in the leaves on the forest floor. And then there was silence.

I stared at Nox. Thanks to my seated position and his semi-suspended one, we were on eye-level with each other, practically face-to-face. His mysterious hazel eyes were narrowed and piercing. Was he trying to hear my thoughts, too? Could he?

I couldn't speak, but Nox did, belatedly answering Lad's order—the first command of his new king—*take her*.

"I will."

AFTERWORD

Thank you for reading HIDDEN DEEP, Book One of the Hidden Trilogy. If you enjoyed it, please consider leaving a review on Amazon and Goodreads. Reviews help authors more than you know!

To learn about upcoming releases from Amy Patrick, sign up for her newsletter. You will only receive notifications when new titles are available and when her books go on sale. You may also occasionally receive teasers, excerpts, and extras from upcoming books. Amy will never share your contact information with others.

Follow Amy on Twitter at @AmyPatrickBooks, and visit her website at www.amypatrickbooks.com. You can also connect with her on Facebook

The Hidden Trilogy continues with Book 2, HIDDEN HEART, coming soon. Here's a sneak preview of the story:

17-year-old Ryann Carroll thought she knew who she was… a small-town Southern girl just trying to survive her parents' messy divorce and find some peace for herself. She thought she knew what she wanted… a summer job, a car, a first date that didn't suck, and NO complications from a serious relationship—any guy in her life would simply be icing on the cake.

But now… she's not only in love, her boyfriend Lad is an Elven prince, and Ryann's learned she's part Elven herself. Things could hardly get more complicated than that.

More importantly, she's learned the world's top celebrities… those actors, musicians, athletes, and politicians who seem a little too beautiful and talented to be true… are actually Dark Elves. And they're using their glamour and the increasing popularity of fan pods to control more and more humans. But why?

With her best friend Emmy leaving soon to join the fan pod of a famous actor, Ryann has to find out the answer. And she can't do it alone. But after the shocking murder of his father, Lad's duty is to the Light Elves, and Ryann's not sure whether his top priority is their relationship or his people.

In this second book of the Hidden Trilogy, true friendship will take Ryann from rural Mississippi to the glittering city of Los Angeles. And true love will take her to places she never expected to go…

Excerpt

It was her, or at least it might have been her, if she'd cut her hair and gotten major highlights, which she probably had. The girl turned, and I saw her face. Another false alarm.

It was my first big Hollywood party, and I was the lame zebra trying to keep up with the stampeding herd, moving through a sea of designer dresses, and beautiful faces, and crystal champagne flutes. Emmy was here somewhere. She had to be, because if she wasn't, I'd have no idea where else to look.

Having already searched the first three floors of the massive, glass-walled modern museum of a house, I walked out onto the roof deck where the sounds of a slick alternative band filled the moist salty air, pumping up the party guests to an even higher pitch.

Scanning the scene, I finally spotted what I was looking for—not Emmy, but the next best thing. The one person who knew for sure where she was, where she'd been the past four weeks. He was leaning against the balcony railing, his perfect form framed by a backdrop of stars over the Malibu beach, and naturally, surrounded by a crowd of adoring young women.

Adrenaline surged through my veins like the surf I could hear in the background. Finally, after everything I'd gone through to get here, I was so close to finding her.

Preparing to charge Vallon Foster—huge Elven bodyguards be damned—I planned to demand Emmy's whereabouts and immediate release. A strong hand gripped my shoulder and slid down to my waist. I was pulled back against the solid warmth of a large male body.

"Calm down, Ryann," a smooth familiar voice murmured at my ear, "and let me handle this."

With considerable effort, I slowed my pace and we approached the movie star together, hand in hand.

"Sweetheart, I'd like you to meet my good friend, Vallon Foster." His voice was comforting, full of loving assurance.

I forced myself to smile and appear something less-than-hostile as Nox introduced me.

"Vallon, this is Ryann... the newest member of my fan pod."

ACKNOWLEDGMENTS

This is an important part of the book for me, because without the people named here, HIDDEN DEEP wouldn't exist.

Huge thanks go to my lovely editor Judy Roth and to Cover Your Dreams for another beautiful cover.

Thank you to my husband, who never doubts my abilities and expects the best, and my precious boys, who make me laugh every day, put the joy in my life, and have to be the easiest kids on the planet.

To my lifelong bubba Chelle, who loves me no matter what, to Margie, for being a cheerleader and wonderful friend in every way, and to the Westmoreland Farmgirls, who are always ready to read and celebrate.

I am constantly inspired (and set on the right path) by my amazing critique partner, McCall Hoyle and special thanks to Kim for all the help on this one. Love and thanks to the rest of the fabulous GH Dreamweavers and Dauntless girls for the fun and friendship, and special thanks to my Lucky 13 sisters for their loyalty, good advice, virtual Prosecco, cupcakes, and cabana boys.

#teamworddomination. Big hugs and forever love to my Savvy Seven sisters. Thank you Mary and CM for all the great book (and life) talks.

No acknowledgments could be complete without mentioning my first family. I've been blessed to have a mother who made me believe I could, a brilliant and loving dad, a funny and loyal brother, and the best sister anyone's ever had. Thank you to Joanne and Larry, for all the support, encouragement, and boy-clothes shopping! And thank you to the rest of my friends and family for your support and for just making life good.

ABOUT THE AUTHOR

Amy Patrick grew up in Mississippi (with a few years in Texas thrown in for spicy flavor) and has lived in six states, including Rhode Island, where she now lives with her husband and two sons.

Amy has been a professional singer, a DJ, a voiceover artist, and always a storyteller, whether it was directing her younger siblings during hours of "pretend" or inventing characters and dialogue while hot-rollering her hair before middle school every day. For many years she was a writer of true crime, medical anomalies, and mayhem, working as a news anchor and health reporter for six different television stations. Then she retired to make up her own stories. Hers have a lot more kissing.

I love to hear from my readers. Feel free to contact me on Twitter and my Facebook page

And be sure to sign up for my newsletter here and be the first to hear the latest news on Ryann, Lad, Nox, and the Hidden Trilogy.

The Hidden Trilogy

Hidden Deep
Hidden Heart
Hidden Hope